DEAD END HOUSE

BRYAN SMITH

Grindhouse Press
PO BOX 540
Yellow Springs, Ohio 45387

Grindhouse Press #092
ISBN-13: 978-1-957504-07-0

This one is for Kristopher Rufty.

Other titles by Bryan Smith

ONE

THE RADIO IN LARA KINCAID'S vintage cherry-red Chevy Nova was tuned to the local classic rock station, with Blue Oyster Cult's "This Ain't the Summer of Love" issuing from the speakers at a low volume. It was a warm night and the windows were partly rolled down. Things were getting hot and heavy in the back seat. It was about damn time.

Lara had been trying for weeks to get into Kevin Malone's pants and had made precious little progress. With most guys the seduction process only took minutes and sometimes only seconds, but Kevin was the straightest of straight arrows. He was the uptight product of a conservative religious upbringing, and early on in her amorous pursuit of him he'd actually told her he was saving himself for Jesus, by which he meant he intended to remain a virgin until after he was married.

Ridiculous.

The boy was a football star. He should be banging chicks left and right and doing keg stands at field parties after the big game every weekend. Instead he had the pious mentality of a timid schoolgirl from a more innocent era. It made Lara want to throw up.

Right from the start, she embraced his mindset as a challenge, his precious purity becoming something she was determined to take from him. She wanted to fuck him in all the dirtiest and raunchiest ways imaginable and leave him feeling like his soul had been indelibly sullied, but that would require actually getting her hands on his equipment, something she'd been trying without success to do for twenty straight days.

Until tonight.

He moaned as her hand moved inside his pants again, making him writhe as she squeezed his rigid cock. She watched his face, fascinated by its contortions and the way he kept his eyes closed as she made him shiver helplessly with pleasure. The weirdest part was the tears leaking from his screwed-shut eyes even as this happened. No penetrative sex had occurred yet, but he was nonetheless consumed with guilt.

The deal she'd made with him minutes earlier was that it wouldn't go beyond what she was doing with her hand, a pact she had no intention of honoring. She had his cock out of his jeans now. It'd be the easiest thing in the world to lift up her skirt, swing a leg over, and mount him. He wouldn't be able to stop her until it was too late, and as soon as he was inside her, he wouldn't want to, she was sure of that.

It was tempting to take him into her mouth first, though.

He would protest, but so fucking what?

She would have her way with him now, every way she wanted after this long period of frustration, and that was all there was to it.

The funniest part of it was what had finally gotten them to this point. In retrospect, it was something so obvious she wanted to kick herself for not thinking of it earlier. There was only so much resistance her ego could take.

So she questioned his sexuality, suggesting maybe he was gay.

That did it.

He became angry, sputtering denials tinged with more than a touch of overcompensation. She laughed at him in uproarious fashion. Some of the mirth was genuine, deriving from a state of high amusement sparked by his frantic defensiveness, but there was a bit of exaggeration involved as well. It was her way of taunting him, playing upon his latent homophobia by making him feel belittled and pushed to the edge.

He told her they could "fool around a little," whatever that meant, but they would have to find a private place to do it. Somewhere out of the way of prying eyes. His house was obviously out of the question. He'd never risk getting caught in the act of doing anything naughty by his fundamentalist parents. Her house was also out, but for different reasons. Kevin feared her aggressively garrulous father, who was almost never sober, and her overly flirty mother made him so nervous he couldn't stand it. Her parents wouldn't give a shit if she banged the football star in her room, but Kevin would be mortified.

Thus why they were now parked on a dead end street on the outskirts of town. The street was a short one adjacent to an old neighborhood where the houses were nearly all decrepit and falling apart. Many were abandoned and boarded-up, like the ones here. There were just three houses on this little stub of a road. Two stood across from each other on opposite sides of the road.

The third house was Dead End House.

The two-story Victorian was infamous, the subject of local legend and rumor. Several brutal murders had occurred there in the distant past. It became a hot subject anew among local kids every Halloween season, with many of them daring each other to break in. Most lacked the guts to ever try such a thing, having been warned against it in the severest terms by their parents. Even rebellious kids normally inclined to ignore edicts from authority figures mostly steered clear of the area. Its reputation was that foreboding.

Also, this was the *bad* part of town.

That never failed to amuse Lara. This wasn't the big, bad city, and this neighborhood wasn't *that* scary. Most of the remaining residents kept to themselves and just wanted to live in peace and be left alone. She'd been out here many times throughout her high school career, bringing a parade of boys—and the occasional girl—to what had become her preferred private make out spot.

She was right on the cusp of taking Kevin's cock into her mouth when he spoke.

"There's a light on in that house."

Lara considered ignoring what he'd said in favor of proceeding with what she was doing, but there was something in the tone of his voice that gave her pause.

3

A quaver that had nothing to do with sexual arousal.

He sounded . . . *afraid.*

But that was ridiculous.

There was nothing to be scared of out here.

Right?

With a reluctant sigh, she sat up and looked at him, seeing that his eyes were open for the first time since she'd pulled down the tab of his zipper. Open wide and bulging with fear.

She followed his gaze and saw that it was riveted to Dead End House.

Her brow creased in confusion as she sat up straighter and shifted around for a more direct view of the house, which was fully visible through the Nova's windshield. He was right. A light was on in one of the second story rooms.

Kevin's voice sounded jittery as he said, "I thought nobody lived there. Didn't you say all these houses were empty?"

She shrugged. "Not this one, apparently."

"But that's Dead End House, isn't it? The haunted murder house?"

"The murders happened a long time ago. Like, fucking *decades* ago. If somebody's moved in, it's nobody who had anything to do with all that."

Kevin's wide-eyed gaze was still pinned to the house. "What did they call the guy who killed all those people, Crazy Calvin or something like that? I heard my older cousins talking about him once. They said he's still alive."

Lara groaned. "Jesus. People and their rumor-mongering. Yeah, he's still alive, but baby, he ain't here. He's been locked up tight in a state mental institution for years and isn't ever getting out. There's nothing to be scared of, okay? Now am I gonna get some action tonight or what?"

Kevin whimpered. "I want to go home. Take me home. I'm getting creeped out."

She smirked as she reached for his wilting member again. "Don't worry, baby. I'll protect you from the big, bad—"

The Nova's back window exploded.

Kevin screamed.

A high and piercing sound that came to an abrupt end as a sharp, curved blade hooked around his throat and tore it open, resulting in an impressive eruption of blood. Much of the blood struck Lara in the face and spattered her leather jacket and the skimpy top beneath.

Then she was screaming too as a pair of strong hands reached for her.

TWO

Five years later...

A MAN DRESSED IN MULTIPLE layers of raggedy-ass clothing came shambling down the sidewalk as Brady Whitmore stepped out of O'Bannon's Tavern, squinting as he emerged into bright late afternoon sunlight. The end of his mid-day shift was less than an hour away, but his replacement was already behind the bar and it'd been too long since his last smoke break. He tapped a smoke out of his dwindling pack of Camels and fired it up as he watched the homeless man approach a utility pole and staple a black-and-white flyer over another flyer advertising some DJ's club gig.

The flyer was a missing persons notice that showed side-by-side images of two attractive young people, a boy and a girl. Below the photos was a number for the local police. The boy was handsome in that stereotypical high school jock way. He looked like a million other kids of that type. The girl, though ... she was something special. There was a hint of something wild in the curl of her mouth and in the direct and challenging way she looked at the camera.

A faint feeling of sadness tinged Brady's thoughts as the man moved away from the pole and continued shambling down the sidewalk. The feeling was reflexive, a mere echo of a much stronger feeling from years ago. He knew those faces. The homeless man was the girl's father. He was once semi-respected in town, but for the last few years he'd been a jobless beggar. The people here had long memories. They pitied him and filled the coffee tin he carried with him with coins and small bills on a regular basis. It wasn't enough money to get him off the streets, but it was enough to keep him in cheap booze and allowed him to make a new batch of those flyers every couple months. Help of a more substantial type had been offered many times, but he didn't seem to want it.

Brady puffed on his cigarette and watched the man approach another utility pole at the end of the block. Before he could reach the pole, the missing girl's father stumbled over an uneven part of the sidewalk and pitched forward. He cried out and made an awkward, flailing attempt to remain upright, but it was no use as his knees hit the sidewalk with an audible crack. The stack of freshly printed flyers flew away from him, the individual pieces of copy paper separating as they went spinning across sidewalk cement. The bulk of them stayed on the sidewalk, but several continued into the street, where they were almost immediately run over by multiple passing cars.

The man remained sobbing and unmoving facedown on the sidewalk as a stiff breeze picked up more copies of the flyer and carried them out to the street.

Flicking his half-smoked cigarette away, Brady jogged down to the end of the block and knelt at his side. "Hey, dude, are you okay? Here, let me help you."

The man turned his head so that one side of his face was pressed against the sidewalk. His one visible bloodshot eye swiveled in its socket until it found Brady, locking on him with surprising intensity.

"Don't fucking touch me. I'm not helpless, boy."

The enraged tone surprised Brady. He'd gently taken hold of one of the man's arms, but now he jerked his hand away as if stung. The gruff rejection of his offer made him consider washing his hands of the situation. He'd tried to do the humane thing and had only gotten cursed out for making the effort. A lot of other people, finding themselves in a similar situation, would already be moving along. Being this close to the man wasn't exactly pleasant. He reeked of cheap booze, a pungent odor enveloping him like a cloud of poison gas.

DEAD END HOUSE

That was bad enough, but the stench of filth permeating his clothes and body was even worse.

Something compelled him to remain where he was a while longer. Despite his protestations, the man made no move to lift himself off the ground, and he breathed in a slightly labored way as Brady eyed him with a worried and wary expression. That bloodshot eye was unfocused now, no longer fixated on him. It was hard to look at him and not see a man on the thin edge of utter defeat, of permanent surrender.

"You know, Mr. Kincaid, I used to know your daughter. We were classmates. I even came over to your house once." He forced a chuckle that contained no real mirth. "It was just the one time, so you probably don't remember me."

Kincaid made a deep and raspy throat clearing sound. "Lot of boys visited my baby. Most only once or twice."

It was hard to miss the bitter edge to his tone.

"She was a slut," he added.

Then he began to weep.

Brady listened to him for a few moments, feeling helpless. He had no idea how to respond to that. In his opinion, the pronouncement was unnecessarily harsh and judgmental, but what good would come of saying that to this broken man?

Not knowing what else to do, he got up and began collecting as many of the remaining flyers as he could before they could get swept away by the wind. After he'd gathered up all the salvageable ones, he glanced at the spot on the sidewalk where he'd last seen Kincaid.

He was gone.

THREE

SHE WOKE UP AND HEARD something moving around in the basement. The absolute absence of light made it impossible to discern what that something was. It might be a rat or a bat or a cat. Wormie had heard no flapping of leathery wings, which likely ruled out the second of those possibilities. Bats did sometimes enter the basement, and she knew they were capable of hanging motionless in their chosen roosting places for hours, but their intrusions here were rare occurrences. They only happened when Calvin got extra careless and left the basement door open. The concrete stairwell led out to the backyard rather than inside the house.

There was also a furtiveness in what she was hearing, a quality she did not associate with rodents. A cat was capable of stealth in some circumstances, but they also tended to move with a light step. This creature was trying not to be heard, but was of a size that rendered total silence unachievable while moving about in a dark and cluttered space. In all probability, the unseen, furtive thing was no rat or bat or cat, nor any other type of wild creature. The longer she listened and analyzed, the closer she came to arriving at an exciting conclusion.

For the first time in a while, Wormie had human company in the basement. Company other than Calvin or his equally deranged family members, that is, though Alma Wilcox rarely descended to the basement these days due to her advanced age and numerous physical infirmities.

Her guess was verified when this new person in the basement bumped into something hard enough to elicit a sharp cry of pain. The sound lasted barely more than a second, because it was stifled with deliberate abruptness by the person who'd produced it. Whoever this new arrival was, they'd already learned the importance of silence, which meant they'd probably spent at least a few days up in the house before being tossed down here. Wormie, however, had heard enough in that split second to deduce some stuff. For one thing, the new person was female, which was not surprising. Calvin and Ursula killed most of their male victims right away. The house didn't want boy blood was what they always said, whatever that meant.

After several moments of absolute stillness, the new girl started moving around again, this time more slowly and with a greater level of care. Wormie's heart sped up a little when she realized the girl had changed directions and was headed her way. She smiled and reached for the narrow fissure in the cement floor she used as a hiding place for important stuff. Her fingers closed around a small sliver of sharpened bone and extracted it from the fissure. She brought her arm forward and held the bone-shiv in front of her face, ready to use it with deadly precision should the need arise. This she accomplished without making any noise at all, at least none detectable to human ears. She was good at being noiseless in her movements, because she'd had years to perfect the skill.

The new girl bumped into something again and started crying. She was still striving for relative silence, but her fear was getting the better of her, an emotion heightened to an unbearable degree by her inability to see anything in the pitch black of the basement.

She'd stopped moving again.

Wormie needed to lure the girl closer and knew just how to do it. It'd been a while since the last time, but her method was time-tested and proven.

It would work again, no doubt about it.

She summoned certain old memories that reliably filled her with a deep and aching sadness, then spoke in the most pitiful manner possible, her voice vibrating with apparent terror and helplessness. "P-puh . . . please . . . is s-suh . . . somebody there? I huh-hear you. Puh-please . . ."

Utter silence from the newcomer for a moment.

Wormie made herself sniffle and sob, effortlessly generating an authentic-sounding feeling of misery.

The new girl remained silent only a short beat longer before saying, "I hear you." She spoke in a voice so soft it was barely above a whisper. Any quieter and it would have been inaudible. "Are you hurt? You sound like you're in pain."

Wormie sniffled again. "I am. Could you puh-please come to me."

The new girl said, "If you're hurt, you shouldn't move. Just keep talking and I'll come to you."

Yet another pathetic-sounding sniffle from Wormie. "O-okay. I'm suh-sorry you're here. So sorry they cuh-caught you. But I'm glad I'm not alone now. Does that make me a buh-buh . . . bad person?"

The new girl's voice was tinged with real compassion as she said, "You poor thing. No, it doesn't make you bad. It just makes you human. Unlike that sick animal who took us."

The whole time she talked, she continued picking her way forward in the dark, making occasional noises of surprise and disgust as she bumped into things or passed through messes of an indeterminate organic nature.

Wormie rose up on her hands and knees, readying herself as the new girl came within grabbing range.

Then she pounced.

The new girl yelped in fright as Wormie landed on her back and drove her to the floor. She pressed the sharp edge of the bone-shiv against the girl's throat and warned her against screaming, telling her that if she did, Calvin and his mother would be upset. They would come down here and there would be consequences. Not for the new girl, though, because by then she'd already be bleeding out from her slit throat.

She pressed her mouth against the shivering new girl's ear and whispered, "Now, are you gonna be good and do as you're told?"

The girl whimpered and promised she would.

Wormie then spent some time enjoying the sensation of her naked, filthy flesh pressed against the much cleaner bare flesh of another human being. Too much time had passed since she'd last experienced this kind of contact with another person. It was comforting and reassuring despite the extreme sense of terror the person lying beneath her was experiencing.

Wormie gently kissed the side of the girl's neck and spoke again. "Listen close and do exactly as I say. If you try anything funny, you're dead. Understand?"

The new girl whimpered again. "Why are you doing this?"

Wormie pressed the bone-shiv harder against the tender flesh of the girl's throat, slicing just deep enough to draw blood. The girl squealed in fright and shivered hard against her for a moment.

"The next cut kills you," Wormie told her. "Now do as I say."

She lifted herself up off the girl, but kept a hand at the small of her back as she guided her forward through the darkness. They stopped as they arrived at an obstruction too large to circumvent. The new girl reached out and touched metal slats with a shaking hand.

"Wh-what is this?"

"It's where you'll be staying from now on, except for when I take you out to play."

She opened the door to the cage and ordered the new girl inside. There was the expected moment of resistance accompanying a sharp new surge of terror, but Wormie jabbed the shiv against her side and got her moving. The girl was sobbing nonstop as Wormie followed her into the cage and latched the door.

Then the girl screamed.

And Wormie smiled, knowing the new girl had discovered the unmoving form of her cellmate. The female corpse curled up at the back of the cage had been there a long time. Months.

Maybe longer.

It was hard to tell anymore.

The new girl screamed again and again.

Someone upstairs stomped angrily on the floor. Wormie and the new girl would have visitors in the basement soon and it was unlikely to be a pleasant experience for either of them. That was okay with Wormie, though. She'd endured a lot of pain over the years and knew she could tolerate a good bit more. Besides, all this empty time spent in the perfect blackness of the basement had gone on for far too long.

It'd be good to shake things up some.

Even if it got her killed.

FOUR

BRADY DROVE STRAIGHT HOME AFTER the end of his shift at O'Bannon's Tavern. He was in a restless mood, unable to concentrate on anything other than his unsettling encounter with the homeless man for more than a few minutes at a time.

Once he was back inside his apartment, he grabbed a beer from the fridge and headed out to the living room, where he sat on the couch and spent some time flipping through channels on his TV. He did this in the most rote, distracted way, paying almost no actual attention to the rapidly alternating images on the large screen. He went through the entire spectrum of channels at least three times before the pointlessness of the exercise became obvious. Realizing there was no room in his head for frivolous entertainment for the time being, he turned the TV off and dropped the remote on the coffee table.

All he did for the next few minutes was stare at the blank screen and sip his beer. He thought of nothing in anything like a focused way, but his face was twisted in a deep frown the whole time. That restlessness was still bubbling under the surface, causing him to fidget and bounce his leg.

He got up and carried his beer out to the balcony.

The apartment complex was located close to the center of town, and from the balcony he could see the lights of the main strip and hear music emanating from that direction. It was Friday night, and there was a significant amount of traffic moving through the area. The town of Elkmont was no bustling metropolis, but it was just big enough to require a decent range of downtown entertainment options. On just about any other weekend night, Brady would be out there on the main drag, having beers with his buddies and hitting on girls at Big Poppa's Place, a popular billiards and dining establishment at the far opposite end of the strip from O'Bannon's.

He knew he should snap out of the mental funk gripping him and start texting his pals to see if anyone wanted to hang out. The question would be only a formality. His buddies *always* wanted to hang out on the weekends. The single ones did, anyway, and because most of his friends cycled in and out of relationships on a frequent basis, enough of the gang was always available to warrant a decent hangout night. Brady himself was unattached and had been for several months. He'd gone on a number of dates during that time, but nothing had clicked in any serious way and he was okay with that. He was young and carefree and content to keep it that way for a while.

He set his beer on the balcony rail and took out his phone. The screen lit up and he saw he had numerous text notifications from Alan Carson and Paul Costa, his two best friends since high school. They were at Big Poppa's and from the obnoxiously profane phrasing of the messages it was clear both already had a few beers under their belts. The texts from Paul included a photo of a big-boobed blonde waitress in a frilly, low-cut top. She was carrying a tray of drinks on an upraised palm and her pretty features were set in an expression of profound non amusement.

The caption accompanying the photo read, "Boobarella doesn't think I'm funny. Maybe because I called her Boobarella."

Brady grimaced.

Paul might have had more than just a few beers already.

He put his phone away and picked up the beer, sipping from it as he resumed staring out at the center of town. On any other Friday night, he'd already be responding to messages like the ones he'd just read and maybe he'd yet do that, but for now he refrained. He couldn't fully quell that restless feeling, and it wasn't long before he fixated again on the encounter with Mr. Kincaid, a broken man he'd met briefly before his downfall.

This inevitably led to sifting through memories of his senior year at Elkmont High, in particular those involving Lara Kincaid. They were never close but were always on friendly terms. She thought he was funny, always laughing at the jokes he made in class, the same ones that made the snooty cheerleader types roll their eyes. He lusted after her, of course. How could he not?

One day when Lara was between boyfriends, she stopped him in the parking lot after school and asked him to go to a movie with her that night. After he got over the shock of being asked out by his greatest crush, he accepted the invitation, declining obviously not being an option.

While driving out to see the movie later, she told him, "This isn't gonna be anything serious. We're just gonna have a little fun, okay? We might fuck, though."

That last bit rendered him temporarily speechless. She laughed at the look on his face, enjoying his inability to play it cool. This made him blush and she laughed about that too, but he couldn't help it. He'd still been a virgin at that point and had never had a girl proposition him in such a blunt fashion.

The two hours they spent in the theater turned into a prolonged hot and steamy make out session. After the movie, Lara drove them out to her preferred private spot for amorous activities and relieved him of his virginity in the backseat of her Chevy Nova. It was perhaps the most significant milestone event of his life up to that point, one that left him happy and emotionally overwhelmed, but it wasn't the memory of his symbolic passage into manhood that caused his mind to drift back to that momentous night. It was, instead, his memory of the spot she'd chosen.

Millhaven Road.

Right in front of the notorious Dead End House.

In the months after her disappearance, he had the opportunity to consult with several of her numerous other lovers and it wasn't long before he realized she'd taken nearly all of them there at least once.

Nothing weird or suspicious happened the night he was there with Lara, but he recalled with great clarity how supremely creeped out the place made him feel. He'd begged her to take them to some other spot, virtually anywhere else in Elkmont that didn't happen to be the location of the town's most infamous murder spree.

Lara refused.

She taunted and teased him, distracted him by beginning to re-move items of her clothing before climbing into the Nova's backseat. The temptation of her luscious bare flesh was all he needed to over-come his trepidation, prompting him to climb into the backseat with her.

Brady thought about Dead End House a lot the first year after high school. There was so much about the disappearance of Lara and that boy she'd been seeing that never added up as far as he was con-cerned. The cops found her abandoned Nova in the parking lot of a grocery store, where it'd apparently been left at some point during the overnight hours. The back window was smashed out and there was blood all over the backseat. The boyfriend's blood, it was later deter-mined. Not a drop of it belonged to Lara.

No other trace of either of them was ever discovered.

People in Elkmont had a lot of wild theories about what might have happened. A few even suggested Lara had killed the boy after some heated lover's spat and had skipped town to start a new life somewhere else. To this day there were people who believed that bullshit. It pissed Brady off. Lara was wild in certain ways, true, but she wasn't evil or violent. He figured what had actually happened was obvious. Some unknown person or persons had attacked Lara and the guy at some other location and had dropped off the Nova at the grocery store to throw off investigators, a tactic that seemed to have worked perfectly because no arrests had ever been made in the case.

Brady went back inside and into the kitchen. He dropped the empty beer can in the trash and took out his phone again, seeing he had several more texts from his inebriated friends, as well as three missed calls. Paul had left a three-minute voicemail. Drunken ram-bling, probably. He'd been ignorant of all of it since his phone was on silent. The thought of responding to any of it felt like more than he wanted to deal with just then.

He put the phone back in his pocket and thought about grabbing another beer from the fridge.

Then a glimpse of something from the corner of his eye drew his attention to the stack of missing persons flyers Kincaid had spilled all over the sidewalk earlier. He'd brought them home with him, with the vague thought of either returning them to Kincaid or putting them up himself at some point. They were on his countertop next to the microwave.

He picked up the one at the top of the stack and stared at the black-and-white image of Lara's face for more than a minute before coming to an impulsive decision. The question of how to spend his Friday night had been resolved, albeit in an unexpected way. After grabbing his wallet and keys, he headed out of the apartment and got in his car.

He was going for a drive.

His destination was a place he'd last seen in person over five years ago.

FIVE

MILLHAVEN ROAD WAS, BY ALL outward appearances, a desolate and abandoned place. The houses there showed more outward signs of decay and neglect with each passing year. The two that faced each other from opposite sides of the short street had overgrown lawns and were partly covered by vines. One had a large hole in its gable roof. Dead End House was different. Its patchy front lawn was almost entirely devoid of grass and no creeping greenery was attempting to overtake the structure. This contrast with its nearest neighbors was so striking it significantly enhanced the long-standing impression among locals of the dead end as a blighted place, one shunned by nature due to the unspeakable evils committed there years ago.

People who lived nearby almost never ventured into the area. Rumors of remnants of Crazy Calvin's deranged family still inhabiting Dead End House continued to circulate. Many who lived in houses on the closest adjacent streets believed the stories to be true. Even if this wasn't the case, the belief that the place was infused with some form of supernatural evil was prevalent in the community. Some had even voiced the opinion that the place should be burned to the ground, perhaps under the cover of night by a group of courageous and civic-minded people armed with gas cans and shotguns.

Thus far, however, no one had ever quite been brave enough to make it happen.

That long ingrained fear of Dead End House itself, and whatever might yet lurk inside it, was still too great.

Friday night, while Brady Whitford was still ruminating about the past in his downtown apartment, a green Range Rover turned down Millhaven and roared straight toward the dead end, blaring loud rock music recorded decades before the birth of its occupants. The music continued to play for a few seconds longer as the vehicle came to a screeching halt right at the edge of the barren lawn in front of Dead End House. The driver then cut the engine off, abruptly silencing Dead Moon's "Walking on My Grave."

The two young women in the Range Rover were identical twin sisters in their early twenties. Their given names were Alicia and Patricia Fullerton, but they were better known as Lexie and Trixie, the TrikTok Twins. Trik, as they were fond of saying, as in the Tricksy side of TikTok, where every day was Halloween. They looked exactly alike with one notable difference, even dressing similarly in ripped fishnets, tight little miniskirts, ankle boots, and midriff-exposing tops. The one way anyone not close to them was able to tell them apart was their hair. Lexie was blonde and her sister had spent the last year dyeing her hair a blatantly artificial shade of bright red.

The deliberately slutty attire was donned only when they intended to record TrikTok Twins material, as was the case tonight. They otherwise kept a low public profile, keeping their hair pinned up under hats and dressing in a more conservative fashion. This was due to the surging popularity of their shared account, which had recently passed the half-million followers mark. It wasn't unusual for them to get recognized when in full TrikTok regalia, and they did everything in their power to keep that to a minimum. There were a lot of creepy dudes out there, many without any functional sense of personal boundaries.

Trixie was in the Range Rover's front passenger seat. She held her phone in front of her face and summoned her trademark sneering smile as she started a recording. "Hey, guys! I'm Trixie."

She turned the phone toward her sister, who sneeringly mugged for the camera while throwing up a metal horns hand sign. "And I'm

Lexie, motherfuckers!"

Lexie cackled in the unhinged, theatrical way familiar to their legions of loyal viewers.

Trixie turned the phone back in her direction. "And tonight we have a special treat for you. Your favorite crazy fucking bitches have traveled a long way from home, all the way out to a little town called Elkmont in the middle of motherfucking nowhere."

Lexie, still off-camera, unleashed another loud cackle.

"And let me tell you fuckers something," Trixie continued, her usual on-camera perma-sneer becoming even more pronounced than usual. "This town is the fucking pits. It's a backwards-ass cesspool filled with ugly, inbred motherfuckers, a disgusting shit stain at basically the ass-end of the universe. So why are we here?"

She again pointed the phone at Lexie.

Her sister shifted excitedly behind the steering wheel. "The deal is that we've already taken you to a lot of this fucked up country's most infamous murder sites. You loved our Bundy and Dahmer tours and dug the fuck out of our Manson clips. But that shit's been done and done a million fucking times, so sometimes we like to take you down these less traveled roads and show you some shit you don't already know about. Fucked up true crime shit has happened just about everywhere in this wasteland called the USA, and some of the worst of it has gone down in places you've never fucking heard of. Places like . . ."

She trailed off for dramatic effect.

Then she turned her face away from the camera to gaze out through the windshield.

Trixie put her phone out the window and said, "Dead End House."

Her sister put on the Range Rover's high beams, illuminating the front of the decrepit old house well enough to get a decent on-camera shot of the structure. They had a lighting rig they would use once they breached the interior of the house, but a murkier first long-range view would serve as an effectively creepy tone-setter for the segment they were recording.

It'd be different if they were doing a live video, in which case they would have gotten in close with the lighting rig deployed before beginning the segment, but the TrikTok Twins didn't do live shoots much anymore. They'd done it often in the early days of perfecting their schtick, but there was too much that could go wrong. Now they preferred to get the footage they needed and then edit it down in a professional way. This allowed them to cut out or drastically shorten all the boring extended shots of them walking around in the dark in abandoned places with nothing exciting happening.

Trixie brought her hand back inside the vehicle and paused the recording. "Do you ever think we're going too far with some of this shit?" She had a look of introspective contemplation on her face, and her tone was somewhere around ninety-eight percent less manic now that she was no longer playing to the camera. "Like, is it messed up to act so excited about seeing places where real people died in horrible ways?"

Lexie shrugged. "Of course I think about that. It's not like I'm some kind of monster incapable of empathy, but at the end of the day, we're mostly talking about people who snuffed it a long time ago. Nothing we say or do changes the fact that they're gone or that they suffered."

Trixie smiled. "Good point. Okay, I feel better. You ready?"

"Yep. Let's do this. I just hope this place isn't too nasty inside."

They gathered the things they needed and a few moments later they were out of the vehicle and trudging their way across the patchy front lawn, never for a moment considering the possibility that someone hidden might be watching them.

Someone lurking inside Dead End House.

SIX

SHIVERING IN A BACK CORNER of the cage with her knees pulled up to her chest, Melissa Cavanaugh was consumed with misery and tortured by a nerve-shredding sense of dread about what might happen to her next. Less than a full day had elapsed since her abduction by the gangly weirdo at the carnival, but after all the horrors she'd endured in the hours since then, her relatively carefree life prior to being taken already felt like an eternity ago.

The carnival was one of those seedy traveling affairs operated by shady individuals with lots of missing teeth, piercings virtually everywhere, and bodies adorned with a profusion of obvious jailhouse tattoos. She had ink of her own, but it was all beautiful work of vastly superior quality done by real artists. Body modification as a concept wasn't something she was judgmental about by any means, but it was different with this particular batch of carnies. Their modifications made them look dangerous and filled her with an instinctive unease, but she'd pushed back against that gut feeling, urging herself to just relax and have a good time. She wished like hell she'd trusted her instincts.

The deranged girl who'd forced her into the cage at the point of some form of sharp implement kept giggling and poking at her with the tip of the knife (or whatever it was). She felt multiple small dots of blood oozing out of the tiny holes the repeated jabs created in her bare flesh. Though she couldn't see the girl in the perfect blackness of the basement, she had the sense she was sitting cross-legged in front of her only a foot or two away. She also didn't need to see the girl's face to clearly picture the crazy grin she was likely sporting while tormenting her.

She was trapped in what might as well be Hell itself with this lunatic and there was no way out, and it was all because she'd made the foolish mistake of going off by herself in search of a bathroom after more than an hour of drunkenly stumbling about on the packed carnival midway with her equally drunken friends.

In a crowd that dense, she figured she'd be safe getting temporarily separated from her friends. She was convinced no one would try anything too egregious in the presence of so many potential witnesses, but she got lost and became disoriented. The feeling worsened as she started to get sick from a combination of the stifling heat and too much alcohol. She began to feel suffocated and paranoid, and when she spied a narrow alley-like opening between carnival tents, she slipped into it and kept going until she'd put some distance between herself and the crowd.

It was when she stepped out into an open area behind the tents that the gangly man with the pitted face grabbed her and held her tight as he slapped a hand over her face. An instant jolt of intense terror cut through the cloud of inebriation and sickness. She screamed, but the sound was muffled by the big, strong hand clamped tight over her face. There was so much noise from the midway that her scream might not have been heard anyway. She flailed and kicked and scratched at the man who'd grabbed her, but none of it had any effect on him. He started carrying her deeper into the dark night, away from the midway and away from the tents.

Soon they came to a place where some of the dangerous looking carnies were hanging out near a dilapidated bunkhouse trailer. She screamed again when she saw them and reached out to them in desperation, waving her hands around, but none of the carnies made any move to come to her aid. They were drinking and showed no apparent concern for her plight. Some even laughed as the gangly man walked by them. She was shocked, unable to believe they could give so little of a shit about the dire situation of a woman in obvious danger.

The gangly man got tired of her thrashing and swept her off her feet, cradling her tight against his chest as he continued carrying her away from the carnival grounds. She twisted her head about and saw a distant parking area filled with cars, but they weren't headed in that direction. He carried her into a nearby stand of trees and her state of terror skyrocketed as the carnival disappeared from view. She thought of her friends back there, still wandering about on the midway, having fun and totally oblivious of her abduction. She started crying then and in response the gangly man snorted in a piggish fashion, amused by her distress.

Eventually they emerged from the woods and the gangly man approached a nondescript brown van parked at the side of the road. The van was a boxy kind, of an obvious 1970s vintage. As they neared the vehicle, the side door came open and a slender young woman with pasty pale skin emerged. She had lank and greasy long brown hair and stood barefoot at the side of the road in a dirty white dress.

The girl smiled when they got close, exposing a mouthful of black and yellow rotting teeth. "Oh shit, Calvin, you got a good one this time. She's so pretty."

The man she called Calvin responded with more of those piggish snorts of amusement.

The girl, as she would learn soon enough, was called Ursula.

She was Calvin's sister.

She tried appealing to the girl on the basis of being another woman, but Melissa would also soon learn the pointlessness of that. The gangly man was a monster, a thing he later proved beyond a doubt, but if anything, his sister was even worse. They brought her to Dead End House and once they were all safely hidden away inside, they went to work on her, violating and torturing her in just about every way imaginable over a long period of time. And now that they were done with her, at least for now, they'd tossed her down into the basement with this other horrible, wretched creature.

Every time the deceitful bitch poked at her, she cringed and tried twisting away from the sharp point of the knife, but there was nowhere to go, no place to which she could safely retreat. Turning one way put her face against a side of the cage, while twisting the other way put her in direct physical contact with the corpse curled up at the back of the cage. She shivered in deep repulsion each time those moments of contact occurred. The corpse had a strong musty smell but not the putrid stench of relatively recent death and decay, leading her to suspect the person had been deceased for quite some time, long enough to become desiccated. Because of the blackness enveloping them, she had no way of knowing with certainty the gender of the crazy girl's deceased companion. Gut instinct, however, told her the deceased was another girl or young woman.

The next time the crazy girl reached out to her it was to tweak one of Melissa's nipples, pinching it between thumb and forefinger and giving it a hard twist. The girl tittered at the yelp of pain this elicited. She did it again, giving the nipple a more savage twist this time. She growled in annoyance when Melissa tried swatting her hand away. This was followed by another jab of the knife, and this time the weapon penetrated her flesh more deeply than before. This resulted in a greater level of pain but also provided insight. The girl's weapon was a makeshift device, something fashioned by hand and not made of metal.

The crazy girl maintained a tight grip on whatever the implement was while keeping the pointed end embedded in Melissa's flesh. "Don't you fight me when I'm having my fun." The girl was leaning much closer now, close enough to feel the spittle flying from her mouth. She gave the sharp end of her weapon a twist. "You hear me?"

Melissa screamed through gritted teeth.

The pain wasn't the worst she'd experienced since being abducted, but it was bad enough. The unknown weapon slid in a little more, to a depth of perhaps a full inch inside her flesh just beneath the rib cage. Melissa screeched through her clenched teeth again and then screeched another time as the crazy girl gave the thing another twist.

The girl laughed at her sounds of agony.

Then she leaned closer still and licked her face.

Melissa shuddered in instinctive repulsion at the sensation of the trail of slimy wetness rising from her jawline up to an eye socket. She again tried twisting her head away, but as always, the gesture provided little in the way of actual relief. The girl just pressed in tighter against her and licked her face several more times, giggling with each useless twist of her prisoner's head. Melissa sniffled and begged the girl to stop.

DEAD END HOUSE

The girl withdrew the sharp thing from the spot below her rib cage, causing a thin stream of warm blood to trickle down her abdomen. A moment of relief lasting barely more than a full second ensued before the crazy girl shifted her grip on the weapon and jabbed it into her side.

Melissa screamed.

Another jab in the side followed.

And then another one.

More screaming ensued, as did more deranged cackling.

The sounds began to annoy the people upstairs, it seemed, because soon the ceiling above them vibrated from a round of angry floor stomping.

The crazy girl pulled the sharp thing out and nipped playfully at the tip of Melissa's nose. "Want another one?"

Melissa sniffled. "No. Please, no."

Another cackle. "Too bad."

The sharp thing went into her side again.

Melissa unleashed her loudest scream yet, her lungs straining as her throat began to turn raw. This resulted in a lot more stomping from upstairs, as well as a lot of muffled shouting. Someone up there was definitely getting pissed. More than one person, from the sound of it. She'd been told to keep quiet or else when they dumped her in the basement, but she couldn't help it. The pain and psychological torture she was being subjected to was just too much.

And the crazy girl just kept poking at her.

It went on for what seemed like forever, an eternity of miserable torment, until the loudest stomping yet from upstairs was followed by the sound of a door slamming.

The crazy girl sighed in apparent satisfaction and retracted the sharp thing. "Finally. They're coming now."

Melissa wailed in despair.

SEVEN

AFTER LEAVING HIS APARTMENT, BRADY had every intention of immediately heading for the northern outer reaches of Elkmont, the part of town inhabited primarily by the rural poor folk of the area. He hadn't visited the blighted neighborhood where Dead End House was located even once since that long ago night with Lara, but he still had an approximate idea of how to get there. Before setting out, he'd tried looking up the physical address of the house online, but was unable to pull up the information.

He might have been able to find what he was looking for by digging a bit deeper, but he didn't feel it was worth the effort. Elkmont wasn't a big town, and he had no serious worries about finding his way to the right place.

A different complication arose before he could even get clear of the downtown area. He'd pulled to a stop at a red light and was whistling in an absentminded way while checking out the area around the intersection and waiting for the light to change. The whistling came to an abrupt halt as he spied a scruffy looking individual swaying in an alarmingly precarious way at the street corner to his left.

"Oh, shit."

It was Lara's father.

He looked like he was about to fall into the street.

The light changed, red yielding to a bright green orb hanging right in front of him. His foot remained on his car's brake pedal as his gaze returned to Lara's father, who stood right at the edge of the sidewalk, swaying so badly now it was amazing he was still upright.

A blare of horns commenced. Brady pulled up tight to the street corner to his right, creating just enough room in the lane for vehicles backed up behind him to go on by. A few drivers shot angry looks his way. There were some raised middle fingers. He ignored it all, seeing no point in responding in kind. Someone might get riled up enough to pull over and fight with him and he wanted no part of any nonsense like that. He put on his emergency flashers, waited until the lane was clear, and got out of his car.

He hurried across the street and caught Kincaid by a wrist, pulling him back from the edge of the sidewalk. The man's reaction was no less belligerent than it'd been the last time Brady tried to help him. He was much drunker now and he'd been far from sober at that earlier hour. The alcohol fumes that rolled out of his mouth as he wheeled toward Brady hit him with almost a physical force, causing him to gag and stagger backward a step.

The part of the man's face visible above his scraggly beard was a sickly bright red. His head wobbled as he looked at Brady in an unfocused way. "Get your greasy hands offa me, you no good punk ass son of a bitch!"

Brady grimaced. "I'm just trying to help you."

The man spat at him, a high-velocity wad of phlegm and saliva that sailed right by Brady's head, missing him by perhaps an inch. "Fuck you. I don't need your goddamn help." His eyes narrowed to slits and he leaned forward a little, making an effort to see him more clearly. "You're the same punk who had his hands all over me earlier. I'll give you a blow job if that's what you're after, but I won't take less than five bucks for it."

Brady recoiled inwardly at the offer, but somehow managed to maintain an impassive expression, reminding himself this was a sick and broken man. A man who'd suffered a devastating loss and deserved sympathy. While it was true that lots of people suffered loss without spiraling out of control, writing off those incapable of that same level of fortitude or bravery didn't seem right. He'd spent years ignoring this man's desperate condition—just like nearly everyone else in Elkmont—but now he wanted to at least make an effort.

He took out his wallet and extracted a twenty-dollar bill. "I'll give you some money, but not for anything like that."

Kincaid licked his lips and eyed the bill with obvious interest, but a tinge of distrust remained. "I won't take it in the ass. That's where I draw the line."

Brady sighed. "I'm not interested in anything like that either. Just take the money and get yourself something to eat."

Kincaid snatched the bill from his fingers. "Fuck you. I'm gonna get some liquor."

He turned away from Brady and started stumbling back up the sidewalk in the opposite direction.

Some inexplicable impulse caused Brady to call out after him: "I think Lara might still be alive."

That was all he said at first, holding his breath as he watched the man come to an abrupt halt some twenty feet away. The man just stood there with his back to him for several moments, not moving, looking as frozen as an ice sculpture. He stayed like that until Brady exhaled and spoke again.

"Or maybe not, but I don't think she was killed the night she disappeared."

Kincaid remained in that frozen posture a moment longer.

Then he turned slowly around and glared at Brady, his eyes more focused than before. He started walking back up the sidewalk, his hands clenched into tight fists at his sides. "You don't have any right to talk to me about her, you fucking punk. You don't know shit. Are you a detective? Got a badge?"

The man kept coming closer. He was just six feet away now.

Brady tensed, readying for a retreat should one become necessary. "No, sir, I'm not a policeman. I knew your daughter, though. Remember, I told you that earlier?"

Kincaid halted his approach after one more step forward. Deep furrows formed in his brow as he squinted again and studied Brady's face carefully. Then he grunted. "Yeah, I remember. But so fucking what? You're nothing special. You didn't mean a damn thing to her. You were a blip on her timeline. There were dozens of you dumb fuckers. A nonstop parade of assholes. Don't talk to me like you really knew her because you didn't. Ain't none of you fit to speak her name. Come at me again with this bullshit and I'll cut your throat."

Kincaid turned away from him and resumed walking back up the sidewalk in the opposite direction, continuing in a more or less straight line for a half-dozen steps before beginning to stagger again. Brady lingered at the corner a couple moments longer, wondering whether he should ignore the man's threat and persist in trying to help him, but in the end he opted against chasing after him. He felt bad for Kincaid, but there was only so much he could do to help someone so dead set against it.

He waited until the way was clear again and jogged back across the street to his car. Once he was back behind the wheel, he sat there parked at the corner a bit longer, doing some more reflecting instead of immediately pulling back into traffic.

Maybe it was foolish of him to continue wallowing in this sudden fixation on a girl no one had seen in more than five years, someone who, despite what he'd told Kincaid, was probably dead and had been the entire time.

Then an image of Lara smiling as she straddled him in the backseat of her Nova on that long ago night flashed into his head. An image of such startling clarity it took his breath away. For a moment, he could almost feel her thighs clenched tight around him.

Brady started his car and pulled away from the corner. He was determined to see Dead End House again before the night was over, though for what reason he wasn't quite sure. Maybe it was mere nostalgia, but he thought it was more than that. The desire was imbued with an underlying sense of urgency, which was a strange thing. Lara was five years gone. Nothing he did tonight would alter anything about whatever sad fate had befallen her back then.

Recognizing this fact in no way reduced that odd sense of urgency.

If anything, the feeling only intensified.

Brady drove faster.

EIGHT

THEIR INTENT WAS TO RECORD another brief introductory segment before attempting to enter the crumbling old murder house, but the TrikTok Twins had hit a bit of a snag. This segment was to be recorded with one of them standing on the porch while giving a quick rundown on the nature of the crimes that had occurred here. The gist of what would be said had already been rehearsed back at the motel. It was pretty simple, just a recitation of the basic facts to set the tone before going inside. They'd then fill in the gory details while documenting their exploration of the interior. The problem was they were now locked in a heated debate regarding who should deliver this last pre-entry speech.

Lexie was up on the porch, standing with her back to the closed front door. Clutched in her hands was a crowbar they would use to break in once they were done recording this bit, providing whether they were able to get past this bullshit of arguing about who was going to do what.

"I don't get what the issue is here." She scowled at her sister as she slapped the curled end of the crowbar against the open palm of her right hand. "We already went over this at the motel. I wrote the lines and you listened while I rehearsed them. It only makes sense that I say them now."

Trixie rolled her eyes. "You always do this, though."

Lexie made a scoffing sound. "What's that supposed to mean?"

"You just did all that without consulting me first." There was an edge of long repressed bitterness in Trixie's voice. She was still in the yard, standing several feet away from the porch. "You wrote the lines without asking for my input and rehearsed them like it was already decided. It didn't used to be this way. This is starting to feel like less of a real collaboration and it sucks."

Lexie gaped at her in disbelief for a moment. "Are you for real right now? Didn't I just let you start the arrival segment in the car?"

Trixie sneered. "Do you even hear yourself? You *let* me start the segment, huh? I really hope you're just oblivious to how demeaning that sounds, because if not, holy shit, the ingrained level of disrespect you feel for me must be off the fucking charts."

Lexie made a sound of aggrieved, weary impatience. "You're being ridiculous."

Trixie snorted. "Like fuck I am. Gee, thanks for letting me start the first segment, sis. I'm ever so grateful for the token fucking gesture. You did most of the talking again, like always lately. You fucking camera hog. We're supposed to get equal time."

Lexie glared at her from the porch for a tense, silent moment.

Then she stepped down to the yard and snatched her sister's phone away, pushing the crowbar into her hands instead. "This is stupid. I don't want to fight. This is supposed to be fun. You do the dumb segment. I'll record it."

Trixie frowned and glanced at the porch before making reluctant eye contact with her sister. "I'm sorry. I know that came out of nowhere. I should've tried talking it over with you earlier instead of waiting until we were here to make a big deal about it."

Lexie's expression again took on a weary aspect as she shook her head. "No, you were right. I think I got so mad because I knew that. I'm sorry. I've got control issues."

Trixie nodded. "And a giant fucking ego to boot. Just like me. This is why I keep saying we need to hire a camera operator again, someone to take care of the technical end so we can both focus on doing our thing."

"Yeah, you're right," Lexie said, laughing. "Only next time we should hire one we can both be sure we'll never want to fuck because that only complicates the living shit out of everything."

Trixie laughed, too.

At last, something they could agree on. And just like that, the tension between them evaporated. The sisters hugged and exchanged more ardently expressed words of apology. Then they separated and Lexie removed her backpack full of gear and set it on the ground.

Trixie had started up the steps when she heard a muffled but unsettling sound that sent a chill down her spine.

The sound came again.

She took her foot off the bottom step and turned toward her sister with a wide-eyed expression. "Are you hearing that?"

Lexie frowned as her gaze went to the side of the house. "Yeah. What the fuck is it?"

Trixie moved away from the porch to stand near her sister. Both were staring in the same direction now, at the deep darkness beyond the side of the house. The sound came yet again. And again.

Lexie's heart felt like it was slamming against her rib cage. "It sounds like somebody screaming."

They stood there without saying anything for another moment as the sound continued to resonate from somewhere to the rear of the supposedly empty abode. The longer they listened, the less doubt there could be regarding the nature of what they were hearing. Those were definitely screams and the muffled nature of the sound strongly implied they were coming from somewhere inside the structure they'd come here to explore.

Lexie's expression was troubled as she glanced at her sister. "This place *is* abandoned, right?"

Trixie nodded, but she looked uncertain. "I mean, I think so. That was the implication in all the stuff I read online. The people who did all the horrible shit are all dead, in jail, or locked in the loony bin."

The sharpest, loudest scream yet made both of them flinch.

Lexie clutched her sister's phone tighter and wondered aloud whether she should call 911. The only reason she hadn't yet was knowing what summoning the police to the scene would mean for them. Their original plans for the episode would have to be scrapped, which would be a shame because they'd invested a significant amount of time and money in traveling far from their home base of

Minneapolis to visit this rural pit of southern hell. That was without even taking into consideration all the research that had gone into selecting this place over dozens of other true crime location candidates.

The screaming continued as they fretted over it.

Trixie groaned. "We have to do the right thing here, I guess. The responsible thing. I mean ... unless ... well, what if somebody in there is watching a horror movie?"

Lexie's expression turned thoughtful. "Hmm, the way it's kind of going on and on does make me think of *The Texas Chainsaw Massacre*. Maybe that's Marilyn Burns we're hearing cranked up really high on a kickass surround sound system."

Neither of them really believed this. The lack of an accompanying chainsaw roar alone took the wind out of the theory, which was unfortunate because it would have been nice to believe in such a benign explanation for what they were hearing.

Trixie grimaced. "That's not a fucking movie. Something bad is happening to somebody in there and we should probably get the hell out of here before it starts happening to *us*. We can call 911 as soon as this place is in our rearview mirror."

Lexie didn't reply right away. Her features still had that contemplative cast and her gaze was still glued to the dark area beyond the side of the house. She almost looked like she was in a trance. Then an abrupt change came over her face, determination displacing uncertainty. She handed the phone back to her sister and snatched her backpack off the ground, carrying it by the strap as she began to move swiftly toward the side of the house.

Trixie gasped and stared at her sister's back in shock before hurrying to catch up. "What the fuck are you doing? Are you crazy?" She spoke in an urgent tone while striving not to raise her voice, belatedly worrying about attracting the attention of whoever was in the house. "Goddammit, are you listening to me? Stop right now. We have to fucking *leave*."

They rounded the corner and proceeded along the side of the house together, Trixie working hard to keep up despite her burgeoning desire to be moving rapidly in the opposite direction.

"Goddammit, Lexie, have you lost your mind? What are we doing?"

Lexie came to an abrupt stop once they reached the rear corner of the house. She peeked around the corner a moment before pulling back and meeting her sister's beseeching gaze. "There's an external concrete stairwell going down to a basement or storm cellar. Pretty sure the screaming is coming from down there."

Trixie snorted disdainfully. "So the fuck what? If you think you're gonna attempt a rescue, think again. I'll tackle you and drag your skinny ass out of here first. This is a job for SWAT, not a fucking internet personality."

Lexie surprised her with an eager, excited grin. "Don't you get it? This could be the opportunity of a lifetime. Call 911 and tell them someone is being murdered. That'll get the cops out here fast. Then start recording me as soon as you're done. If the timing works out, we'll get amazing footage and look like badass action movie bitches. And who knows what the cops might find in this place this time. Imagine being the first ones on the scene of another Dahmer type story. It'd be so fucking massive."

Trixie frowned. "Fuck. Oh my God."

Lexie nodded excitedly, smiling now. "Right? Now you're getting it. Go on, summon the pigs."

Before Trixie could make the call, another startlingly loud sound distracted them, an enraged bellowing coming from somewhere inside the house. Though she hadn't realized it on a conscious level until now, it hit her that the person screaming was a woman. A man might sound like that if sufficiently terrified, but in the case of this other sound, there was never any doubt. It was endowed with a deep and thunderous bass quality that made her heart start pounding the instant she heard it. In her experience, there was nothing quite so terrifying as the sound of a truly enraged man.

Another terrifying sound was audible underneath the bellowing, some kind of heavy pounding noise. Someone in there was repeatedly hitting or stomping on something. The sisters locked eyes again, and this time Lexie's expression was lacking its previous avidity.

She looked scared.

"Fuck everything I just said. Let's go."

Trixie felt almost dizzy with relief. Her sister's considerable powers of persuasion had briefly overwhelmed her better judgment, but now she was right back to wanting nothing more than to get away from this place as fast as possible. Anything else was sheer insanity.

The unmistakable sound of a door being thrown open at the back of the house intruded before they could get going, and for a moment, before the door flapped shut again, the thunderous roar of the enraged man could be heard with an even more stomach-curdling level of clarity. Instead of prompting her to finally start running away, a surge of profound morbid curiosity caused Lexie to peek around the corner again.

Trixie experienced the same disorienting mixture of fear and curiosity. She pressed in close against her sister and peeked too.

The first thing she saw was a distorted rectangle of light painted on the ground at the back of the house. This patch of light was on the opposite side of the external stairwell her sister had mentioned. The source of the light was from somewhere inside the house, presumably the kitchen. It was streaming through the windows of a screen door overlooking a small back stoop.

They saw a slender, barefoot woman in a loose white dress descend the steps of the stoop to the ground and storm her way over to the stairwell. The look on her face was one of murderous fury, an impression enhanced by the presence of the machete gripped tight in her right hand. In her other hand was a long silver flashlight.

The screaming from the cellar had tapered off some in the last few moments, but it renewed and rose in volume again as the woman in the white dress began to descend the concrete stairs. Another sound that also seemed to issue from the cellar became audible as the door at the bottom of the stairs was kicked open.

It was the insane cackling of a madwoman.

Trixie clutched at her sister's wrist, pulling her away from the house. There was no time left for debate. Active retreat was the only sensible remaining option. Her sister came willingly and without resistance.

That was good.

What wasn't good was the unexpected obstruction awaiting them once they reemerged into the desolate front yard.

An obstruction in the form of an ugly, gangly man in denim coveralls aiming a double-barreled shotgun at them.

NINE

THE SOUND OF THE BASEMENT door crashing open made Melissa shriek in fearful anticipation of an even greater level of torment to come. The crazy girl giggled and jabbed at her again with the sharp thing. This time the blood-slicked tip went into her hip. There was an audible snap as the implement broke in half with a piece of it still embedded in her flesh.

A faint level of ambient light penetrated the enveloping darkness when the door opened. Not enough to see well, but Melissa was able to discern the shape of the scrawny woman squatting in front of her. The woman's head was turned away from her now and tilted to one side as she listened to the additional crashing sounds of someone blundering their way through the cluttered basement. A bright circle of light appeared in the midst of the darkness as the approaching person snapped on a flashlight. The light got steadily brighter as the person came closer, the beam sweeping jerkily over many discarded pieces of antique furniture, tall and unwieldy stacks of boxes, and piles of assorted junk. As the woman threading her way through the haphazard mess neared them, she hurled a torrent of angry epithets and threats.

Hearing that voice made Melissa whimper and shiver uncontrollably. It belonged to Ursula. She loathed Calvin for the things he'd done to her, but she feared Ursula more. The immediate sexual violations committed by her brother were awful in soul-shattering ways, but they were of short duration. There would be trauma to process later, if she survived, but when Ursula was torturing her, she wasn't sure she even wanted to survive. The cauterized nubs of two amputated fingers and three missing toes were the physical legacy of those initial torture sessions. The prospect of enduring another one so soon afterward felt like more than she could take.

She saw the swirling hem of Ursula's dirty white dress as she stepped around an old steamer trunk and shined the flashlight at the cage. The beam lit up the crazy girl's head and Melissa gasped loudly when she got her first good look at the person who'd been tormenting her. Her mouth was hanging open and she was missing at least half her teeth as well as her entire bottom lip, which left blackened, swollen gums exposed. One of her eyes was gone and in its place was an ugly mass of cauterized flesh. The teeth that remained were yellow and jagged. One side of her scalp was devoid of hair, the skin badly scarred from burns. Lank, dirty blonde hair grew from the other side of her scalp and hung to her bony shoulder. Her jaw looked slightly out of alignment, as if it'd been broken and left to heal without being properly set. She was missing multiple fingers and toes, something they had in common now, though her digits appeared to have been removed much longer ago. Much of her body was covered in other scarring and in huge and splotchy purple bruises.

Sensing the scrutiny, the crazy girl looked at her and tittered. "You want me now, don't you?"

Melissa felt bile rise into her throat. Even the vaguest thought of physical intimacy with this pitiful wreck of a human being made her sick to her stomach. The worst thing was knowing this hideous thing was the end-stage result of a process that was just beginning for her. If she couldn't either escape or somehow take her own life, there would be no avoiding it.

Ursula kicked the front of the cage and screamed at them, calling them worthless little slag bitches for causing such a disturbance. Words of apology gushed unbidden from Melissa's mouth, hot tears flowing ceaselessly from her eyes as she tried to explain how the crazy girl forced her to scream by stabbing her with something over and over.

The flashlight beam shifted as Ursula leaned over the top of the cage and directed the light at Melissa, who was again pressed tightly into the rear corner with her legs pulled up to her chest and her arms wrapped over her knees. "Drop those hands and stretch out those legs. Let me see what she's done."

The crazy girl tittered again as she looked back and forth between them, but she said nothing.

Melissa sniffled and continued to tremble and did as she'd been told. The circle of light above the cage shifted again, the beam playing slowly over her violated flesh. "You're all bloody."

A helpless whine escaped Melissa's lips. "I told you, she wouldn't stop stabbing me with something." She shifted around on her ass, turning her hip outward. "It broke off in me the last time."

The tips of Ursula's long brown hair dangled through the slats at the top of the cage as she bent even closer. "Goddammit, Wormie, look what you fucking did. How many times have I told you not to do anything to them until I say you can?"

The crazy girl looked up at her, her upper lip—the only one she had—twitching in a reflexive sneer. "That ain't no fun, though. They're all used up by the time you say I can play with them."

Ursula slapped the top of the cage, making it rattle. "That don't matter none. You get scraps, that's all. You aren't fit for anything else. You know that."

Wormie reached up with a trembling hand, her fingers brushing the dangling tips of Ursula's hair. "Remember when I was your favorite? Remember the things we used to do together, how I could make you scream?"

Ursula made a sound of disgust. "Those days are gone. You're too ugly now. You're fucking repulsive. You know that, right?"

A tear trickled from a corner of Wormie's eye. "I miss you. It gets so lonely down here in the dark."

Ursula laughed. "Tough shit. That's fresh meat you've taken liberties with. You know better. There's a price to pay for that, something else you already fucking well know."

The long blade of a machete abruptly jabbed in through the slats at the top of the cage, slamming into Wormie's open, upraised mouth. There was a crunch followed by a wet, squelching sound as the machete pierced the back of her throat. Wormie gagged and gurgled and clutched at the blade, but it was no use. Ursula set the flashlight atop the cage and gripped the machete's handle with both hands, shoving down again with twice the level of force. Blood gushed from the corners of Wormie's mouth, spilling in twin crimson streams down the twitching front of her emaciated body.

Melissa whined as she again pressed herself into the corner and watched helplessly as the brutal act of murder occurred a few feet away. She closed her eyes and waited for the horror to end, keeping them shut while Ursula worked the machete free with a series of grunts. When the blade at last came loose, the fresh corpse fell over on her, making her shriek in disgust.

Ursula laughed as she again directed the flashlight beam at Melissa's tear-streaked face. "Kiss her."

Melissa had been in the act of shoving the body away from her as Ursula uttered these words. Now her face contorted in confusion as she looked up at Calvin's demented sister. "Wh-what?"

More evil laughter from Ursula. "You heard me. I'm leaving her in there with you. Pull her into your arms and kiss her on the mouth. Make out with her. She's your new girlfriend." The laughter abruptly ceased and her tone became harsh. "I'm serious. Do it. If you don't, I'll hurt you way worse than I have so far. You know I'm not lying."

Melissa's body shook with sobs.

That was the bitch of it, the evil hook already embedded deep in her battered psyche. Things could always get worse thanks to Ursula's relentlessly cruel and creatively sick imagination. She didn't want to do this obscene, repulsive thing, but she had no choice.

She shifted around and grabbed hold of Wormie's corpse, grunting and struggling in the tight confines of the cage as she pulled it into her arms. Then, once she had the dead woman wrapped up in a necrophiliac mockery of a lover's embrace, she pressed her trembling lips against the ruined mouth and fought hard against the urge to recoil. More tears spilled from her eyes as she tasted blood that was still wet and warm. She whimpered and forced herself to keep her lips pressed to the dead woman's mouth for several more seconds, hoping that would be long enough to appease Ursula.

It was not.

The instant she broke off the kiss, the blade of the machete again punched in through the slats at the top of the cage. This time the edge of the blade sliced a bloody trench down the side of her right arm, a wound that stretched from her shoulder down to her elbow. It wasn't a deep slice, but it was plenty painful. She screeched and Ursula matched her volume with a shrill scream. The scream was followed by a renewed volley of threats, along with a demand for silence. She was warned that if she screamed even one more time without fulfilling her obligations, she'd be pulled out of the cage and punished in the most horrible way she could imagine.

Ursula thrust the blade in through the cage slats again and rattled it around, forcing Melissa to flinch away from it several times.

"Stop. Please, please stop. I'm begging you."

"Are you going to be quiet now and do as you're told?"

Melissa nodded rapidly, trembling with pitiful eagerness. "Yes, yes, yes, I promise!"

Ursula grunted. "I hope you mean that. If you don't, I'll fuck you in the cunt with my machete. I'll fuck you hard and deep, make you take every inch. Do you want that?"

Melissa whimpered. "No."

"Then cease your blubbering and start kissing Wormie again." Ursula leaned closer, shifting the flashlight so that the beam illuminated her own face. The visage looking down at her was hard and unforgiving, filled with an unreasoning hatred. "I told you to make out with her. I want to see you give her some tongue."

Melissa felt queasy at the thought of sliding her tongue into the dead woman's mouth, but she would have to do it. No other acceptable option existed because she knew that Calvin's sister did not make idle threats. If she failed to do anything other than what she'd been told, Ursula would drag her out of the cage. Melissa would fight against her, of course, but she was in a weakened condition and in the end Ursula would subdue her and then proceed to violate her body in exactly the way she'd described.

She pulled Wormie close again and slid her tongue into the dead woman's mouth. Making out with her was the task she'd been assigned, and she shunted aside the instinctive repulsion this spurred within her and did exactly that. She tilted her head and pressed her lips harder against Wormie's mouth, making wet, smacking sounds as she continued to probe the bloody interior of the mouth with her tongue. The dead lump of Wormie's unmoving tongue sent more tremors of revulsion through her every time she touched it, but somehow she continued, forcing herself to feign sounds of arousal. They sounded little different from the real sounds of arousal Ursula was making as she stood at the side of the cage with the hem of her dress hiked up and a hand thrust between her legs.

TEN

BRADY DROVE THE REST OF the way out to Millhaven Road in silence. He was still too lost in introspection and memories of the past to cope with the distraction of music and voices on the radio. His head felt cluttered enough without filling it with additional noise.

He also spent some of that time questioning what he was doing. His desire to see Dead End House had its roots in a notion he'd harbored since shortly after Lara's disappearance. The generally accepted view was Lara and her boyfriend were murdered at another location before the unknown killer dropped her Nova off at the grocery store.

Well . . . what if that other location was Dead End House?

She'd gone out there often with many of her other beaus. This was a known, established fact. Another established fact was that many years ago some really horrible things happened in that house. In his opinion, the notion that members of the murderous Wilcox clan might still reside in the supposedly abandoned house wasn't so preposterous that it didn't at least warrant some cursory level of investigation.

Even if Crazy Calvin's surviving kin could all be accounted for and dismissed as valid suspects for whatever reason—too old and feeble, incarcerated, or dead—that didn't preclude the possibility of someone else sinister living in Dead End House. Many of history's most notorious serial killers had ardent admirers every bit as devoted as the fans of rock musicians and movie stars. Despite not being as widely known as Dahmer or Bundy, Calvin was no different in that regard. There was ample proof of this on the internet. So maybe one or more of his more unbalanced fans were squatting in the old Wilcox homestead, demonstrating their devotion by maintaining the legacy of horror and evil.

He'd gone to the cops at the time and told them all about his nagging suspicion that the house was somehow connected to Lara's disappearance. The detective he spoke to laughed at him and strongly insinuated he was a crackpot, a dumb kid with an overactive imagination that came from watching too many horror movies. Brady persisted and tried taking the matter higher up the ladder of authority.

The tactic didn't work.

One day on the way to his old job at the pizza parlor—this was the summer after high school graduation—he was pulled over by a couple of cops in an unmarked cruiser. They handcuffed him and put him in the back of their car. He was freaked out because he hadn't been speeding and had never been in any trouble with the law. Then, as they took him on a long, silent drive out to a secluded pier at the lake, it came to him that this had something to do with pestering the detectives about Lara and Dead End House.

The cops in the front of the cruiser were not the detectives he'd talked to at the station. They steadfastly refused to respond to his questions. By the time they pulled into the little parking area adjacent to the pier and stopped there, he was close to convinced they meant to put a bullet in his head and dump him in the water. The men sitting up front sat there and stared out at the lake for at least ten minutes in absolute silence. That time spent trapped in the back of the cruiser still counted as by far the most terrifying experience of his life.

Then, at long last, the cop in the passenger seat broke the silence, speaking without looking back at him. "People in this town like to gossip and spread stories. Wild, unfounded stories that only make our jobs harder than they already are. Dead End House is empty and has been for a long time. You're not going to bother us with your harebrained ideas ever again. Matter of fact, you'll never share your theories with anyone at all. Isn't that right?"

There was no option other than total acquiescence. He was just a kid in way over his head. He told them what they wanted to hear, and they took him back to his car, dropping him off and driving away without uttering another word.

Brady never told anyone about the incident and he never spoke of Lara again in connection with Dead End House. Thoughts of it preoccupied him to the point of obsession at times, the way existing in the aftermath of any traumatic experience can preoccupy a person. Then time passed. Years went by and slowly the terror of that day at the pier faded, along with the indignation he'd felt. After half a decade, he'd gotten to a point where he barely thought about any of it anymore. He'd pushed the matter from his head, suppressing it with effective deliberateness.

Until today.

He was still lost in his memories when he turned down Millhaven Road and drove up the short street toward Dead End House. In a neighborhood designed with a keener sense of aesthetics, a closed-end street would culminate in a cul-de-sac, a wide circle with a concrete curb that would make it easy for lost motorists to turn around in a wide loop and head back the way they'd come. This street was not like that. It was a straight lane that merely came to an abrupt end at the edge of the ugly, desolate front lawn of Dead End House. There wasn't even a driveway, a detail he remembered from his one previous visit to this place five years ago. He supposed that back in Calvin's day visitors or people who lived here parked either in the yard or in the street.

The driver of the green Range Rover had chosen the latter option.

Brady stomped on the brake the instant his headlights lit up the back of the other vehicle. He sat there staring—mouth agape—at it for a few moments, his hands tightly gripping the steering wheel as his mind worked to process what he was seeing. Someone else had arrived here ahead of him. That much was obvious, unless the Range Rover was a stolen or abandoned vehicle. According to official records, no one had lived on this street in many years. It was feasible that a ditched car could remain here for a considerable period of time without being noticed or reported, but the pristine outward appearance of the SUV meant the odds of it being an abandoned junker were virtually nil.

DEAD END HOUSE

The more likely explanation was whoever owned the Range Rover had driven it here for the express purpose of visiting Dead End House. He leaned forward and squinted at the Minnesota license plate. The northern state was a considerable distance from Elkmont, several hundred miles at least, which made the SUV's presence here even harder to understand. He hadn't expected to encounter anyone else here, much less anyone from so far away.

Then again, in another sense, perhaps it wasn't so strange a thing after all. Locals mostly shunned this place, even those living in the populated adjacent areas. This was considered tainted ground by many, even among that segment of the citizenry that wasn't superstitious about other things. Haunted if not hallowed ground. Some said the ghosts of Calvin's victims walked this street at night. Brady didn't believe that, but he did believe that precious few people who lived in Elkmont would ever voluntarily set foot here, especially at night.

But someone from far away—someone thus not overly burdened with the weight of local history and emotion—likely wouldn't harbor similar fears or feel that same hesitation. And the story of Calvin Wilcox and his murderous kin was far from unknown outside the local area.

There'd been no movies made about the local boogeyman's exploits, no multi-part prestige documentaries produced for Netflix or HBO, but it'd all been documented extensively on various true crime websites, as well as by YouTubers and podcasters. It was entirely possible a true crime aficionado (or aficionados) on a long road trip had decided, what the hell, while we're passing through here, let's take a detour and check this place out.

A few minutes had passed since Brady's arrival on Millhaven Road, and he was still mired in indecision about what to do. The impulse to back up, turn around, and head back toward town strongly tempted him. His theory about out-of-state interlopers was plausible enough on the surface, but it was only a theory. It remained possible that the driver of the Range Rover was up to something shady. Something dangerous.

Like dumping a body in the abandoned murder house.

Unlikely, sure, but that didn't matter much to a guy sitting alone in his car in the dark on a dead end street, circumstances conducive to shattering rationality in favor of illogic and flights of morbid fancy.

Brady sighed.

Goddammit. Fuck it. I'm outta here.

He felt deeply annoyed with himself. The sense that this had been a fool's errand from the start became overwhelming. What was he even thinking? He was no genius amateur detective or anything remotely like that. He wasn't going to solve the mystery of Lara's disappearance by snooping around the grounds of a crumbling old house. No, what he needed to do was join his friends at Big Poppa's, have a bunch of beers, and shove all his troubling ideas about the past into some deep, dark corner of his mind, abandoning them there forever.

His right hand went to his gear shifter, but before he could put the car in reverse, a sharp, piercing sound cut through the stillness of the night. His hand tightened on the knob of the shifter as he sat there and waited to hear the sound again, barely aware he was trembling the whole time as at least a full minute elapsed. The trembling subsided slightly as another minute passed.

The sound did not repeat.

He took his hand off the shifter and let out a breath. He tried replaying that sharp, piercing sound in his head and asked himself whether that was really a scream he'd heard or something else. He wanted to believe it was anything else, perhaps the shrill caw of some large bird, something misinterpreted by his frayed nerves and overdriven imagination.

That seemed the most likely explanation, but even if that was a scream he'd heard, what did it really mean?

Someone out there might be screwing around.

It might have been a loud cry of passion.

But it might also have been something else. Something far worse.

He was overcome by impulse again, this time in the opposite direction. An impulse driven by the memory of his run-ins with Lara's broken father today as well as by a rebellion against cowardice. He was tired of turning away in the face of things that seemed scary or dangerous, tired of being haunted by Lara's face in his dreams.

He left the engine on as he got out of his car, the better to facilitate a quicker escape should it become necessary. After letting out a big breath, he took a tentative first step in the direction of the Range Rover. This thing he was doing wasn't something he thought of as courageous because there was no visible evidence of anything truly amiss here. This was just a case of him acting on a powerful compulsion, one he needed to purge from his system before he could move on. More than likely it'd soon be revealed as a pointless gesture. He nonetheless vowed to himself he would bolt at the first sign of real danger.

More annoyed with himself than ever, he abandoned the slow, cautious approach in favor of expediency. He hurried forward and put his face against the Range Rover's back window, squinting into the vehicle's dark interior. The lack of functioning street lamps made it difficult to know for certain without opening the vehicle, but there didn't seem to be anyone inside it. He could make out the shapes of seats and headrests, but no shadowy outlines of bodies, an impression reinforced as he circled the vehicle and peered in through the other windows.

There was no one in the Range Rover.

The dashboard was dark, but the hood felt warm when he touched it. Whether this indicated recent engine operation was hard to say. It'd been another middle of July scorcher today, and the nighttime temperature was still a shade south of ninety degrees Fahrenheit. If the vehicle had been parked here all day, the hood would feel like this.

He tried the front driver's side door.

It was locked. So were the rest of them.

Done with his examination of the Range Rover, he moved to the edge of the yard and stared at Dead End House. It looked as dark and foreboding as he remembered from that night with Lara. No lights burned in any of the windows, which was a relief in more ways than one. Seeing a light on in there would have been kind of terrifying, despite offering confirmation of his long-held suspicions about the place. That sense of relief deepened as he stood there and stared at the dilapidated old house, which was literally falling apart in places and clearly was no longer fit for human habitation.

He shook his head and laughed softly, amused now by the storm of conflicting emotions that had held him here for the last several minutes. The cops he'd labeled as incompetent assholes years ago had been right all along. It was a humbling and slightly uncomfortable truth, but one he'd needed to face. He was glad he'd come here tonight. Maybe now he could finally let it all go and purge those old ghosts from his subconscious.

He was smiling as he turned away from Dead End House and began walking briskly back in the direction of his car. His newly carefree mood lasted until the moment he moved past the rear of the Range Rover. He glimpsed the man who'd been lurking, crouched down there in his peripheral vision an instant too late, dumb instinct causing him to turn toward the flash of movement instead of running away.

It all happened too fast.

There was no time to prepare himself for conflict or react in any effective defensive manner. There wasn't even time to think about where his assailant had come from or how he'd been able to maneuver into this position with such tremendous stealth.

The axe chopped through Brady Whitmore's neck with the ease of a butcher knife cutting a stalk of celery. His head came free of his body and went flying away from it, eventually landing against the windshield on the hood of his car. His brain continued to work a few seconds longer, allowing him to bear witness to the horror of his headless body briefly remaining upright as his hands clutched uselessly at the air while blood shot up in a fountain from the stump of his neck.

Then he saw the big, gangly man in denim coveralls as his body toppled forward.

It was Crazy Calvin himself.

Which made no sense, because the murdering motherfucker was supposed to be locked up in a state mental hospital a hundred miles away, but there was no time left to theorize or consider the implications of that.

For Brady, it was all over.

ELEVEN

THEY COULD HEAR HIM STOMPING around and bellowing insensibly, but the big man was no longer in the living room with them. He was restless, roaming all over the decrepit house, upstairs and downstairs. At times the noise he was making sounded close, as if he might be lurking in the hallway adjacent to the living room. Other times he sounded muffled and farther away. The heavy tread of his feet was accompanied by the loud creaking of rotting floorboards. The stairs sounded on the verge of splintering and giving way at any moment, though the thumping of the man's booted feet as he went up and down them suggested a distinct lack of concern.

Lexie raised her head and looked at her sister, hoping she'd finally make eye contact with her, but Trixie's face was still pressed against the filthy area rug in front of the sagging couch. Her scarlet hair was fanned out around her head like a pool of blood. She was crying and trembling, and an acrid stench of fresh urine was detectable from her vicinity. The odor blended in seamlessly with the overall rotten stench permeating the interior of the house. Some of the putrid smell was clearly attributable to biological decay. Lexie figured there were corpses in various stages of decomposition stashed here and there throughout the house, maybe a lot of them, but there was also a heavy overlay of dirt and must, likely accumulated over multiple decades. There were cobwebs everywhere. The stench was cloying, suffocating, a situation worsened by the stifling level of heat facilitated by the lack of air conditioning.

She attempted verbal communication with her sister, but the words were muffled by the dirty rag stuffed in her mouth, which was also covered by a strip of duct tape. Trying again, she carefully enunciated Trixie's name several times, adding extra vehement emphasis to those syllables, but each time her twin failed to acknowledge her.

Beyond the dire nature of their predicament, what worried Lexie the most was the thought of her sister blaming her for it. She was more afraid than she'd been at any point in her entire life, could barely stand to think about what else might yet happen, but she believed she could face anything if only Trixie would look at her and reassure her in some small way. Just some tiny gesture. A look of compassion. A flicker of love in her eyes.

It still wasn't happening.

Lexie's eyes filled with tears.

The worst thing was she knew she didn't deserve to be absolved of responsibility. If not for her, they would have been safely gone from this place long before the big, gangly man could get the drop on them. She was the one who'd insisted they should not only investigate the source of the screaming but should also attempt to exploit it for social media clout. She'd been so heavily invested in thinking of what they did as the TrikTok Twins as mere entertainment—no different from scripted crime stories on network TV—that she lost sight of the truth. True crime stories were about real people who suffered horribly and died. It was ugly and depressing, not sexy and exciting. The victims were dead and rotting in the ground, not safe behind a screen. She'd always known those things on a detached, intellectual level, but she'd never fully grasped the real truth behind any of it until now.

When it was too fucking late to matter.

And now here they were, hogtied and gagged in the living room of this awful place, stripped of their clothes save for their fishnet stockings. They'd already been groped and abused, punched repeatedly and smacked around while their tormentor chortled again and again, a sound that was strangely animalistic, barely like real human laughter at all. Lexie had the sense that he wasn't very bright, an insight that provided no comfort at all. A stupid man could hurt them just as easily as an intelligent one.

The man stomped back up the stairs again, his third trip up there since leaving them bound and gagged on the living room floor. His state of intense agitation was only getting worse. The sound was so alarming it prompted Trixie to finally lift her head off the floor. She glanced in the direction of the foyer before groaning and turning her head to at last look directly at her sister. There was a sustained moment of eye contact. Her emotions were hard to read beyond the obvious surface level of terror, but Lexie detected no anger or recrimination directed at her, just a hint of what might have been a weary sadness.

Tears again blurred Lexie's vision. She swallowed a lump in her throat and tried her best to enunciate the words "I'm sorry" from behind the gag.

Trixie appeared to understand.

She nodded and rested her face on the grimy rug again.

The big man was still upstairs when the sisters heard a door slam on the first floor. It seemed to come from somewhere toward the back of the house. There was a brief silence after that, a shift that felt eerie in the wake of so much belligerent noise-making. Then came a sound of soft footsteps as someone came into the living room.

Lexie turned her head and saw a barefoot woman in a white dress. The loose, knee-length garment billowed around her slender frame. Her skin was so pale it'd be easy to believe it'd never been touched by the sun. She said nothing as she walked over to a big floor model tube television, the kind encased in a cabinet made of real wood. A number of jagged cracks radiated outward from a small hole in the center of the dark screen. Even if the piece of vintage technology were in working condition, watching it wouldn't be an option, given the apparent lack of electrical power.

The interior of the house was lit by a combination of oil lanterns and a vast profusion of candles. The candles were of varying shapes and sizes, many of them crooked and wedged into numerous ill-fitting antique holders. They gave off a greasy smell that caused Lexie to suspect they were homemade tallow candles. Relying so heavily on candles for illumination seemed dangerous in a musty old dump like this, especially in the middle of a hot summer.

The gangly man had set their belongings on top of the television, stuff he'd retrieved from the Range Rover and the things they'd dropped while trying to flee. These items included the lighting rig they'd never gotten around to using, Lexie's backpack, their purses, and their phones. The woman in the white dress carefully examined each item one by one. She opened the backpack and took out everything in it, sorting through the mundane assortment of urban exploration provisions with a look of profound boredom, an expression that changed when she saw the battered old paperback copy of Vincent Bugliosi's *Helter Skelter: The True Story of the Manson Murders*.

A smile slowly spread across her face as she turned the book over and read the copy on the back. She then put the book down, picked up the phones, and came over to them, sitting cross-legged between them on the floor.

She smirked as she glanced at each of them in turn. "Let me guess. Y'all ain't from around here. Know how I know that? No? Well, you see, most local folk ain't stupid enough to come snoopin' around Dead End House at night, or any other time, to tell you the truth. But not you bitches. You don't know any better because you're from somewhere far away."

She smiled and looked slowly back and forth between them again, her eyes appearing to twinkle with mischief in the flickering light of the candles. The playful quality lent her face an appealing aspect that wasn't there when her expression was flat. She wasn't unattractive, Lexie realized, had perhaps even been pretty at one time, but that had been a while ago. Clear traces of her former beauty remained, but her unusually pale skin and lumpy, battered face made guessing her age almost impossible. She might have been anywhere between twenty and forty, though Lexie supposed the truth was probably somewhere in the middle of that range.

She abruptly stopped glancing back and forth between them and fixated on Lexie. "Hi, cutie. I get the sense you're a smart little thing. I can almost feel the strong brain waves beaming out of your pretty little noggin. That big brain of yours is workin' overtime tryin' to figure a way out of this mess, I bet. Well, I hate to break it to you, doll, but that shit is pointless. You and your mirror image here ain't ever gettin' free."

The woman in the white dress was far more articulate than the rampaging man in the coveralls. She was also much smaller than him, a difference in physical stature so pronounced she'd obviously be no match for him in a fight, yet Lexie found it interesting that he was silent now. There'd been no more bellowing or stomping around since she'd come into the house. She had a hard time believing a man like that might actually fear this relatively petite woman, but she didn't know how else to explain it.

The woman ripped the strip of duct tape away from Lexie's face, giggling at the squeal of pain this produced. "I'll take out that rag now, but no biting or I'll knock your teeth out with a hammer. You don't want that, do you?"

Lexie shook her head.

"Didn't think so."

The woman reached into her mouth and pulled out the rag, which had been pushed in deep, almost against the back of her throat. She coughed and wheezed as soon as it was gone from her mouth, the rotten taste of it still coating her tongue with its foulness.

At the same time, Trixie started sobbing again.

The woman in the white dress mimicked her muffled sounds of distress, which had the effect of intensifying Trixie's sobbing. The woman slapped her thighs and threw her head back as she laughed like she'd never heard anything so funny.

Lexie seethed with hatred for the woman. She yearned to say something defiant or scathing, and there were words that came to mind, but they never made it past the tip of her tongue. The way she was mocking her terrified sister pissed her off, but her own terror of being reprimanded in some awful way kept her quiet.

The woman's laughter soon subsided.

She picked up one of the phones and started swiping at the screen, the mirth fading from her face as she began to frown again. "Which of you little bitches does this one belong to?"

She held it out for them to see.

The sparkly purple case that housed the iPhone identified it as Lexie's own, but before she could say anything the man came running down the stairs again. Lexie's head turned toward the sound just in time to catch a glimpse of him as he passed through the foyer and went running toward the back of the house.

He'd had a tool of some kind gripped in his hands. She thought maybe it was an axe, but her glimpse of him had been too fleeting to be sure. In another moment, they heard the clap of the back door being thrown open again. The woman in the white dress turned her head and stared in that general direction, as if she could see through walls, her brow knitting in contemplation of something.

She looked at Lexie. "Well, that was mighty curious. Gonna guess someone else has come snooping around. Damn unusual for that to happen twice in one night. Might this be some tardy friends of yours showing up late for the party?"

Lexie allowed herself only a fleeting moment to weigh her response. There might be some way to leverage this new development to their advantage if she had any additional information at all, but she did not. The only thing she was certain of in that moment was it'd probably be a bad idea to attempt any kind of bluff only for it to be exposed as a lie shortly afterward.

She shook her head. "We came alone."

The woman shrugged. "Well, whatever's happening, I reckon we'll know soon enough. Where were we? Oh, yeah. Whose phone is this?"

She gestured with the iPhone in the sparkly purple case.

Lexie sighed. "It's mine."

The woman smiled. "Appreciate the honesty, doll. How do I get into it? There a code or something?"

She wasn't thrilled about the idea of the woman browsing the private contents of her phone. There was all the sensitive security information stored on it, for starters, but she was more apprehensive about her captors perusing the many questionable photos stored on her camera roll. Some would only be mildly embarrassing, such as all the photos of nude women, while others would be hard to defend given their current circumstances.

The woman's smile vanished. "Stop thinking about it, bitch, and tell me before you wind up real fuckin' sorry."

Lexie winced at the woman's harsh tone. "There is a code, but you can also just hold it up to my face."

The woman blinked in surprise. "What, really?"

"Yes."

"Huh. Let's see."

The woman held the phone up to Lexie's face and then made a sound of pure glee when she pulled it away and looked at the screen again. "Well, I'll be dipped in shit, it's like magic."

Several minutes passed as she swiped repeatedly at the screen, making occasional grunts of mild interest. Lexie knew the exact moment she started scrolling through her camera roll because that was when she made the first of numerous exclamations of surprise. The woman also looked askance at her several times, one eyebrow raised as she chuckled and shook her head.

Then she heaved a sigh and lowered the phone, her expression turning speculative as she looked at Lexie again. "That's an interesting collection of pictures you've got there, girl."

Lexie didn't say anything.

The woman laughed. "What is it you're most embarrassed about? All the naked ladies or the pictures of dead people?"

Again, Lexie said nothing.

"Answer me before I get up and kick you in the face."

Lexie sighed. "The crime scene photos."

The woman nodded. "Figured as much. It's kind of funny, huh? I bet you've spent a lot of time looking at them. In all that time, did you ever once think you might one day end up just like those people?"

A new surge of terror made Lexie's guts twist and clench. "You can't kill us."

The woman sneered. "You're wrong about that."

Trixie lifted her head off the floor and made an emphatic attempt at speech, but the words came out muffled.

The woman in the white dress glanced at her briefly before looking at Lexie again. "You get the gist of that?"

Lexie's guts kept clenching, but she almost smiled. "Yeah. She's saying you can't kill us because we're famous."

The woman laughed. "Come on, now. You expect me to believe that?"

Before Lexie could say anything else, they heard the back door open and slam shut again, a sound followed by the heavy tread of the man's footsteps. The sound got louder and closer and in another couple moments he emerged through the hallway entrance into the living room. The thud of his booted feet made the floorboards vibrate as he approached the three of them.

Trixie screamed behind her gag when she turned her head to look at him.

Lexie choked back acidic bile.

The man stepped between them and presented the woman with the severed head of a young man.

She took it from him and held it between her hands, a strange expression coming over her face as she tilted the head first to one side and then the other. There was a melancholic quality to the cast of her features, as well as perhaps a faint twinge of regret. That a person like this sadistic woman could feel such things seemed impossible, yet Lexie believed it was so.

The woman sighed. "Oh, Brady."

Her eyes watered and there was a hitch in her breath as she said the words.

Then she brought the severed head closer and kissed the dead man's lips.

TWELVE

Five years ago

THE NIGHTMARE WAS A BAD one and Lara woke up with a scream on her lips. She felt tendon-straining tension in her jaw and a weight of terror swelling within her to the point where she felt like she might burst from it. Her whole body was shaking as she recalled the image of the monster from her nightmare, still so horribly vivid in her mind. The monster was the same one she always saw when the bad dreams tortured her fitful sleep, a monster she could not escape even in her waking life, because she lived with it now, here in this rotting, putrid house.

Her fingers curled into claws and her body contorted as she fought to push the image away and suppress the scream her battered psyche so desperately yearned to unleash. She clenched her jaw shut, grinding her teeth so hard they felt close to cracking. Little by little, she was able to ease the tension gripping her body, allowing her swollen lungs to slowly deflate, the air passing between her clenched teeth as if from a punctured tire.

The only question now was whether she'd screamed before waking. If she'd made any audible noise, the old lady who was the boss of the house would come to her room soon. Within seconds, she would hear lurching footsteps hobbling down the second-floor hallway. Then would come the rattling of the key in the lock, followed by the loud creaking of the ancient hinges as the door swung inward.

The pattern was familiar because the old lady had come to her many times in the weeks she'd spent imprisoned in the dark room. Alma Wilcox would scold her first for the noise before proceeding to berate her again for tempting her poor, innocent boy with her nubile young body. The scolding would be fierce and hateful, and it'd be followed by a savage beating. Her nude form was covered in bruises and welts from being whacked so many countless times by the woman's wooden cane.

Calvin was never in the room with them when these beatings were administered, but the old woman didn't need him to restrain her. Heavy chains bolted to the walls held her in place, rendering resistance not only futile but impossible. The shackles clamped tight around her wrists and ankles were encrusted with rust, but age had not weakened the iron.

Enough time passed for Lara to begin feeling safe again, at least for the time being. She heard no hobbling footsteps out in the hallway, and no one had yelled at her from downstairs. The house was as quiet as it ever got in the periods between Calvin's intermittent psychotic outbursts, those times when he'd go rampaging around downstairs and upstairs, stomping his feet and screaming incoherently about things that enraged him.

The windows of the second-floor room were painted black and covered with black curtains, leaving her cocooned in perfect darkness whenever she was left alone. She existed in a state of ceaseless misery, feeling scared and depressed during all her waking moments, and yet she felt grateful for this state of solitary confinement every time Calvin had one of his episodes. The memory of how he'd taken off Kevin's head with the scythe after smashing out the window of her car was never far from her mind.

Her first glimpse of Calvin had come seconds later, and it was an image that left an indelible scar on her psyche, that ugly, malformed visage leering at her, enjoying her terror. That was almost as bad as the memory of the things he'd done to her after dragging her into Dead End House, vile violations performed in the filthy living room of the house right in front of his family members. After that, he beat her so severely she drifted in and out of consciousness for hours.

She tried her best not to think about what had happened to Kevin. It'd been the single most shocking and horrifying experience of her life, but what bothered her more than the essential fact of his death was the overwhelming sense of guilt. The spot at the end of Millhaven Road had creeped him out and he'd asked her to take him home, but she'd refused. She'd felt such contempt for him in those last moments before Calvin's assault, thinking less of him for his fear and dismissing his concerns as having no merit.

She'd thought he was a pussy.

That was the blunt reality of it. The old version of herself could never have been with a guy like Kevin long-term. He was too serious about too many things, especially his religion. She'd fully intended to dump him in favor of someone else after getting what she wanted from him. The night of the attack she'd spent some time mulling over a list of replacement boyfriend candidates, seeing their faces in her head even as she groped him and stuck her tongue down his throat. It pained her to recall how little real regard she'd had for him.

The heavy links of the chain clanked as she shifted her body on the wooden floor. There was some slack to the chains due to their length, allowing a limited range of motion, but the floor's lack of padding ensured she could never have a truly comfortable moment so long as she remained imprisoned here. Splinters from the rotting floorboards pricked her bare skin any time she moved, making her feel like a human pincushion at times.

She longed for her comfortable bed at home and wished with fervent intensity for a chance to rewind time and do things a different way. There were even times when she tried bargaining with God, vowing to marry Kevin and live an exemplary life of moral purity if only she could be granted that magical second chance. She'd never been a believer, but hell, it was worth a shot, wasn't it? Nothing came of her desperate plea for divine intervention, which didn't surprise her. What self-respecting deity would bestow favors on hypocrites?

In her mind, for perhaps the millionth time, she yet again saw Kevin's head come free of his body.

She clenched her teeth in frustration.

Stop thinking about it!

But that was impossible.

She felt on the verge of a sobbing fit until the sound of a key sliding into the door's lock intruded, dispersing the feelings of guilt along with the memories that triggered them. Of more immediate concern was the strong likelihood of enduring another prolonged period of pain at the hands of one of these monstrous sadists. She whimpered and trembled in anticipation of what they might do to her.

The key rattled and then there was a click.

Lara lifted her head off the floor and turned it slightly to watch the door swing inward. A person holding a glowing lantern stood framed in the doorway for a moment before entering the room and shutting the door.

A soft pad of footsteps approached.

She looked up and whimpered again when she saw who it was. "Oh, no. God, no. Not you."

Ursula smiled. "Hi, sweet thing. You don't sound happy to see me. That's a shame." She set the lantern on the floor and sat down. "Are you mad that I've been neglecting you these last few days? I apologize for that, but I've been busy breaking one of our other girls, a real feisty one, but I'm ready to give you my full attention again."

Lara sobbed.

Ursula laughed. "Oh, come on, stop being so dramatic. Maybe I won't hurt you too bad this time if you make me feel real good when I sit on your face."

She laughed again.

Lara sniffled. "I'll do anything."

Ursula leaned close and patted her on the cheek. "I know you will. What choice do you have? But we both know I'm lying again, just like I always fuckin' do." She giggled. "I'm gonna hurt you, bitch. I'm gonna hurt you a lot." She turned her head, glancing at one of the room's dark corners a moment. "I think my bag of tools is still in here. Let's see."

In a display of natural athleticism, she surged to her feet from the sitting position without first bracing her hands on the floor. As she scurried away, darkness briefly obscured her slender form, almost seeming to swallow her for a moment. A fleeting fantasy that the woman had been devoured by a vengeful shadow monster offered a moment of illusory hope, but Ursula quickly emerged from the darkness with her sack of tools, the lantern light making her look like an apparition drifting out of the shadows as it touched her pale skin. She smiled as she again sat cross-legged near Lara and set the lumpy sack on the floor.

She rubbed her hands together in exaggerated excitement. "Let's see what we have here."

Lara sniffled. "Just kill me, please."

Ursula laughed. "Don't be ridiculous. You've only been here a few weeks. I ain't gonna be killin' you for a long time yet. Hurting you is too much fun. Why would I deprive myself of that?"

Lara's face contorted as she wailed in anguish.

Ursula smirked. "You know what really pisses me off about you? It's how pretty you are. You're almost as pretty as me."

The assertion almost made Lara laugh in spite of her terror.

She knew people generally found her attractive—or at least they had prior to the start of this descent into misery and madness—but her ego in that department was not so large that it allowed her to deny obvious reality. Ursula Wilcox was a deranged sadist who lived in squalor, but she also had been blessed with one of the most naturally beautiful female faces she'd ever seen. She was so pretty it hurt to look at her because beauty on that level should not exist in so ugly a setting. It was obscene, like seeing a big, shiny diamond at the top of a ten-foot-tall pile of rotting aborted fetuses.

Ursula reached inside the burlap sack and grabbed hold of something. "What I've gotta do now, I think, is work on making you just a little bit less pretty. Not so much that you don't still turn me on, but enough to knock you down a few notches on the ten scale. Right now you're about a nine. I'm thinking you need to be a six." She paused, pursing her lips. "Hmm, or maybe a five."

Lara wailed in desperate distress again. "No. Please, no."

Ursula's hand came out of the bag with a heavy-duty pipe wrench. "Yes."

She raised it and brought it down with significant force, fracturing one of Lara's cheekbones.

Lara screamed and tried rolling away from her.

Ursula snarled like an animal and scurried after her, crawling atop her and then straddling her, pinning her to the floor.

Lara opened her mouth wide to scream again.

The pipe wrench came down again, her mouth filling with blood an instant later as the impact shattered several of her teeth.

THIRTEEN

THE SUN WAS SHINING WHEN Sterling Kincaid awoke sitting up on a bench inside a sheltered bus stop. His mouth was dry and his head was throbbing as he squinted against the mid-morning brilliance of the big yellow ball hanging in the bright blue sky. He had no memory of falling asleep in this spot, but that was not unusual. Living in a perpetual alcoholic haze meant that a good chunk of his days and nights were lost to memory blackouts, and by now he had a long history of waking up in unusual or unexpected places.

On more than one occasion he'd woken up inside a dumpster, covered in trash with rats crawling all over him. Another time he'd emerged from a blackout naked and handcuffed to a radiator inside the squalid apartment of a meth addicted prostitute who was convinced he was the devil. How he'd talked himself out of that predicament was yet another thing he couldn't remember. All things considered, waking up with no recollection of passing out on a bus stop bench was one of his more mundane post bender experiences. He considered himself lucky not to have been rousted and chased away by some bored patrol cop already.

He felt weak and his body ached in many places. This also was not unusual. Some of that could be attributed to getting older—he'd passed the half-century on Earth mark during his first year of living on the street—but the way he lived his life was the larger factor by a considerable margin. He couldn't remember the last time he'd slept on any sort of padded surface, much less an actual bed. Living rough was taking a heavy toll, weakening his body and robbing him of his dignity. There were times when he wished for an end to it all, for this act of slow suicide by alcohol to finally reach its inevitable conclusion. He had frequent fantasies of speeding the process up by stepping in front of a speeding bus or perhaps by antagonizing a police officer. The bastard cops of Elkmont had no love of the homeless, and he was certain any of them would be more than happy to indulge the self-destructive impulses of an unhoused man who came at them swinging an empty liquor bottle. There was only one reason he hadn't yet availed himself of either option.

Lara.

The memory of his missing daughter was the only thing that kept him going, along with the remote possibility she might still be alive. Contrary to what people thought, he wasn't completely delusional. He knew it was likely she'd been dead since the night she went missing, yet the lack of conclusive proof prevented him from fully accepting the grim truth. It might have been easier if even one drop of her blood had been found in the Nova, but that hadn't happened.

Early on he'd focused his grief in more positive ways, hiring a private investigator and leading the civilian effort to look for Lara while the cops did nothing. The lack of official law enforcement progress in the case became a major source of rage and frustration for him. He'd always been a drinking man, but after a while of getting nowhere with the investigation, he started hitting the bottle harder than ever. After another six months of spiraling, he found himself jobless and homeless. Things only got worse from there.

And now here he was, a societal outcast and a wreck of a human being no one on this planet gave a shit about anymore, reeking of piss because of course he'd voided his bladder while passed out. It'd been happening more often than not for a long time now and he was beyond feeling shame over it. It was just part of the way things were now, another item on the endless list of reasons why no one would mourn his worthless ass when he finally kicked the bucket.

A few respectable-looking normal people were standing at the edge of the sidewalk, just outside of the bus stop shelter. One was a well-dressed elderly woman who glanced back at him with a look of utter contempt. Nobody was standing inside the shelter itself or sitting on the bench with him, yet another thing that was not surprising. He couldn't even bring himself to be mad about the way they shunned him or for their lack of compassion. It was nothing less than exactly what he deserved, as far as he was concerned.

Sterling's knees cracked as he got to his feet with a groan. He began walking down the sidewalk. The people he encountered as he began making his slow way back toward the center of the downtown area did their usual avoidance thing, giving him a wide berth. As usual, more than a few did abrupt wide swerves to move out of his path after glancing up from their phones.

He took no special note of the young girl who stepped away from the entrance of a record store and started walking alongside him until he belatedly realized she was remaining close to him on purpose. One glance at her was enough to tell him she was no addict or any other type of street person. Her clothes were clean and she didn't stink. She was some kind of rebellious kid, dressed all in black except for a short black-and-white checkered skirt. Black top, black leather jacket, black tights, black boots. Even her hair was dyed black. Her lipstick and eyeliner were also black. It all made for a pretty dramatic contrast to her ghostly pale skin.

She smiled when he looked at her. "Hi."

Sterling frowned. "What are you, some kind of day walking vampire? Get away from me. You're freaking me out."

She laughed. "Freaking people out is my specialty. I live for it."

His frown deepened and twisted, becoming a scowl. "Isn't a leather jacket a little uncomfortable this time of year? It's hot as a motherfucker."

She arched an eyebrow as she looked him up and down. "I could say the same for you. So many layers of filthy rags. And all that hair. You look like some kind of garbage can Jesus. Messiah of the apocalypse."

Sterling grunted. "Okay, I get it now. You get your kicks by fucking with bums. Well, consider me officially fucked with. Go away."

Her smile vanished. "No way, dude. That's not me at all. This is just my sarcastic personality. Look, I need you to do me a favor."

Sterling glanced at her again. There was a fearlessness to her that reminded him of his daughter. It was evident in the way she'd shown not even the slightest trace of trepidation in approaching him. He was a social pariah accustomed to people recoiling in disgust, as if terrified they might catch some awful contagious disease just by walking past him on the sidewalk. This girl, however, seemed blissfully unbothered by any of the many things about him that repulsed most other people. It was an impression he didn't fully trust, and he suspected a thus far unrevealed ulterior motive.

"I don't know what you're playing at here, but I'm not as stupid as you think. Used to run my own business years ago. A successful one, too. Some pretty little jailbait bitch coming to someone like me for a favor ain't anything but bad fucking news. So run along and find some other old bum to hassle."

The girl smiled again, unfazed by this gruff response. "Dude, it isn't even anything crazy. ABC Liquor is up another block on this street. My proposal is simple. I give you money, enough to get me a bottle of whiskey and something for yourself. That's it. No hidden agendas at all. No weird sexual manipulation. I just want to get my drink on. So what do you say?"

Sterling frowned. Her proposal was straightforward enough, but he still felt uneasy, thanks in no small part to the thoughts of his daughter she'd stirred. That he should feel this way at all surprised him. He'd long ago passed a point where he harbored moral qualms over just about anything, and he needed to procure the day's ration of booze some way or other.

"How old are you? Be honest."

She laughed. "I turn nineteen next week."

Sterling's frown deepened. "But why come to me? You must have legal age friends who'd get you a bottle."

She groaned in an exasperated way. "Holy shit, stop being so fucking paranoid. I'm not a cop or a narc. This isn't the world's lamest ever sting operation. I just moved here a few weeks ago and don't have many friends yet. Or any, to tell you the truth."

Sterling came to an abrupt stop on the sidewalk. He had other questions for the girl, starting with why would a young person such as herself, apparently already out of the familial nest and living on her own, choose to move to a place as unremarkable as Elkmont without already knowing people there?

All of that was temporarily forgotten, however, because of

something he'd glimpsed in his peripheral vision. He turned and stared at a utility pole near the edge of the sidewalk. A tattered remnant of one of his own Lara flyers was stapled to the pole, one he'd put there weeks ago judging from its weathered condition, but that was not what had caught his attention.

The young goth girl had continued down the sidewalk for several more paces before realizing he was not still walking alongside her. She turned and came back to him now, a puzzled look on her face. "Hey, thought I'd lost you. Something wrong?"

A deeper sense of unease gripped Sterling now, one wholly unrelated to the prospect of buying booze for someone not legally old enough to drink it. The worst thing about it was he was not immediately sure why he should feel so unsettled by the new flyer stapled to the pole directly above the tattered piece of the old Lara flyer. The flyer showed a black-and-white photocopied image of a young man's face. It stirred a flicker of recognition, but at first he wasn't sure why the visage should seem so familiar.

Printed above the image of the man's face were the words, *Have you seen Brady?*

Beneath that was a phone number.

Then it came to him and his heart gave a sudden lurch inside his chest.

The constant daily influx of alcohol kept his memory of recent events fuzzy, but now he vaguely recalled how the kid—apparently one of Lara's many short-term boyfriends from years ago—had tried to help him on more than one occasion. His days passed in a blur for the most part, one largely indistinguishable from any other, but he had the feeling these run-ins with the young man had happened very recently.

The girl stood beside him and made a noise of recognition when she saw the poster. "Oh, yeah. Sad, huh? Did you know him?"

Sterling couldn't help noting her use of the past tense, but he elected not to remark on that. "Not well, but he knew my daughter." He looked at her, a growing curiosity showing in the deep lines of his sun-bronzed face. "What happened?"

She shrugged. "Oh, man, you haven't heard? It's been a big story."

Sterling grunted. "My lifestyle isn't exactly conducive to keeping up on current events."

The girl laughed. "I guess not. Well, the dude went missing almost a week ago. Cops found his car parked behind an abandoned warehouse. There was no sign of him, except for some traces of blood on his windshield."

Sterling felt unsteady on his feet.

He staggered away from the utility pole and started looking for a place to sit. A queasiness overcame him and his vision blurred. The girl made a sound of alarm and took hold of him by an arm, steering him away from the edge of the sidewalk. She was still talking, but the sense of her words was lost to him as the world continued to spin.

Then it dropped out from under him as he fell into darkness.

FOURTEEN

THE BODY OF THE WOMAN who'd tormented Melissa during her first night in the basement was deep into the bloat stage of decomposition. Because most of her time was spent in darkness, she was largely spared the disturbing visual evidence of the physical changes the corpse was undergoing. To her great dismay, however, it'd not been possible to avoid catching occasional glimpses of Wormie's swollen form. She received visits from residents of Dead End House at least once a day when it was light out. The door at the bottom of the stairwell was always left open when this happened, letting in enough sunshine for her visitor to negotiate the daunting landscape of junk without the aid of a flashlight.

She'd seen enough in those moments to experience a deep sense of existential horror and dread that lingered long after any visitor departed, taking the sunshine with them. Not because she mourned the loss of Wormie. She was incapable of lamenting the death of a woman who'd tortured her and might eventually have killed her had they spent more time together.

The thing that really bothered her was knowing that one day—a day perhaps not too far into the future—she would likely die in this cage. Just like Wormie. Just like the other woman at the back of the cage, a person she'd never known. Also just like them, her body would be left to rot down here. She would bloat and begin to emit a stench worse than a backed up big city sewer. A dark substance would ooze from her mouth and nose, and that too would carry a horrendous odor. She'd seen the substance leaking out of Wormie the last time the door opened. Then that stage would pass and she'd enter a more advanced state of decay, her skin turning black and mushy, maggots crawling in the gashes in her flesh.

She couldn't help vividly visualizing the changes her body would undergo, how she would look as her corpse bloated. The visualization became so intensely clear during those long hours in the dark that she could almost feel the maggots that would one day squirm inside her empty eye sockets. During her bleakest moments, the prospect made her hope that, in the event she did expire in this place, the authorities would never recover her remains from the property.

She wasn't a conceited person, but she had always taken justifiable pride in her appearance. Her prettiness was something she liked about herself, a thing for which she'd always felt a deep level of gratitude. She didn't believe it made her better than anyone else. It was just a fact of her existence. She enjoyed being pretty. Guys complimented her on her looks often, as one would expect, and that was nice, but she liked it even better when other girls said things to her like, "Wow, you are so pretty." She felt it came from a place of greater sincerity and so it meant more. It hurt her heart to imagine a policeman or crime technician gazing upon her corpse someday and feeling the same things she felt whenever she glimpsed Wormie.

Feeling repulsed by the ugly thing she'd become.

Even worse than that was the utter impossibility of escaping the horror every facet of her existence had become. There was a padlock on the cage now. And the slats were thick, more like the bars of a jail cell than the slender slats of a dog crate. There was no give to them whatsoever. Someone with a bolt cutter could possibly snip through the padlock from the outside, but she was trapped inside and there was no such tool at her disposal anyway.

Because she couldn't get out, she spent most of her time at the front of the cage, gripping the slats and resting her head against the locked door. She did this because it was as far away as she could get from the corpses, but in truth the distance wasn't nearly enough. The putrid stench emanating from Wormie was made worse by the oppressive summer heat. Her body was slathered in perspiration on a constant basis, and she held her mouth open almost all the time, panting like a stray mutt desperate for even one taste of something cool and refreshing. She wanted—*needed*—water so badly she knew there was precious little she wouldn't be willing to do for it, including debasing herself in virtually any manner the creative sadists upstairs could devise.

She thought she was probably now at a point where she might even kill for it, and until this day she'd sworn to herself that was a line she could never cross. That would constitute the ultimate level of defeat, becoming like them, tainting her soul forever. She believed in an afterlife, believed in Heaven, and she knew if she allowed herself to sink to the level of her tormentors, she would never ascend to paradise and be with her mother and grandparents again. Instead, she would descend to Hell, where her torment would last forever.

The thirst was so bad now, though. Being stranded in the middle of an endless desert couldn't possibly be any worse. The inside of her mouth was so dry and raw. Her tongue felt like it might turn to ash at any second. It was unbearable. She didn't want to die, remained enthralled to the miserable will of the human body to persist despite being pushed far beyond the limits of physical endurance, was as much a prisoner to that as she was to those who'd taken her.

So, yes, she thought she might kill now if they asked.

They'd asked before and she'd refused.

But now?

I'll do it, she thought. *I'll do it and I won't fucking hesitate. I'll do it because I am so miserably fucking thirsty and I literally cannot take it even one more minute!*

She allowed herself some moments to wallow in the stark undeniability of this new conviction. Her eyes closed soon thereafter and she lapsed into a brief period of fitful sleep.

Her eyes snapped open again after enduring yet another nightmare about making out with Wormie's bloated corpse, only this time she knew it wasn't the nightmare that woke her up. She heard the familiar creaking sound that always accompanied the opening of the door at the bottom of the stairwell. Enough light streamed in for her to know it was still relatively early in the day. A visitor was already

71

navigating their way through the haphazardly piled up heaps of junk, uttering annoyed curses each time they bumped into something.

She looked up as her visitor moved past the huge old steamer trunk near the cage, her face drawing down in a frown of surprise when she saw who it was. "Where's Ursula?"

The new girl smiled. "You miss her, huh?"

That of course was not true, but Melissa only groaned in reply.

The new girl's smile gave way to a grimace. "Oh, Jesus, I don't know how you stand being cooped up with that awful smell." She laughed when she saw the weary but withering look Melissa directed at her. "Yeah, it's not like you've got a choice, I know. I don't either, for what it's worth. Ursula has decided it's time for another loyalty test." She rolled her eyes. "You'd think the stuff I've done to my sister would be more than enough, but I guess not."

Melissa groaned and clutched the cage slats tighter. "Please go back up there and tell them I'll do anything they want now. *Anything.*"

The girl smirked. "Yeah, I bet."

She squatted in front of the cage and set the backpack she'd brought with her on the floor, flipping her long, scarlet hair out of her face as she unzipped it and reached inside. The hair was an obviously artificial shade, the dye job a recent one that wasn't showing roots of her natural color yet. She was dressed in denim cutoff shorts and a green halter top. These were Melissa's own clothes, the ones that'd been forcibly stripped from her body after they put her in the van. She shuddered at the sudden memory of their hands all over her once they had her stowed inside the vehicle, all their enthusiastic groping and sounds of excitement.

Melissa whimpered. "Trixie . . . please don't. It's just you and me. They won't know if you don't do anything this time."

Trixie's hand came out of the backpack gripping an iPhone with a sparkly purple case. She stared at the screen with a look of concentration for a moment as she swiped at its screen a few times.

Then she looked at Melissa and smiled again. "Here's the thing. They want visual confirmation that I've done what I said I'd do." She laughed, her face flushing with genuine amusement. "That's not normally an option for these backwards fuckers." The smile vanished with discomfiting abruptness. "Get ready to scream a lot."

She poked at the phone's screen again, got to her feet, and approached a rack of metal shelving that stood against the wall directly opposite the front of the cage. The shelves were crowded to the point of overflowing with junk, boxes of things and piles of forgotten knick-knacks. After moving some things aside and sweeping others to the floor, she propped the phone against a large glass jar filled with what looked like beer bottle caps.

Once she was satisfied with the position of the phone, she moved back a step and began speaking in a bright, cheery voice that made her sound like a vapid TV morning show announcer, albeit one without an internal profanity filter.

"Hey, Dead End House pals! It's Trixie, your favorite crazy fucking bitch again, and have I got an extra special treat for you today. It's the debut episode of *Tearing Up Slaggie*, soon to be everyone's favorite new sitcom. And who is Slaggie, I hear you asking? Well, allow me to introduce her."

She turned away from the shelving, moved a step to the side in order to not block the camera, and swept her hands toward the cage in a showy way.

"Ta-da!" She giggled. "Say hi to Slaggie, the bitch I'm about to fuck up beyond all recognition."

Melissa sobbed.

Trixie came at the cage fast, kicking the front of it with the sole of a sneaker that'd once belonged to some other unfortunate girl. This happened too quickly for Melissa to unwrap her hands from the slats. She screamed in pain as the shoe smashed against the fingers of her left hand, the ones that still remained.

Trixie laughed. "Save your energy, Slaggie. We're just getting warmed up. That's your new name, by the way, in case you hadn't figured that out already. Because you're a total fucking ugly slag. You know that, right?"

Melissa moaned, but said nothing.

Trixie sneered. "I want to hear you say it. Tell me what your new name is."

Terror at what was to come surged inside of Melissa, but rather than surrendering to it, she screamed in defiance: "*Go to Hell!*"

Trixie grunted. "Fine. Be like that. But you're gonna say your name before we're done here." She squatted and reached a hand inside the backpack again. "Get ready to scream again."

Her hand came out of the backpack with a burlap bag cinched shut at the top with a knotted drawstring. Something was squirming around inside the bag, desperate to get out. Melissa's eyes widened in abject horror as Trixie held the bag over the top of the cage and untied the knot.

In another moment, Melissa was screaming again. She didn't stop for a long time.

FIFTEEN

Earlier that week

THE CORRUPTION OF TRIXIE, PART ONE:
INKLINGS

AT THE END OF THEIR first night in Dead End House, the sisters were locked inside a room upstairs. An odor of human waste and rot permeated the room's interior. Heavy chains with shackles attached were bolted to the walls. In one corner was a pile of skeletal human remains, and it was impossible to tell whether the bones were all that was left of just one person or if they'd belonged to multiple individuals who'd rotted away to nothing without ever again glimpsing the world outside these walls.

Ursula secured each of them in the rust-encrusted shackles. Before leaving them alone in the dark, she administered a last series of savage slaps and backhanded blows while they sat trembling on their knees. She did this in eerie silence, a stark and disquieting contrast to her frequent laughter and verbal exuberance of earlier in the evening. The only sounds in the room during those minutes were the loud cracks from the repeated impacts of her hand against their faces, and then afterward the pitiful, wretched sobbing of the sisters.

After retrieving her lantern from the floor, Ursula departed the room without a word. They heard the rattle of a key in the lock and then the sound of footsteps moving away down the hallway. The miserable sobbing continued without interruption for at least several minutes thereafter.

Then Lexie made a halfhearted attempt to pull herself together. She took a deep breath and tried to speak in a whisper to her sister. This was only the first of several attempts, all of which went unanswered. Though she couldn't see because the windows in the room were painted black, she retained a sense of her sister's location, which should still be a few feet to her immediate left. If Trixie had moved, there would've been a clanking of chain links, and that had not happened.

She tried reaching out to Trixie and felt her fingertips brush across a slender forearm. Her sister shrieked in surprise and scuttled away from her, dragging a length of the heavy chain across the floor with her. At first Lexie believed this was because her sister's psyche was experiencing an overload of terror and paranoia. Perhaps she believed there was someone—or something—else here in the darkness with them, but this was revealed as a false impression when Lexie tried to offer her reassurance.

Trixie was furious.

That was not a surprise, given the dire nature of the circumstances. What did surprise Lexie was that most of that fury was directed specifically at her rather than at their captors. It was the realization of everything she'd feared during their time trussed up in the living room. She apologized for the unthinking rashness of her actions earlier that night, admitting it was her fault they were in this predicament, even if there was no way she could have foreseen anything this crazy happening. That qualifier at the end of her apology further enraged Trixie, who unleashed a stream of bitter invective that left Lexie stunned.

"Don't talk to me again," Trixie told her at the conclusion of the vicious rant. "Not even one fucking word, or I swear I'll strangle you with this chain as soon as you fall asleep."

Lexie took those words to heart and did not speak again that night. But her sobbing resumed and went on for hours.

They both fell asleep at some point late that night and when they awoke again, the room was still cloaked in darkness. During those first moments of hazy semi-consciousness, Lexie experienced a dim hope that all of it had only been a terrible nightmare. Then the baked stench of human piss and shit invaded her nostrils, and she felt the heaviness of the shackles clamped tight around her wrists. That was in addition to sleeping naked on rotting wooden floor planks, which left her feeling stiff and sore as she came fully awake and sat up with a groan. She felt she'd slept a considerable amount of time, but because the darkness of the room remained absolute, it was impossible to tell what time of day it was.

After a few moments, she became aware of Trixie's breathing and could tell from the sound of it that she too had awakened.

"Have they been back?"

A silent moment elapsed.

Then Trixie said, "Everything I said before still stands. Don't say a fucking word to me or I'll hurt you."

These words stabbed at Lexie's heart, the viciousness of her sister's tone wounding her as deeply as the words themselves. Her mouth opened, her jaw working for a moment as she struggled with the need to again spew words of earnest apology. There was also a contrary underlying urge to speak in defiance, to remind Trixie they were both innocent victims here. She was truly sorry, but she could not have known any of this awfulness would happen. The memory of how Trixie had reacted the last time she said these things stilled her tongue.

They then spent a long stretch of mostly silent hours awake in the darkness. Their own breathing and the clanking of the chains as they occasionally shifted around on the floor were the only sounds during that time. Until, that is, Lexie heard what she initially believed was a sound of running water. Then came the belated realization that this was actually her sister pissing on the floor. Hearing it triggered something in Lexie, made her painfully aware of how strained her own bladder was feeling. She didn't want to piss on the floor, an idea that was dehumanizing on the most basic level. That was the kind of thing an animal did when its owner waited too long to let it outside.

I am not an animal, she told herself. *I won't let them make me sink to that level.*

This belief was, of course, nothing but desperate delusion.

The need became too physically overwhelming and before much longer she did as Trixie had done, the urine coming out in a warm, fast stream. As it happened, it struck her that by doing this she was contributing on a sensory level to the unfolding history of horrors that had transpired in this room, deepening and further enriching that pervading odor of stale piss.

At some point after they'd both been awake for several hours, they again heard a key rattling in the door lock. Lexie had been lying on her side, but upon hearing the sound, she sat up with a sharp intake of breath. The door creaked as it swung inward. Ursula stood framed in the open doorway, still attired in the same raggedy white dress.

She came into the middle of the room and set her lantern on the floor. "It's playtime again, bitches. Y'all are coming downstairs with me after I let ya out of them chains. Calvin's waiting at the bottom of the stairs, so be smart and don't try anything stupid. Got me?"

There was a brief, wary pause followed by murmurs of assent from the sisters.

Ursula approached Lexie first. "On your feet. Be quick about it."

Lexie did her best to comply, but moving with anything approaching quickness while in chains wasn't easy. The soreness of her body didn't help matters. It took her around a half minute to get fully upright. As it turned out, this was not nearly fast enough to satisfy Ursula, who punched her in the face, splitting her bottom lip and eliciting a shriek of pain. She whimpered and tasted blood while her tormentor laughed at her.

Ursula roughly took hold of her and told her to be still. The shackles slipped away from Lexie's thin wrists as they were unlocked. One struck the bare toes of her right foot as they fell to the floor, the pain severe enough to draw out another shriek of agony.

This earned her another closed fist to the center of her face, causing her to take a staggering step backward as blood gushed from her nostrils.

Ursula laughed.

Then she moved on to Trixie, who surged to her feet without being told. Ursula touched her face, caressing her cheek with surprising gentleness. "Good girl."

She removed Trixie's shackles, taking a notably greater level of care in doing so. "You are both miserable little worms, lower than gutter trash. As such, I'm gonna need you to crawl like worms, all the way down the hall and down the stairs to the living room."

Trixie looked directly at her sister for the first time since the door was opened. One corner of her mouth curled sharply upward in a sneer of contempt. She dropped to her belly and began wriggling her way toward the open door. A broad smile stretched across Ursula's face as she watched this happen, and again Lexie could see clear traces of the battered woman's former beauty.

The radiant smile faded when she looked at Lexie. "The fuck are you waiting for? Start crawling, worm, before I take a hammer to your fucking kneecaps."

Lexie's vision blurred.

All she wanted to do was cry, but there was no time for tears now, not in this unforgiving corner of Hell.

She dropped to her knees and went to her belly.

Then she began to crawl.

Ursula followed along behind her, laughing and offering up a nearly nonstop stream of derogatory comments. When she wasn't doing that, she was spitting at Lexie, who cringed each time she felt those splashes of saliva against her skin.

The hallway floor was devoid of carpet and there was no coating of varnish to smooth the rough floor planks. As Lexie crawled toward the stairs, numerous tiny wood splinters became embedded in her flesh. She tried to focus only on moving forward, but now and then she would lift her head slightly and see her sister's nude form crawling ahead of her, almost seeming to glide smoothly down the passageway with little in the way of obvious physical effort or discomfort. This was at least partly an illusory perception, she was sure, one enhanced by her own struggle to keep going, but there was no doubt Trixie was moving at a somewhat faster rate. Something more than fear was driving her, perhaps some twisted element of spite directed at her sister, as well as maybe a desire to prove something to their captors.

Trixie reached the end of the hallway and began her careful descent down the creaky stairs. Several seconds later, Lexie arrived at the same spot and lifted herself up slightly in preparation of doing the same.

Before she could, Ursula spoke in a low voice. "Gonna need you to raise your ass up and brace your knees on the edge of the stairs there."

Lexie frowned. "What? But why—"

"Shut up, worm. Just do as you're told, and keep your ass up in the air."

Lexie did as instructed, raising her rear end up and bending her torso forward to brace her hands on the second step down. Trixie was still descending step to step with the utmost care, taking the time to be sure of where she was placing her hands and knees with every movement. Calvin was waiting at the bottom of the stairs, leering at her in his dopey yet terrifying way.

Trixie was about halfway down the stairs.

Ursula braced one of her rough-soled bare feet against Lexie's ass, maintained pressure against it for a moment of gut-twisting apprehension. Then she let out a loud grunt of exertion as she shoved forward with her foot, sending Lexie tumbling down the stairs. She felt ribs crack as her body bounced off the railing and smashed against the edges of steps. She was like a boulder falling down the side of a mountain. There would be no stopping until she reached the bottom. The only question was whether she would still be alive once she got there.

Hearing the clatter and commotion of her sister's tumbling body, Trixie ceased descending and glanced backward in time to gape in horror at the nude form hurtling toward her. There was no time to think about what was happening or get out of the way.

Lexie crashed into her sister and then they were both falling.

Seconds later, they landed in a heap of sprawled limbs in the foyer, with Lexie lying sideways across her sister's midsection. She was in a tremendous amount of pain, and judging from her pitiful moaning, so was her sister. The sources of throbbing agony felt innumerable, with the worst of it issuing from her ribs and her left wrist, which felt broken. She figured this was how it must feel to survive going over Niagara Falls in a barrel. Every inch of her body felt battered and bruised.

Then she looked up and saw a smiling Ursula looming above her. She couldn't see Calvin from her current perspective, but he was somewhere nearby, snorting and giggling in his usual dumb way.

Ursula stepped on Lexie's stomach, making her scream.

Calvin mimicked the sound, then did more of that piggish snorting.

Lexie screamed again as Ursula applied her full weight to her stomach, lifting one foot off the ground to balance atop her for several moments. The pain in her ribs became unbearable, like dozens of little knives digging into her chest. This latest exercise in torture lasted less than a minute, but each second felt like an eternity of agony. The degree to which the pain lessened after Ursula finally stepped down was barely measurable. She'd believed she'd experienced the highest level of misery imaginable at multiple points prior to now, but that belief had been exposed as false.

As if reading Lexie's mind, Ursula said, "You think that hurts? It's nothing compared to what's coming. Calvin, drag these bitches into the living room. I think they're done crawling for now."

Ursula moved away and in the next moment Calvin's leering, goony face filled Lexie's field of vision. He scooped her into his arms and carried her swiftly into the living room, dumping her on the couch. The impact of her body against the cushions caused puffs of dust to rise into the air, making her gag as her eyes watered. Before leaving to retrieve her sister, the big man made her scream again by grabbing hold of her fractured wrist. Instead of relinquishing the wrist upon hearing this expression of pain, he squeezed it and elicited an even louder scream. Then his other hand was on her, hefting her up and forcing her into an uncomfortable sitting position at one end of the couch.

Ursula came into the living room. "Get the other one in here and then go fetch Mama."

Calvin's leering grin disappeared, his bottom lip pooching outward in a display of petulance.

Ursula slapped him, making him yelp. "Just do it, you dumb ox."

Calvin roared something incomprehensible and ran out of the room, returning with Trixie cradled in his arms seconds later. He dumped her on the other end of the couch, then bellowed again as he stomped out of the living room, disappearing down the first-floor hallway.

Ursula rolled her eyes. "I swear, he's such a baby sometimes."

Lexie sniffled. "I'm hurt. I need a hospital."

Ursula cackled. "Bitch, how stupid are you? I hate to break it to you, but that ain't gonna happen."

Lexie trembled as she raised her left arm and examined the unnatural angle of her swollen wrist. She knew if she didn't receive proper medical care soon, the wrist would heal wrong, if it healed at all. There might be serious additional complications, including gangrene or infection. She wondered if she might be able to set and care for the broken limb on her own, but didn't know if she possessed the mental strength she'd need to even attempt such a thing. That wasn't even likely considering the strong likelihood of her captors hurting her so much worse that her broken wrist was rendered irrelevant.

Ursula giggled. "Shit, did you hear what I just said? 'Break it.' That's fucking funny as shit." She giggled again. "Do you get it? It's funny because your twig is broken."

Lexie sneered. "I get it. I just don't think it's funny. You're not as clever as you think you are, you psycho cunt."

The look of mirth faded from Ursula's lumpy face. A corner of her mouth curled and her hands clenched into fists.

She took a step toward the couch.

At the other end of the couch, Trixie sat up with a groan and said, "*I* thought it was funny."

Ursula glared at Lexie a few moments longer.

Then she let out a breath and slowly unclenched her fists.

She was smiling again by the time she turned her head to look at Trixie. "Yeah? You mean that?"

Trixie sat up straighter, grimacing as she nodded. "I do. I respect what you did. It's what we deserve for being so pathetic."

Ursula raised an eyebrow. "Huh. Well, I kinda suspect you're kissing up for obvious reasons, but that's interesting. We'll see if you still feel the same way in a while."

A muffled sound of voices emanated from the hallway not long thereafter. One of the voices belonged to Calvin, more of his insensible mumbling, and the other had a creaky feminine quality to it, suggesting a speaker of advanced age. A moment later, Calvin rolled a wheelchair bearing an elderly woman of considerable girth into the living room. Lexie couldn't help cringing when she saw the woman. Not because she was ugly—even though she was—but rather because the only thing she was wearing was a large adult diaper.

Calvin parked the wheelchair in front of the couch and locked the wheels.

The old woman licked her lips as she leaned forward and looked Lexie up and down before speaking in a warbly voice that made her sound like the world's most demented grandma. "You are so cute. I've always had a thing for blondes."

There was a pause.

Then Ursula giggled.

Calvin followed suit a moment later.

Trixie grinned as she studied each of their faces.

Then she started giggling, too.

The collective sound of deranged mirth went on for several more moments, only stopping when Ursula raised her voice to cut through the cacophony. "You can have your way with whatever's left of her later, Mama, but we've got a lot to do before then." Her revived grin remained in place as she approached the couch, putting herself between Lexie and the old woman in the wheelchair. "Calvin, go fetch my tools."

Calvin started moving away from them, but Ursula had one final instruction for her brother.

"And while you're at it, go ahead and drag the Bad Girl Chair in here."

SIXTEEN

Five years ago

THE GAPS BETWEEN VISITS FROM her captors got longer as Lara's period of confinement in the perpetually dark upstairs room dragged on, and she surpassed the one-month mark locked within its four walls without her even realizing it. At least two full days had gone by since either Alma or Ursula had dropped in to check on her. The good thing about that was there had been no punishments, no beatings or exercises in humiliation. She'd endured a lot of pain, more than any person should have to experience over the course of several lifetimes, and she was grateful for any respite.

She was less thrilled about the physical effects of the deprivations she was experiencing. Lengthy periods of no food and water only served to worsen her already weakened state. It didn't help that her body still sought to fulfill all its normal functions. This included the attempted purging of waste even when there was nothing of substance left to expel. Her stomach would seize up with cramps as her straining anus released only a thin stream of brown liquid. She'd become so thirsty in the sweltering heat of the musty room that she'd taken to licking her piss off the floor every time her bladder voided, even though there wasn't nearly enough of it to quell the thirst.

She was fantasizing about strangling herself with one of the rusty chains when she heard someone insert the key in the door lock and begin to rattle it. There was a sharp click a moment later and then the door swung inward with its usual loud groaning of hinges.

She sat up and sniffled softly as Ursula padded into the room and set her lantern on the floor. "Please . . . I need water. I'm so thirsty."

Ursula grunted. "Yeah. I bet you're hungry, too."

Lara's only response was a despairing moan. Deducing the actual intentions of her captors had become an exercise in futility. It was possible Ursula was only here to torment her on a psychological level with the mere prospect of receiving water and nourishment without actually providing those things. That would not have surprised her, because they'd shown over and over, that there was no bottom to their cruelty. She did, however, believe there was some chance she'd be given what she needed, if only because she'd die without receiving it soon. It all hinged on whether they were still interested in keeping her around, and despite the fantasies of suicide that consumed so much of her waking time in isolation, she knew she wanted to keep on living.

Ursula made a sound of disgust. "Good Lord, you sound pathetic. Get over here and pay your respects."

Lara went to her on her hands and knees. She kissed each of the woman's dirty bare feet, mumbling the words of obsequious praise she'd been instructed in all the other times. When Ursula raised the hem of her white dress, Lara raised up on her knees and pressed her face to the wet place between her legs. She felt Ursula's fingers at the back of her head, clenching and pressing against her while she licked and probed with her tongue.

After Ursula decided she'd had enough of the oral ministrations, she shoved Lara away from her, making her whimper as she hit the floor with a thud. She left her lantern on the floor as she walked out of the room, a scraping sound signaling her return a moment later. Lara had landed on her side, facing away from the open door. She rolled over and frowned when she saw that the source of the scraping noise was the legs of a sturdy wooden chair being dragged across the floor. Ursula set the chair upright near the lantern and walked out of the room again, returning seconds later with a paint-stained metal bucket and a hammer.

She smiled when she saw Lara's look of confusion. "I want you to build something for me. If you do a good job, you'll get food and all the water you can drink." She set the bucket on the floor. "Come see what I have for you."

Lara felt apprehension, but she sat up again and waddled on her knees until she was close enough to the bucket to peer inside.

She frowned when she looked up at Ursula. "I don't understand."

The bucket was filled with nails of varying sizes, most of them slender and only an inch or two in length. She saw a small scattering of longer, thicker nails. A high percentage of them were brown with rust. Some were coated in some type of viscous substance she thought was possibly motor oil.

Ursula patted the top of her head. "Of course you don't understand, darlin'. You're dumber than a tree stump. I'll explain." She moved away from her and picked up the chair, turning it upside down. "What you're gonna do is take a bunch of them nails and hammer them through the underside of the seat." She tapped the indicated area and set the chair upright again, then swept her hand over the seat in a waving motion. "I want the points of the nails sticking out all over this thing, leaving a space of no more than an inch between all of them. Then when you're done with that, do the arms and the back. You follow so far?"

The chair had wide armrests and the back was comprised of three wide, thick slats. This job would not be an easy one. Completing it would require a significant amount of time, at least an hour or two, and she wasn't sure she had the strength or stamina for it.

She met Ursula's gaze. "I follow. I'll do my best, but I just don't know if I'll be able to get it done if I don't at least get some water first."

Ursula's expression hardened. "I already told you, bitch. You'll get your water after you're done. You have my solemn fucking word. But you better get to work." She moved closer and touched Lara's face with the back of a hand, making her tremble and flinch. The pain from the assault with the pipe wrench remained significant. "I like your new look. You're definitely not nearly as pretty as me now."

Lara sniffled. "I never was."

Ursula laughed. "I know."

She picked up the lantern and moved away from her. At first Lara thought she was leaving already, but instead she set the lantern on the floor again, this time just inside the open doorway.

Then she said, "I'm gonna leave the door open and the lantern right there so you have light to work by. There should be enough slack in them chains to do what you need to do. Holler when you're done."

She stepped out into the hallway then and was gone.

Lara looked at the hammer and wondered if she could smash her way out of the shackles with it, but she knew even pondering that was another exercise in pointlessness. Smashing open the shackles might be possible in theory—though she was far from convinced—but she knew she'd never be able to get it done before the denizens of Dead End House would come rushing into the room to subdue and punish her.

Ursula yelled at her from somewhere downstairs. "*I don't hear any hammerin' up there!*"

Lara turned the chair over and set it upside down on the floor, with the underside of the seat facing upward at an angle. She reached into the bucket and came out with a single two-inch nail.

Then she picked up the hammer and got to work.

SEVENTEEN

THE CORRUPTION OF TRIXIE, PART TWO:
FULL IMMERSION

ANOTHER PERSON THEY HADN'T SEEN previously came into the living room while Calvin was off fetching things for Ursula. This guy was tall and skinny, but not as awkward or gangly as Calvin. He had long, greasy brown hair and a beard to match. Lexie guessed he was somewhere in mid-to-late middle age. This was something she detected in the gauntness of his features more than anything else, as there were no telltale gray strands intermingled with the brown in his hair. He wore dirty blue jeans with holes in the knees, sandals, and a white t-shirt with a small rip in the front at chest level. The words *Cyber Freak* were emblazoned across the front in a retro computer font. He wore glasses with thick black rims, and they were held together with a piece of white tape in the middle.

The look on his face as he came into the room was one of mild curiosity. There was something about him that made Lexie uneasy, something beyond the mere fact of his apparently uncoerced presence in this horrible place. Compared to the other residents of this putrid den of insanity, he looked almost normal, like a hippie in dire need of a shower after a summer spent following around a traveling music festival in a van. Something else about him, however, some hard to identify quality, just seemed . . . off.

The man made no attempt at stealth, coming all the way into the living room to stand next to the old lady's rickety wheelchair for a few silent moments. He looked back and forth between Trixie and Lexie, his brow furrowing as he studied them. Ursula and the old lady paid him no mind whatsoever, not glancing at him even once the whole time. He walked back out of the living room when Calvin returned, disappearing into the foyer. The stairs creaked as he went up to the second floor.

Lexie and her sister exchanged a puzzled glance. The animosity Trixie felt for her was still evident, but it was clear she too was left feeling slightly discomfited and confused by the strange man's brief visit to the living room.

"Who was that fucking weirdo?"

Ursula raised an eyebrow. "You'll have to be more specific."

Lexie's look of confusion deepened. "You know who I mean. The greasy hippie who was just in here."

Ursula shrugged. "I don't know what you're talking about. You've got bigger worries anyway, bitch."

Calvin approached the couch with the handle of a large metal toolbox clutched in one hand, while with the other hand he dragged in a sturdy wooden chair studded with the points of what had to be at least a hundred nails. The points protruded from all over the seat, as well as from the armrests and the slats in the back. Several necklaces and pendants that had once belonged to young girls and women who'd either been kidnapped or lured into Dead End House dangled from some of the nails, in particular along the armrests. The seat was stained a dark crimson in the spaces between the nails. Leather straps were attached to the arms, legs, and back. Nailed to the top slat of the seat's backrest was an irregularly cut piece of stained wood, its shape a jagged semi-circle. Adorning it was a skillfully rendered painting of a young woman in tears.

Lexie could only assume this was the so-called "Bad Girl Chair." The sight of it triggered another wave of stomach-churning dread. Most of the nail points protruded from the wood by only about a half-inch, some less than that. Its purpose was to torture rather than kill, but she knew the distinction was one that would scarcely matter to anyone forced to sit in it.

Calvin turned the chair so that it was directly facing the couch from a distance of about three feet. The toolbox he simply dumped on the floor, a number of metallic implements inside it audibly clunking together as it landed with a heavy thump on the filthy rug.

The top of the toolbox consisted of two cantilevered parts that when pulled apart revealed trays filled with various items. After opening it, Ursula reached into the main compartment and removed a heavy pipe wrench.

She stood up and looked at Lexie. "This is for asking impertinent questions."

The hand gripping the pipe wrench whipped around in a flash, leaving Lexie no time to jerk her head out of the way. The impact of it against her cheek resulted in a devastatingly intense burst of agony. She heard her sister gasp and say "Oh, no" even as the wrench flashed around again, this time striking the other side of her face. Once again, the pain was extraordinary. An audible crack accompanied the second impact, and she knew her cheekbone had been fractured. It was just another step in a systematic process of brutalization she feared wouldn't end until she'd been reduced to a quivering blob of insensible organic jelly only faintly resembling a human being. This thought filled her with fresh terror, but even in the midst of it what mattered most was her sister's startled gasp of horror.

Oh, no.

Their situation was hopeless. She was resigned to that now. The only future remaining to her was one filled with torture and humiliation. She'd be maimed and violated again, and a miserable death at the hands of these heartless sadists would be the inevitable, inescapable conclusion to this season in Hell. She nevertheless decided she could accept all of that knowing beneath all the sneering anger and resentment her sister still loved her.

Ursula lowered the pipe wrench. "How did that feel, bitch?"

Lexie could only moan in response.

Ursula turned toward Trixie. "How did it feel to see your sister get fucked up like that?"

Lexie's eyelids fluttered at half-mast as she turned her head to observe her sister's reaction to this query, which was understandably guarded. Even if she'd experienced a genuine renewed sense of sympathy for her sibling, she would also be concerned about how her tormentor might react to any answer she gave.

Ursula approached the other end of the couch, raising the pipe wrench as if preparing to strike again. "You've got about two seconds to answer."

Trixie cringed at the sight of the heavy wrench hovering high above her head, pressing herself against the back of the couch as she at last blurted out a response. "She fucking deserved it! You should hit her again."

The emotional pain caused by these words was nearly as debilitating to Lexie as her state of physical agony. She knew what her sister was saying was driven by overwhelming terror of being subjected to the same savage treatment. It contained an element of cowardice, but it was hard to condemn a person in her position for that. In her place, she might react in much the same way. There was a part of her that didn't want to believe that—recoiled from even the suggestion of it, in fact—but the primitive lizard brain part of her psyche knew better.

She closed her eyes and allowed her head to tilt backward until it lay against the top of the backrest. Even breathing had become almost too painful to bear, causing more of those stabbing sensations behind her ribs as well as intensifying the throbbing in her cheek. She worked hard to keep her breathing shallow, an endeavor that required most of her concentration.

"Do you mean that?" Ursula asked Trixie, her tone aggressive and suffused with a range of implicit threats. "Do you swear it on your worthless fucking life?"

Trixie whimpered. "I mean it. I swear to fucking God I do!"

"God don't live in this house, you stupid cunt! Don't you ever invoke that name again! This is the devil's domain. Every drop of blood we spill is in *his* name. You best remember that." Ursula was raging at her now, screeching at an ear-piercing volume. "What if I said I was gonna kill one of you bitches right here and now, which one should it fucking be?"

Trixie screamed back at her: "*Her! It should be her! Fuck that fucking cunt!*"

Ursula howled with demonic laughter.

Calvin joined in with some of his loudest snorting and snuffling sounds yet.

Lexie kept her eyes closed and her head tilted back as she tried her best to relegate the madness to the background. She also tried to expunge her mind of anything resembling organized, coherent thought. Death seemed imminent and she decided the only sane way of dealing with that was to detach from reality. She became so immersed in this effort she was barely aware of someone gently taking hold of her un-injured hand and lifting it up. That only began to change when she felt one of her fingers slide into a moist space. Her eyelids fluttered slightly, but her head remained tilted backward.

Then came the snap of teeth crunching down on her finger.

Her eyes snapped open wide and she screamed, heedless of the way this amplified her internal pain. The old lady had a firmer grip on her hand now and was engaged in a furiously determined effort to bite off her forefinger. Lexie tried jerking her hand away, but that only made things worse. The old lady growled and wrenched her head back and forth like a rabid dog. Blood spilled from between her lips and down over her chin and the wattles beneath. There was a crunch-ing sound as she redoubled the effort, causing more blood to burst forth from her mouth. Lexie screamed when she heard the old woman's teeth clack together, having chopped all the way through her finger. She screamed again as she jerked her hand away from the woman's blood-spattered mouth. Then she gaped in disbelief as she held up her hand and watched blood spurt from the stump of her finger, which had been raggedly severed just above the second knuckle.

Had she really believed she'd reached her ultimate threshold of pain at any point prior to this moment?

Well, she'd been wrong about that.

She did some more screaming while Trixie looked at her and smiled. At the same time, Ursula was yelling at her kin, instructing Calvin to get the wheelchair away from the couch and to go fetch the torch. Her brother was initially too fascinated by the way blood con-tinued to jet out of Lexie's finger stump to respond to this command, but he jumped into action when Ursula yelled again and started swat-ting him. He rolled the wheelchair backward several feet and locked the wheels again. Then he ran out of the living room, returning only moments later with a slender metal canister Lexie at first thought was a fire extinguisher, only that made no sense at all.

Then the meaning behind some of Ursula's words belatedly pen-etrated.

Go fetch the torch.

She shook her head. "No. No-no-no-no-no-no . . ."

Ursula snatched the canister from her brother and approached Lexie. "Gonna have to cauterize that finger. It's the only way. We ain't surgeons here."

The old woman cackled from her wheelchair. "You could just let the little bitch bleed." She had the severed segment of Lexie's finger clamped between her teeth in a corner of her mouth and was gnawing on it. "When she dies, we'll slice all the meat off her bones and have a big ol' summer feast. Been too long since we had a proper backyard cookout."

Lexie was still shaking her head. "No. Please don't."

Ursula glanced at her brother. "Hold her down, Calvin. Ain't gonna be able to do this right otherwise. Best to sit on her, I reckon. She's apt to do a lot of squirmin'."

Lexie tried shrinking away from the hulking form of Calvin Wilcox as he loomed over her, but there was nowhere to go, and she was in no shape now to get up and run. He grabbed hold of her and forced her to lie flat on her stomach, facing away from Trixie. She tried rising up, but he shoved her down again and straddled her backside, with her right arm hanging over the side of the couch. Blood continued to drizzle out of the finger stump, further staining the rug.

Calvin clamped a hand around her wrist and raised the hand up.

Ursula moved closer. "I advise you to spread them fingers out and hold still while I do this, otherwise your whole goddamn hand might get burned up."

There was a whoosh as the torch ignited.

Lexie turned her head and saw the thin column of red and blue flame rising from the nozzle. She felt the heat from it long before it touched her skin. Her gaze shifted briefly to Ursula's face. The madwoman was grinning, her eyes alight with anticipation. She realized then the woman wasn't doing this merely out of medical necessity. The opportunity to scorch her flesh excited her. Her deranged brother was excited, too. She could feel his erection pushing against her ass from behind the fabric of his coveralls.

Her eyes flooded with tears as she spread her fingers and turned her head away.

Then she screamed as the flame touched her bleeding finger stump. The pain was massive, worse again by far than the previous highest threshold, and she was unable to keep her hand from shaking. This caused the flame to touch the adjacent fingers, and she screamed into the filthy couch cushion beneath her face, her mouth stretched open as wide as she could get it. The pain was mind-shredding, but she did her best to fight through it and keep her hand as still as possible. She smelled smoke and the sweet odor of her own cooking flesh. The old lady rocked wildly in her wheelchair, cackling and remarking on how hungry the smell was making her.

It seemed to go on forever.

Then the whooshing sound of the torch abruptly ceased.

Ursula chuckled. "There ya go. All fixed up."

Lexie sobbed in between moans of agony, barely noticing now as Calvin continued to grind his crotch against her. This went on until Ursula ordered him off her a few moments later. A reflexive pang of gratitude made Lexie whimper, although she knew gratitude was useless in this scenario. The idiot's sister didn't do things like that out of the goodness of her heart.

Only evil lived in the heart of that ruthless bitch.

Ursula confirmed this belief beyond any doubt seconds later when she looked at her brother and said, "Now throw the bitch in the Bad Girl Chair."

Lexie tried to get up.

She'd been seized by the notion of trying to make a run for it. Yes, the attempt would have virtually no chance of success, but she meant to try anyway because she was long past the point of having anything left to lose. No one was sitting on her now. There were no restraints holding her in place.

She *had* to try.

She got up on her knees and tried swinging a leg over the side of the couch. Before she could get any farther than that, Calvin scooped her up and dropped her in the Bad Girl Chair. She screamed louder than ever as she felt the points of countless nails pierce her ass, her back, and the backs of her legs. She tried rising up and instinct caused her to grip the chair's armrests, which were also studded with nail points. She wailed in unrelenting agony as the points punched into her palms and fingers. Before she could try rising up again, Calvin went to work securing her to the chair with the straps. The endless screams that tore out of her throat became painful, making it feel raw and jagged. Her bulging eyes sought her sister, desperate for even the faintest sign of sympathy or help.

Trixie met her gaze, but her expression was blank.

She looked numb. In shock.

Ursula snapped her fingers in front of Trixie's face, causing her to look almost dreamily up at her. "You, snap out of it. Go sit in your sister's lap and make out with her."

Trixie frowned. "Huh?"

Ursula's expression radiated disdain. "You want to prove yourself to me, show me you shouldn't get the same treatment? Then do as I fucking tell you."

Trixie stared at her a moment longer before nodding.

Then she rose up from the couch and approached the Bad Girl Chair. At first she only stood in front of it, staring down at Lexie with that blank expression again. Then she crawled into her sister's lap, taking care to avoid the nail points as best she could, though her skin did get nicked in a few places. The added pressure further inflamed the already intense pain Lexie was experiencing as the nail points pierced deeper into her flesh. She trembled and wept continuously as she felt Trixie's lips touch her face, first gliding over her swollen cheeks and then pressing against her mouth.

Next came the warm intrusion of her tongue.

Then Trixie was biting her bottom lip.

Hard, drawing blood.

All while the family of crazies that called Dead End House home looked on and made loud noises of approval, hooting, whistling, and clapping with the fervor of rowdy, drunken hooligans at a sporting event.

EIGHTEEN

THE CORRUPTION OF TRIXIE, PART THREE: RATIONALE

THE GIRL IN THE CAGE had given up begging for mercy. She lay curled up on her side, naked and shivering with her arms wrapped around her knees. In the early stages of Trixie's solo session with her in the basement, she'd been quite vocal, shrieking and screaming as her body was subjected to various abuses. Some of her loudest screams had come after Trixie had opened the burlap sack, allowing the rat snake to slither out of it and drop into the cage through the slats at the top. The snake was long and black and scary-looking, but it was also non-venomous, according to Ursula.

The non-venomous part was something she'd been uncertain about, if only because there was always ample reason to doubt the truth of anything Ursula said. The woman was a manipulative sadist who was often upfront about the terrible things she intended to do to her captives, but she also wasn't above telling lies when it suited her. This was especially true when the lies were deployed in a way that made them believable and contributed to the psychological

96

disintegration of the person being tormented.

Such was the case with the girl she'd rechristened Slaggie, whose immediate reaction of shrieking alarm as the snake entered the cage confirmed she had little in the way of working knowledge regarding different species of slithering reptiles. If she'd known it wasn't venomous, she might have spared herself some pain by remaining calm, but instead she frantically swatted and kicked at the creature, earning herself multiple bites in the process. Her wails of panicked distress reached ear-piercing volume and didn't let up until well after the snake slithered out of the cage and disappeared into the dark recesses of the basement.

The girl took seemingly forever to calm down. She grabbed the slats at the top of the cage and rattled them as scream after scream came ripping out of her lungs. The noisy display of unhinged terror simultaneously irritated and pleased Trixie. The shrillness of the endless screams hurt her ears, but she knew the people upstairs could hear them, which was to her benefit as they helped cement the impression she was striving to create. She wanted them to believe she possessed a capacity for cruelty equal to their own.

This was how she would survive, her only chance at not winding up like her sister and all the countless other girls who'd been tortured and murdered at Dead End House down through the years. She had to become one of them, a process that was part performance and part reality. She wasn't actually like them. She didn't enjoy inflicting pain, causing injury, and engaging in acts of extreme perversion, but she was fully committed to giving the *appearance* of enjoying those things. That meant throwing herself into her performance with unhesitating gusto. If Ursula told her to do something, she did it right away, regardless of how outrageously disgusting it might be.

Among other things, this included engaging in sexual activity with the obese old woman Ursula interchangeably referred to as grannie and mama, which was confusing as hell, but she didn't question it. She'd also been required to change the woman's adult diapers and wipe the caked mounds of shit off her massive bottom on a regular basis. Performing oral sex on her was almost a pleasure in comparison to that. There'd also been sexual interactions with Ursula and her brother, sometimes both at the same time. The only non-imprisoned resident of Dead End House who hadn't been intimate with her was the nerdy beanpole with the greasy long hair. She hadn't even seen that guy again since that night in the living room.

DEAD END HOUSE

Then there were all the evil things she'd been required to do to her sister in the days that followed Lexie's first period of confinement to the Bad Girl Chair. The process of degradation her twin was subjected to was methodical and devoid of even the slightest trace of mercy. It also never seemed to end. She was beaten countless times with fists and blunt implements. At times it was her own fist punching Lexie in the face a dozen times in a row. She cut her knuckles on her sister's teeth again and again. She whipped her with a belt and scalded her with boiling hot well water.

The transformation of Lexie's face had been a particularly terrible thing to behold over the course of the last few days. Her visage was no longer a radiant example of natural beauty. Instead, it was bloated, bruised, and ugly. One eye seemed permanently swollen shut from all the beatings. Sections of her flesh looked melted from the hot water scaldings. She was missing half her fingers now, two of which Trixie herself had removed. Her broken wrist was at least twice its normal size and had turned a livid shade of purple. Ursula was saying they might need to amputate her arm below the elbow to keep her alive a while longer, but that determination had not yet been made. They might go the simpler route, allowing the limb to wither and rot. If any associated infections caused by the lack of proper care caused her to perish, well, so be it.

Trixie stared at the quivering mess in the cage, a mess that had once been a normal young woman with hopes and dreams and dignity, a person who had friends and family who loved her. People who were probably sick with worry right now, wondering where she'd gone and what might have happened to her. They likely harbored fears of abduction and the cops probably suspected they'd one day find her corpse dumped in the woods or in a river, the victim of some more mundane class of serial killer than the people who lived in this house.

A similar scenario might even now be playing out among people in her own social circles back home if not for the carefully orchestrated scheme of subterfuge she'd been conducting over social media for the last few days. At least a couple times a day she'd go sit in the Range Rover and record videos for TikTok, doing her best to present a believable illusion of normality. The videos went out to TrikTok Twins subscribers after careful editing to avoid including glimpses of anything that might arouse suspicion. In the videos, she talked about traveling with her sister to various locations in the southeast, describing the journey as a vacation as well as an opportunity to mentally recalibrate and think about what they wanted to do with their show in the future.

The Range Rover was being kept behind Dead End House for the time being, parked at the tree line and hidden beneath a canopy of camo netting. The tree line was a good distance from the back of the house, somewhere around the length of a football field. A person would have to walk most of the way out there to notice the hidden vehicle. Ursula always accompanied her when she went out there to record her videos. They often spent an hour or more in the SUV before returning to the house, turning the engine on and letting the air conditioning run while the phones charged. It made for a nice break from the oppressive atmosphere inside the house.

Satisfied she'd performed adequately again, Trixie retrieved her phone from the shelf and stopped the recording. It was time to take it back upstairs and let Ursula review her work, which she was confident would be deemed satisfactory. Prior to stopping, she'd gotten a lot of good footage of the various cruel things she'd done to Slaggie.

Trixie squatted in front of the cage and showed the woman the ragged ear she'd sawed off the side of her head. "Believe it or not, I don't like this. No, seriously, I mean it. The lack of symmetry bugs me, fucks with my sense of aesthetics. Maybe I'll come back for the other one soon."

Slaggie moaned.

Trixie laughed. Then she frowned.

She wasn't sure why she was laughing or saying these things. No one who mattered was down here to bear witness to them, and she'd stopped the video, so there'd be no recording to show Ursula. Not being observed meant it was no longer necessary to continue indulging in these additional gestures of cruelty, yet something compelled her to do it anyway. It made her wonder if by committing herself so intensely to the performance she was becoming one of them for real. She hadn't killed anyone yet, but at this point, after all the horrendous things she'd done, it wouldn't be a huge leap.

Of course, there was also the blackmail element to consider. She wasn't the only one making videos. Ursula still had the other phone and at this point she had hours of incriminating video that showed Trixie doing a number of shockingly brutal things to her sister. The footage guaranteed that even if Trixie got free of this place somehow, she could never go to the authorities.

The way she saw it, she had two options at this point.

She could fully assimilate and live out the rest of her days as part of the psychotic Wilcox clan.

Or she could bide her time and eventually kill them all in some perfect, vulnerable moment. Just fucking slaughter them, including the elusive, greasy-haired weirdo, provided she could find him. Then douse the place in gasoline and drive far the fuck away before going to the cops with some made-up story about what had happened to her sister. Before doing that, of course, she'd delete all the videos from their phones—as well as from the fucking cloud—and hope like hell she'd eradicated every trace of her own wrongdoing. Even if she managed to do that, however, the cops might find whatever story she told dubious. There was likely no getting around that.

The second option was tempting as hell. It'd be wonderful to return to living in a clean, air-conditioned environment, removed from the company of lunatics and the ever-present stench of death and decay. For all the reasons she'd mentally reviewed a million times already, though, engineering a way to make it happen without becoming a person of interest in her sister's disappearance would be complicated.

The first option might actually be easier, although it would entail permanently lowering her standard of living and embracing a lifestyle of depravity and predation. It would also mean never seeing her friends and family again, which would suck, but there was a flip side to that, wasn't there?

Yes, there was.

If she stayed and assimilated, she'd never have to look her loved ones in the eyes and commiserate with them over Lexie's disappearance while knowing her true fate all along. Not just knowing it, but knowing that she'd contributed significantly to the suffering of the missing girl they all loved.

Trixie groaned.

Goddamn. I am absolutely fucked no matter what.

"I'm heading out, Slaggie. I'll see you again soon. In the meantime, you just remember what I said while you were going down on Wormie. You gotta keep treating her right. Let her know how much you love her. Then maybe one of these days you'll get to make an honest woman of her."

She tossed the severed ear into the cage and laughed as she walked out of the basement.

NINETEEN

THE DOORBELL RANG JUST AS Nancy Kincaid was finishing up washing the dishes. It wasn't a big job because there were never many left stacked in the sink at any one time. She kept a tidy house, believing that maintaining a clean and sanitary environment in the home was one of the most important keys to good mental health. Also, it gave her something to do every day. This was important because she knew from sad experience how dangerous depression could be, especially combined with too much idle time.

She'd spent a lot of time consumed with bitterness over her former husband's willful descent into full-blown alcoholism. When they were still together in those last months, she'd scolded him relentlessly for it. There'd even been some physical altercations, and she'd been the instigator each of those times.

The truth was Sterling wasn't the only one who'd gone off the rails, but her method of chasing oblivion was vastly different. She'd always been a shamelessly flirty woman, but after Lara's disappearance, she became aggressively promiscuous, sleeping with a string of men without ever trying to hide what she was doing from Sterling. One of them introduced her to cocaine and she went through a period of throwing away too much money on her new habit. This included frequently dipping into the funds that had been raised online to aid in the search for Lara. She later estimated she'd gone through more than half the total amount. Some creative bookkeeping on the part of one of her lovers kept her from getting in serious trouble, but that only came after the near-fatal OD that landed her in the hospital for several days.

That was her wakeup call. She began a methodical and unforgiving process of setting her life in order as soon as she was discharged from the hospital. This included issuing an ultimatum to Sterling. He could either sober up and work with her to move on with their lives in a healthier way or he could get the hell out.

Sterling left that day and never returned.

Her existence became a lonely one, but at least she felt relatively at peace. She never stopped missing her daughter and praying for a miraculous return, but she'd come to terms with the strong likelihood of that never happening. The reality was that the best and happiest days of her life were behind her, but so were the worst ones and that had to count for something.

The doorbell rang a second time as she moved through the living room on her way to the front door at an unhurried pace. Her curiosity was aroused because she wasn't expecting a visitor, which meant there was a good chance she'd soon have to spend an annoying few moments shooing away a solicitor. They could be extra pushy sometimes when you were a woman, especially if they sensed you were alone in the house.

In the living room, she stopped at the long table behind the sofa and opened her purse, taking out her can of mace just in case. This was a nice neighborhood, and she was unlikely to encounter real trouble in broad daylight.

Still, it never hurt to be prepared.

She went into the foyer and approached the front door, where she paused to glance through the peephole. A slender and stylish young woman who looked as if her main ambition in life was to look like an extra in a Tim Burton movie was standing on her front porch. She didn't appear threatening in any obvious way, but Nancy found her unexpected presence here mystifying and thus automatically unsettling.

She frowned.

Maybe she should wait for the girl to go away.

A car she didn't recognize was parked in the street in front of her house and someone was sitting slumped down in the front passenger seat. Nancy's sense of unease ticked sharply upward. There seemed to her a strong chance the person in the car was trying to remain unseen. If true, there was a real possibility of some shady partnership existing between these two strangers.

Nancy's grip on the can of mace tightened.

She considered hurrying back into the living room to snatch her phone out of her purse. She was already drifting backward in that direction when the girl raised her voice and spoke clearly from the other side of the door. "Mrs. Kincaid, I know you don't know me, but I'm a friend of your husband's and I need to talk to you."

Nancy stopped in her tracks and frowned again.

Until this moment, she hadn't once thought of the person on her porch in connection with Sterling. She was far too young and cute and put together to have any association with the hopeless and pathetic bum her ex-husband had become during his years on the street. The notion was absurd to the point of being laughable.

And yet this was what she was saying.

Nancy thought again of the person slumped down in the front seat of the car and felt a fresh tingling of unease, but underneath that—no use denying it—was an incipient curiosity. Could that person really be the man who used to share her life and bed, and if so, how and why had he sent this alluring young woman as his messenger?

She unlocked and opened the door, holding up the can of mace and pointing it at the girl. "Sterling Kincaid hasn't been my husband for years, as I suspect you know. I only kept the name because it was easier than changing everything. Who are you and why are you actually here?"

The girl arched an eyebrow as she eyed the slim canister with a bemused smile. "You don't have to mace me. I swear I'm not dangerous. My name is Agatha Winchester. I ran into Sterling on the street by chance a few days ago and wound-up taking care of him after he had a small medical emergency. He wants to talk to you about something and I think you should listen. Hear him out, and if you think there's nothing to what he has to say, we'll leave and never come back. That's a promise. What do you say?"

She spoke in an earnest way that came across as genuine rather than manipulative, but instead of setting Nancy's mind at ease, the impression had the opposite effect. She became even more concerned than she was before, but this time it was on the girl's behalf.

She sighed. "Agatha, I believe you mean well, but you don't know Sterling like I do. He was a good man once upon a time, but those days are long gone. Even if he's managed to string together a couple of sober days, I can promise you that will not last. If you're feeling sorry for him, the sad fact is you're wasting your time."

Agatha shrugged. "Okay, I get it, but I'm not here to convince you that he's changed his ways, and he hasn't come here to beg you to take him back."

"Is that so?"

Agatha nodded. "It is."

A deep line creased Nancy's brow. "Then why *are* you here?"

"It has to do with your missing daughter."

Nancy felt a first stirring of anger. It didn't feel like anything dangerous quite yet, not like years ago when any mention of this subject could have her trembling on the brink of volcanic rage within seconds, especially if it was broached in the wrong way. Sterling's perpetual drunkenness had caused him to frequently ramble on regarding various crockpot theories related to Lara's disappearance. All of it was far-fetched conspiratorial nonsense that never brought them one inch closer to uncovering the truth.

For a long time, he'd been convinced she was taken by sex traffickers and forced into a life of prostitution and drug addiction. Sometimes, when he was at his most paranoid and delusional, he suggested that shadowy people in positions of power were involved. He kept vowing to track her abductors down, exact vengeance, and bring their little girl back home. The drunken fool had fantasies of being like Liam Neeson in *Taken*, but in reality, he was like an even more pathetic version of the Nicolas Cage character in *Leaving Las Vegas*.

So she felt a deep wariness now.

She didn't want to see Sterling again. Not now and not ever.

She knew that as clearly as she'd ever known anything.

"You seem like a sweet girl, and I'm sorry my ex-husband has dragged you into his world of delusion, but—"

"Just hear him out," Agatha said, interrupting with a loud resoluteness that startled Nancy. "He told me you wouldn't want to see him and he explained why. I know he used to have pretty crazy ideas about what happened to Lara. And yes, now he has a new theory, but before you jump to any conclusions, I want you to know I think there might actually be something to this one. Could we please have just a few minutes to lay it all out for you? Like I said, if you think it's bullshit, we'll leave and never come back." She grunted. "Or at least *I* won't. That much I can guarantee."

Nancy was quiet for a few moments after this speech concluded. Once again, her instinct was to reject with prejudice any idea of willingly allowing Sterling to spend time in her presence. His years-long total absence from her daily life had improved her mental health almost beyond measure. His basic energy as a human being was corrosive and toxic. She did *not* want to expose herself to it again, yet it seemed to matter so deeply to this girl that saying no was harder than it should have been.

She was still fretting over what to do when she heard a car door open and shut. Tilting her head, she looked past the girl and saw a ghost from her past. Not really, but that was how it felt to see Sterling strolling across the front lawn toward the house. She sometimes caught glimpses of the barely human looking wreck he'd devolved into when she was downtown. He was so far gone he was close to unrecognizable. The man walking toward her now did not look like that. He was too gaunt to be mistaken for his former self, but he'd undergone a transformation so radical and surprising that the mere sight of it brought tears to her eyes. Gone were the wild mane of filthy hair and the scraggly beard. Also gone were the layers of putrid, raggedy garments. He was clad now in jeans, a tucked-in green polo shirt, and sneakers. She could tell the clothes were second-hand thrift store items, but they were clean and fit him reasonably well. His gait as he crossed the lawn was steady and purposeful, without a hint of drunken stagger. His eyes were clear and focused.

It was like some kind of goddamned miracle.

She hated herself for the tears that spilled from her eyes. They made her feel weak and vulnerable, and yet she was powerless to halt them.

Agatha turned in time to watch him near the porch. "Thought you were gonna wait for me to wave."

Sterling smiled as he glanced at her. "I get impatient sometimes. Just ask my former better half about that. So, what do you say, Nance? Can you spare us a few minutes of your time?"

DEAD END HOUSE

She gave it another few seconds of consideration before sighing in exasperation and stepping aside as she opened the door wider for them. "Oh, the hell with it. Come on in, both of you, but you better not be wasting my time with some load of pure horseshit."

Holding her gaze again, Sterling nodded. "I don't reckon we are, but that'll be up to you to decide."

He climbed the steps to the porch and the three of them went inside.

TWENTY

Five years ago

AFTER LARA COMPLETED WORK ON the torture chair, she endured another long stretch of time spent alone in the upstairs room. The room's door was still open and the lantern remained where Ursula had left it. Per the instructions she'd been given, she'd loudly declared work on the chair finished.

No one responded.

She tried hollering several more times, worsening the sensation of painful strain in her throat each time she made the effort, but the result remained the same. No response. No faint mumble of distant voices. No perceptible sounds of any kind emanating from anywhere. She nonetheless kept trying until her throat hurt too much to continue.

After giving up, she curled up on the floor and spent some time crying, stopping after only a few minutes. There was no one around to hear the aural evidence of her misery, and the tears never helped anyway. She'd cry again, she was sure, because she knew they weren't done torturing her. The work she'd been coerced into doing was something Ursula had undoubtedly conceived of with her in mind. She'd lost count somewhere in the midst of the process, but she estimated she'd driven at least one-hundred nails into the thing. A time would come when Ursula would force her to sit in it, and she'd have no shortage of tears when that happened.

She drifted off to sleep. When she awoke again she knew a significant amount of time had passed, hours at least. Someone had at last come up to the room while she was off in dreamland, taking the lantern away and closing the door. A new level of hopelessness took root inside her upon finding herself enveloped in darkness. She couldn't help feeling as if Ursula had done this on purpose. Physical torture was the thing the woman loved most, but it was clear she enjoyed mind games as well. It'd be just like her to linger somewhere out of sight, waiting to come back to the room after she was asleep.

This distressed Lara, but she felt she was close to reaching a point of no longer caring. She was too tired and too weak. Let Ursula play her cruel little games. Unless she received relief soon, a time was coming when Lara would expire from thirst. This was scary, but the upside of the possibility was that if it happened soon enough, she might never have to experience sitting in the fucking nail chair.

More time passed.

Hours.

Then just as she was starting to become drowsy again, she heard footsteps out in the hallway. She sat up with a groan as she heard the key rattling in the door lock. As the door began to swing inward, she turned her head and spotted the hammer. It was on the floor near the chair. She considered making a grab for it, but decided against it, knowing she was far too weak now to wield it as a weapon.

Ursula came into the room and set her lantern on the floor. She squatted next to Lara and smiled, flipping a ring of keys around on her forefinger. "Looks like you did a solid job on the chair. You're a worthless little pile of shit, but I do have to give you credit for that."

Lara reached toward her with a shaky hand. "Water."

Ursula laughed and slapped the hand away. "No."

Lara sniffled. "You promised."

Ursula nodded. "I know I did. But haven't you noticed? The only promises I keep are about hurting you."

"I'll die if I don't get water soon."

Another nod from Ursula. "Yeah, probably." She shrugged. "But it's not really a big deal, is it? I could let you go right now, let you walk out of here and never lay another finger on you, and it wouldn't matter. Death comes for all of us eventually, no matter what."

Chain links clinked as Lara raised a hand to wipe more useless tears from her face. They'd returned, just as she knew they would, and it hadn't even taken another act of physical torture to make it happen.

"I'll do anything to get out of here."

Ursula flipped the keys around on the ring again. "I'm sure that's true. So what?"

Lara grimaced as she shifted on the floor, trying to get more comfortable but failing again as she always did. She'd become scrawny during her many weeks locked away in this room. And bony, with hardly any meat left on her hips, which made always being on the uncovered wood floor even more torturous.

"But I mean it. Anything at all. I'll kill for you."

Ursula smirked. "You think I haven't heard that before? I've had at least a dozen girls like you in here. Hell, more than that. And every one of them bitches had one thing in common. They all wound up just like this, begging and promising. It means shit."

Lara shook her head. "I'm not like them."

Ursula laughed.

Lara reached out and touched her on the arm, an impetuous act that made her heart skip a beat when she saw the way the woman's face contorted with sudden fury. She kept her hand where it was, though. "No, I mean it. Bring me one of the other girls I know you've got in this house. Bring me *anybody*. A kid. A baby. I don't give a shit. Some kind of fucking sacrifice. Give me a knife and I'll fucking skin a bitch alive. Or cut open a baby and eat its little heart."

Her grip had tightened on Ursula's arm as she said these things, something she hadn't been conscious of until falling silent again.

Ursula's mouth twitched. "Take your hand off me."

Lara pulled her hand away. "I'm sorry. I meant what I said, though."

Ursula stared at her in silence for a long time, and there was something haunted in her expression, a faraway look with a strong hint of unexpected melancholy. "I guess maybe you do mean it," she said at last, her weary tone matching her expression. "And maybe we'll put that shit to the test soon. I don't think you appreciate yet the weight that word carries in this house. 'Sacrifice.' Sacrificial blood is a powerful thing. But we'll come back to that. First you need to see something."

She stood up and went to the door, where she slid the room key into the lock and left it there as she came back into the middle of the room. Lara tensed as she watched the woman approach the nail-studded chair. She suspected Ursula was about to make her sit in it. Even after all the hell she'd been through, she didn't feel ready to endure something that awful.

Ursula turned and faced Lara again. That strange melancholic quality was present in her expression again. She smiled thinly as she pulled the white dress off over her head and allowed it to fall to the floor.

She held Lara's gaze for an extended moment as she stood naked before her. In that moment, Lara had no expectations beyond enduring yet another forced sexual coupling with Calvin's sister.

But that was not what happened.

Ursula took two steps backward and dropped into the nail chair. Her mouth opened wide and her head tilted backward as her entire body quivered in agony. With unmistakable deliberateness, she gripped the armrests, driving the abundance of nail points embedded there into her palms and the undersides of her forearms. She then held on tight, the quivering of her body becoming so pronounced it made Lara think of scenes from old movies in which condemned prisoners were shown receiving a lethal jolt of electricity at the moment of their execution. Small trickles of blood began to spill down the sides of the chair as Ursula's mouth opened wider still, so wide her jaw looked on the verge of coming unhinged. A rising, shrill sound began to issue from that opening, and at first Lara thought it was the beginning of a scream.

She was wrong, though.

Ursula was laughing.

She tilted her head forward until she was looking Lara in the eye again. The pain she was experiencing was obvious from the continued shaking and in the tense rigidity of her muscles, but she looked almost happy.

Tears spilled from her eyes.

But she kept smiling, kept laughing.

Lara frowned. "What's wrong with you?"

Ursula shook her head. "Nothing. I'm finally feeling something real again."

Lara had no idea what to say so she said nothing at all. The woman was obviously even crazier than she'd already imagined. So she simply sat there on the floor and watched her tremble until, with a deliberateness equal to what she'd displayed when wrapping her hands around the armrests of the chair, Ursula began the process of disengaging herself from it. She pushed her ass up off the seat and then pried her hands loose from the armrests. Once she was fully upright, she began moving toward the door, her gait slow and shuffling as she left the room without glancing in Lara's direction again.

A trail of blood drops followed her to the door.

And then she was gone.

The door remained open with the key still inserted in the lock, but it was beyond Lara's reach. She sat there and stared at the opening as she tried without success to divine any special meaning from what Ursula had done. In the end, all she could do was remind herself there was no point in looking for sense in the things crazy people did.

Some more time passed, perhaps as much as a half-hour.

Then she heard footsteps in the hallway again and, in another moment, Calvin came into the room with a jug of water. He held the jug out to her, and she snatched it from his hands, raising it to her mouth immediately to guzzle from the liquid in the container. The sensation of water against her tongue was glorious, but then she sputtered and spat something out. She frowned as she looked into the jug, examining its contents, her stomach twisting when she saw that it contained more than just water. There were also clumps of dirt threaded with blades of dead grass and what she needed a moment to recognize as fresh ejaculate, undoubtedly the product of Calvin's filthy loins. There were also some squirming earthworms and who knew what else.

It didn't matter.

Calvin's piggish laughing didn't matter.

The water was all that mattered and Lara drank every drop she could.

TWENTY-ONE

LEXIE FELT ONLY A SMALL flicker of apprehension when she saw her sister come into the room. It wasn't that she no longer believed she had anything to fear from Trixie. Each of her sibling's increasingly rare visits to the upstairs room resulted in some new level of pain and trauma inflicted on her body, and she had no reason to suspect there would be any deviation from the established trend this time.

She believed she was nearing the end of her ability to experience anything resembling an elevated level of terror. A numbness had infected her spirit, diminishing her natural human will to endure a little more with each passing day. She no longer fantasized about escape or rescue. Escape simply was not possible in her advanced state of physical deterioration, and she was sure she'd be long dead should the day ever come when the authorities decided to raid this place.

She also no longer feared the infliction of additional pain. Yes, as long as she remained alive, she would continue to react to it in the normal way. That came with being a helpless slave to sensation and human instinct. She could be made to cry and perhaps even scream again should the agony become especially intense. The fear of experiencing those sensations was absolutely gone, though. One could only endure so much pain over a prolonged period of time without becoming inured to it, at least to some degree. The sensation of physical misery would come and then it would fade again, just as it always did, and then the cycle would repeat, again and again seemingly without end, until the inevitable day arrived when her body could no longer tolerate the trauma and she died. It was coming no matter what, so why fear it?

Likewise, there was no trace of emotion in her sister's blank expression as she kicked Lexie in the stomach, causing her to whimper and curl up in a tighter ball. The next kick was to the center of her face, and she yelped as she felt her lips split open again.

"Roll over on your back."

Lexie looked up at her. "Why?"

Trixie held the handle of a lantern in one hand and a burlap sack in the other. She set these things on the floor and said, "Because if you don't, I'll put bleach in your eyes. In the one that still works, anyway. Do you want that?"

Lexie sniffled. "No."

"I didn't think so. Now roll the fuck over."

Despite the harshness of her words, her sister's face remained an unreadable mask. Any actual human emotion that might be occurring behind the mask was a mystery. She suspected Trixie had trained herself not to feel emotion at all, a coping mechanism she could understand even if she didn't respect it. In truth, she didn't actually know if the insight was accurate. It was possible Trixie enjoyed degrading and hurting her every bit as much as she outwardly showed whenever members of the Wilcox family were around.

Not that the distinction mattered much anymore. She'd arrived at a point a while ago where she no longer thought of Trixie as her sister. In all the ways that mattered most, she was fully one of *them* now, an outwardly remorseless and merciless member of their deranged clan.

Lexie forced herself to stretch out and roll onto her back, an act of basic physical exertion that should have been easy, but for her that was no longer true. Her body had endured too much abuse and trauma. Even simple movements were excruciating. It was why she'd ceased bothering to sit up and squat when she needed to piss and shit.

Now when bowel and bladder relief became necessary or unavoidable, she went wherever she happened to be, even if she was curled up on the floor, as she was most of the time. The indignity of soiling herself over and over was another thing that no longer distressed her. Dignity itself had become a laughable notion, an illusory concept that would never be available to her again.

Trixie set the lantern and sack on the floor.

Then she straddled her sister's midsection and raised an open hand high above her head.

Lexie stared at the hand's open palm and again felt no fear. Her sister had administered countless beatings during their long weeks in this place. The feel of that palm crashing across her face had become as familiar to her as the new gaps between her teeth, which she was always probing with her tongue, a helpless compulsion that occupied much of her time now.

On most such occasions, she endured the beatings without comment, merely waiting for them to be over. This time an out-of-nowhere impulse caused her to speak before this one could commence. "What would Dad say if he could see this?"

As usual, there was no change in Trixie's expression, not even the smallest spark or twitch of anything resembling regret. "I stopped thinking about that a long time ago."

The hand came down and smashed across her face, snapping her head hard to the opposite side. An instant later, the back of her hand came around and drove her head back in the other direction. The beating continued thereafter without pause until it was over, which did not happen for a period that felt like forever. In reality, it was more like ten minutes, but during that time existence itself felt entirely composed of Trixie's hand and her face. In the midst of it, she sensed clearly the beating was not being doled out in a cursory or rote way, nor merely out of obligation or as a means of appeasing their new masters. The emotion that couldn't be read in Trixie's face came through in the force behind these blows. Where Lexie felt depleted and near the limits of her ability to endure much longer, her sister felt healthy and invigorated. Barely any trace of the beatings she'd taken during that first night in Dead End House remained. The swelling had gone down and the bruising had faded.

She wasn't just surviving here.

She was *thriving*.

As the beating neared its end, Trixie changed gears, her hand curling into a fist to deliver punches instead of open-handed blows. Lexie felt another of her teeth come loose from the gum and fall into the back of her throat, causing her to gag and splutter until she at last was able to spit it out between blows. Her mouth filled with blood again, making her gag and cough. Her nose already felt pulverized, but it endured more abuse as well.

The quickening flurry of punches came to an abrupt end. Still straddling her sister, Trixie reached over for the sack and pulled it close. She opened the cinched top, reached inside, and came out with a length of thick rope, the end of which was fashioned into a loop.

She tossed the sack aside. "Lift up your head, cunt."

Though it pained her to do so, Lexie obeyed. There was no longer any point to defiance, hadn't been for a long time. "Are you finally going to kill me now?"

Trixie slipped the loop over her head and pulled the rope taut around her neck. "You should be so lucky." She climbed off her sister and stood up, pulling roughly at the rope. "Get up."

In this case, immediate obedience was more difficult. It'd been a long time since she'd gotten fully to her feet. How long was hard to say, but she suspected it'd been at least a week, which roughly corresponded to when they'd ceased keeping her in chains, a thing they'd done because she was no longer strong enough to present any kind of threat. Her muscles had gotten so weak, and each step in the series of movements necessary to accomplish this task required an extraordinary level of effort. The dying arm hanging uselessly from her left side didn't help matters. They kept threatening to amputate it, but Lexie suspected the time when they might actually have done that had passed. Little sensation remained in the arm, and from the point of view of her psychopathic tormentors, there wasn't much point in performing an act of maiming that caused little to no actual physical agony.

Rising required placing extra stress on her one functioning arm as well as her feet, which felt barely capable of supporting her full weight, depleted though that was. She felt lightheaded and close to passing out at numerous points in the process, but she kept at it, knowing that allowing herself to collapse would only delay getting to the next phase of her torture. And causing delay was as pointless as disobedience. Might as well get on with whatever this was and get it done.

At last, she managed to get all the way upright.

Her legs were shaking like those of a disease riddled ninety-year-old in dire need of a walker, but she was on her feet. Just accomplishing that felt like enough of a miracle that tears came to her eyes.

Trixie whipped a hand across her face, knocking her to the floor again.

Lexie screamed.

Trixie pulled on the rope again, drawing it so taut this time that it choked her. She wheezed and clutched weakly at the rope with the three remaining fingers of her "good" hand, her vision blurring as her sister continued to pull the noose tighter and tighter. Then, just as she felt on the verge of losing consciousness, the rope slackened and became loose around her neck. She gagged and sucked in ragged gasps of air.

She whimpered. "Please kill me. If you have any love left for me in your heart, please just do it."

Trixie chose not to respond to that.

Instead, she grabbed hold of Lexie under her arms and hauled her back to her feet, holding onto her until she was able to stand on her own. Once she'd accomplished that, she stepped away from her and gestured toward the door. "Move."

Lexie groaned as she glanced in that direction. The door was less than ten feet away, but in her condition the distance seemed more like ten miles. She couldn't imagine traversing it without falling down. "I can't."

Trixie gave the rope a slight tug. "Do it or I'll knock you down again, and we'll start this process all over."

More tears spilled down Lexie's face.

Had she really believed she'd reached a point of total resignation, of absolute numbness to misery and pain? She saw now that'd been nothing more than a willful act of self-deception. That state of perfect numbness would only be achieved with death.

She took a first step toward the door and almost fell.

Trixie grabbed hold of the hair at the back of her head and pulled hard on it, making her stay upright as she tugged on the rope with her other hand. She forced Lexie to continue moving forward, pulling and tugging again each time she stumbled. The journey toward the door and then down the hallway toward the staircase felt as torturous and never ending as a barefoot stroll across a field of broken glass. She had to fight with everything she had to stay on her feet, and each step forward felt certain to be her last before collapse, but against all odds they arrived at the top of the staircase and stood there for a few moments, staring down.

Trixie put a hand on her waist. "Remember how we went down that first time?"

Lexie whimpered. "That would kill me."

It really would, she was sure of it.

She considered throwing herself down, but rejected the idea only because she knew she lacked the strength to do it right. Trixie would sense it was happening and stop her, if only because she had something else terrible in mind for her.

Trixie's hand slid down and caressed her bony hip for a moment. "I know."

She lifted Lexie off the floor and cradled her in her arms as she began to carry her down the loudly protesting stairs. They soon arrived safely at the bottom of the stairs and then passed through the foyer into the living room, where the others were waiting for them. The deranged matriarch leered at them from her wheelchair, shifting around noisily on the creaking seat as she scratched at one of several inflamed red patches of skin on her torso. Ursula sneered from the couch, where she sat swigging homemade hooch from a ceramic jug. Calvin had a hand inside his coveralls and was playing with himself again, as usual.

Lexie whimpered when she saw the Bad Girl Chair.

Alma Wilcox, the old lady, sneered as she wiped snot from her nose. "Aw, poor thing sounds pitiful. Let her have a good, long sit." She cackled.

Ursula set the jug of hooch on the floor and got to her feet, swaying slightly. "Nah. We're running out of time. Come on."

She headed toward the hallway entrance and Trixie followed, turning as they arrived at the open archway so as not to bang her sister's head against the frame. They continued down the hallway and into the kitchen. Like everywhere else in the house, it was lit with lanterns and homemade candles. The smell of putrescence was especially strong in here and it was immediately apparent why. Against one wall was a long, rectangular wood table. Its surface was stained a rich, indelible shade of dark crimson, deriving no doubt from the many bodies hacked to pieces on it over the years. On the opposite side of the room was a wood stove and standing next to that was a non-functioning refrigerator, the door to which was standing open. Crammed inside it were plastic wrapped hunks of rotting human meat. Lexie wasn't sure how they could eat any of it without becoming violently ill. Perhaps they fired up the wood stove and cooked it to a point far beyond "well-done."

Her stomach cramped at the thought.

She hadn't eaten in several days.

Ursula opened the screen door at the back of the kitchen and they went outside. Trixie followed her down the stoop steps and out into the yard. Calvin wheeled Alma out onto the porch and stopped there.

Lexie craned her head around.

It was her first time seeing the area behind the house during the daytime. The backyard was larger than she'd ever imagined, extending to a distant tree line. No houses were visible from back here, which didn't surprise her. These people wouldn't be able to carry out the atrocities they regularly committed if they'd had any close neighbors. She knew from her reading about the Wilcox case there were just two other houses on Millhaven Road, both of which were abandoned. They could do anything to her back here, right out in the open, and no one would ever know, unless other people as stupid as she and her sister happened to come snooping around at the wrong moment.

Though it wasn't quite nighttime yet, the sky was overcast and the air felt charged in the way it always did ahead of a storm. Lexie looked up and saw ominous black clouds stacking up in the sky. The wind was stiffening, and she saw the tops of the distant trees swaying in an alarming way.

They kept going until they reached a point midway between the house and the trees. Ursula came to an abrupt stop and swayed on her feet again as she turned toward them. "Set her down right here."

Trixie lowered her to the ground with surprising gentleness.

It was then Lexie noticed the metal stakes pounded into the ground and the thin lengths of strong nylon rope threaded through holes in each of them. There were four of them arrayed around her. Her sense of alarm intensified.

"What's happening?"

Trixie removed the frayed old rope from her neck and forced her to lie on her back. Lexie made a feeble effort to resist, but of course she lacked the necessary strength. Trixie didn't even have to try very hard. Ursula grabbed Lexie by a wrist and stretched it toward one of the stakes. She whined and tried tugging her hand away, but Ursula held fast and went to work securing the hand to the stake.

The woman laughed. "We're letting you spend the night outside, that's what's happening. Out of the goodness of our hearts, of course."

She laughed again.

Then Trixie laughed, too.

Soon they had all of her limbs stretched out and tied to the stakes. Trixie then used a hammer that'd been left nearby to drive the stakes deeper into the ground. Lexie squirmed and pulled at the stakes, but they would not budge. She suspected she wouldn't be able to budge them even with her strength and health fully restored.

She looked at Trixie. "Don't do this."

Trixie spat in her face.

Ursula laughed and they went away for a few minutes. While they were gone, Lexie stared up at the sky and saw it was darker than it'd been only moments ago, those massive black clouds rearing up like the shadows of angry, vengeful gods.

She felt a single drop of water hit her forehead.

Then another on her cheek.

A slow rumble of thunder preceded a louder crack. The droplets of moisture began falling at a steadier pace, turning into drizzle. She began to shiver as water covered her nude body, feeling hot and cold at the same time.

Then Ursula and Trixie were back.

Ursula had a roll of duct tape, Trixie a wad of camo netting.

Lexie started shaking her head in a frantic motion, "No. No, don't."

They giggled like naughty schoolgirls and went to work again as the drizzle became rainfall. Ursula wound the duct tape around the lower part of her head multiple times, fully and firmly covering her mouth while leaving her nostrils unobstructed. The same nostrils that were, however, partly clogged with dried blood and mucus. Trixie covered her entire body with the netting, which adhered to her bare skin like glue as the rain began to fall harder.

Then Ursula and Trixie were up and running back toward the house, holding hands and giggling again.

Lightning flashed, briefly lighting up the darkening sky.

Then came a massive crash of thunder, like the detonation of a bomb.

The sky opened up and the rain fell in endless torrents.

No one anywhere heard Lexie's muffled screams.

TWENTY-TWO

THE SNAKE WAS BACK IN the cage with her when Melissa emerged from another long period of sleep. She saw it curled up right next to her when her eyes fluttered open, and the primal terror that flashed through her in that first moment of recognition was so intense it instantly dispelled any lingering vestiges of sleep. The knowledge of what had happened the last time failed to keep her from repeating her previous visceral reaction. She screeched and tried flinging the thing away from her, and once again she received multiple bites, this time to her forearm and one to her face before the creature slithered out of the cage and disappeared into the maze of junk.

The places where she'd been bitten pulsed with pain, especially the bite punctures on her cheek. She knew by now that what she'd been told about the snake being non-venomous was true, as she hadn't died from the bites she'd received several days earlier. This was assuming the snake was the same one, but she thought that was a safe assumption. It'd looked exactly the same, and even if she was wrong, so what? A lethal dose of venom circulating through her veins wouldn't be the worst possible thing that could happen at this point.

She was trapped in a cage with a corpse that was still drawing a significant amount of buzzing flies. There were so many of them they kept landing on her and crawling all over her sweat-slicked bare skin. The maggots squirming in Wormie's wounds were grosser, though at her most desperate she'd considered eating some of them. She needed sustenance of some kind and her captors had little interest in providing it, at least not on a consistent basis.

Several minutes went by before she felt calm again, and only then did it hit her that she'd been able to see the snake and could make out her surroundings. She turned her head and glimpsed the daylight pouring in through the open door. Someone had been down here to check on her while she was asleep, but unless that person was hiding somewhere amidst all the junk—entirely possible—they were gone now. It was unusual for any of them to leave the door open when they left, though, unless maybe they were planning to return right away.

She leaned against a side of the cage and waved flies from her face as she stared at the sliver of bright sunlight. The brightness of the light told her last night's storm system had fully passed out of the area. She experienced a tinge of melancholy at this realization. The storm had been the first notable weather event to occur during her weeks of imprisonment. It'd gone on for hours and listening to the endless booms of thunder and the pouring rain had provided a strange kind of comfort. The sounds were proof a living world still existed beyond the confines of this horrible basement. Now she heard nothing at all save for the relentless buzzing of the flies.

As was often the case of late, she felt symptoms of sickness she could not directly attribute to any individual wound out of the many inflicted upon her flesh, none of which were quite severe enough to create a lethal result on their own. She'd been beaten, bludgeoned, burned, whipped, maimed, and sexually assaulted over and over, and yet the people victimizing her always took care to never sever any important veins and to always cauterize any open wounds that might otherwise allow her to bleed out.

Therefore, it was unsurprising that she constantly drifted in and out of a low-grade fever and often experienced flu-like chills and throat soreness. These symptoms never became too severe and sometimes seemed to abate entirely for a few hours before recurring. That they kept coming back had to count as the least surprising thing ever. She'd been living for weeks now in deplorable conditions, confined to a small space with two rotting corpses as her only constant companions, along with some rats, cockroaches, and other pests that were always passing in and out of the cage. The only surprising thing was she wasn't far sicker already.

She was still mulling all this over when she turned her head and finally noticed something that should have captured her attention right away. The cage door was closed, but the padlock normally used to secure it was not hanging from the hasp. Instead of immediately surging toward the door, she stayed where she was because she didn't trust what she was seeing.

She found it hard to believe the padlock's absence from the hasp was anything other than purposeful. She was being taunted or tested again, made to play along with some new form of psychological manipulation. One or more of them were probably somewhere in the basement with her, hiding away and waiting to see what she would do. The maze of junk offered no shortage of potential lurking spaces. Or they might be sitting out there on the concrete stairwell, waiting to crush her hopes of escape in particularly cruel fashion after allowing her to get that far. The latter possibility was precisely the type of diabolically evil shit she expected from Ursula.

She also knew she had no choice but to play along with these wicked machinations. Opening the cage door and venturing into the area outside the cage would likely be tantamount to inviting a deeper level of torture and pain into her already miserable existence, but she would do it anyway. Even the tiniest, most remote chance of escape compelled it.

Melissa groaned as she pushed away from the side of the cage and went on her hands and knees to the door. Before pushing it open, she took another quick look around to check for anyone peeking out at her from behind one of the piles of junk. Seeing nothing of the sort, she opened the door and crawled out of the cage. She groaned again as she tried to stand for the first time in weeks. Her disused muscles ached and her legs trembled as she slowly rose to her full height, but after taking a first few cautious steps away from the cage, she decided she was in no immediate danger of toppling over.

Knowing any window of time to affect an actual escape was likely to be a small one, she kept moving, picking her way through the precariously stacked piles of junk with as much speed as she could muster. More than once she bumped into the piles hard enough to cause items to slide to the floor, some landing with a louder clatter than others as they struck cement. Each time it happened, her anxiety soared to new levels and, fearing her captors would soon arrive to investigate the noise, she willed herself to move even faster. Before much longer, she arrived at the open door and stared up the length of the concrete stairwell.

The *empty* stairwell.

She glanced over her shoulder and saw no one creeping up behind her, which caused her to whimper in relief.

This is really happening, she told herself, still hardly able to believe it. *So get moving, bitch.*

She began to ascend the stairs more quickly. The stairwell was narrow so she braced her palms against its concrete walls to better maintain balance as she put all her energy into forward momentum. She paused for a moment once her head was above ground level, searching for signs of anyone in the vicinity. To her right was a small back stoop and a closed screen door. A line of tall trees stood well off in the distance. There was no sign of Ursula or any of the others.

Move!

Melissa climbed the rest of the way out of the stairwell and stood barefoot in the yard, blinking against the sunlight. It was blinding after so much time spent in darkness. Judging from the position of the sun, it was early in the day, noon probably still hours away.

She'd come to this place as a captive in the back of a van, arriving under the cover of night at a house devoid of exterior illumination. She hadn't been able to see shit. The entirety of her knowledge about the surrounding terrain was limited to what she was seeing now, which left her with a decidedly ill-informed decision to make. Should she head for that distant line of trees, or should she creep around the side of the house and check out the lay of the land out front?

Her eyes began to adjust to the bright sunshine as she tried to make up her mind, and she saw that there was something out there on the ground midway between the house and the woods. Spurred by helpless curiosity, she took several steps in that direction before coming to a sudden halt. The form was a spread-eagle human shape staked to the ground and covered by netting that was still damp from last night's storms.

The shape beneath the netting was not moving.

Melissa shook her head. "No way. Fuck this."

DEAD END HOUSE

She felt bad for whoever that was, but she could not help them, not without probably sacrificing herself in the bargain. In the past, when she'd believed in concepts like the obligations inherent in being a decent member of society, the notion of turning away from another person in distress would have appalled her, but the weeks of torture and misery had changed her outlook on a lot of things. She now valued self-preservation above all else, and if that entailed condemning another person to death through her own inaction, she was okay with that. In this case, it didn't seem to matter, as she felt strongly that the person hidden beneath the netting was dead.

She turned away from the unmoving form and started moving toward the side of the house, which existed in an advanced state of decrepitude that was shocking in the bright daylight. The putrid condition of its squalid interior was a vivid memory even after her weeks in the basement. It still stunned her that anyone, no matter how desperate or depraved, would choose to live like that. As awful as the place was on the inside, the structure's crumbling exterior was even worse. It was clear that no maintenance of any kind had occurred here for decades. She saw shingles on the ground she assumed had been blown off the roof by the storm. How the place was still standing was a mystery. It was almost like a feat of strange magic. She suspected, however, that a day would come when it would finally succumb to the elements, the next big storm maybe causing it to collapse.

Maybe.

But she hoped to be long gone from here by then.

She crept along the side of the house below the level of the first-floor windows. The windows were painted black and covered with curtains, which didn't make her feel any safer. The residents still had ways of surveilling the outside world, and fear of being noticed added extra fuel to the sense of urgency gripping her. No one had come bursting out of the house to chase after her yet, but of course that remained subject to change at any given second. She wouldn't feel safe until she was sitting in a warm police station surrounded by angry officers who'd soon return here to round up the human vermin who called this place home.

After a peek around the corner in front to confirm there was no one in the yard or on the porch, she moved away from the house and started advancing across the patchy lawn toward the street. She felt a little stronger with each step and willed herself to move faster and faster. The hope she'd restrained out of fear of having it dashed bloomed fully to life, providing an extra jolt of adrenaline.

She glanced over her shoulder as she neared the street, fear causing her to whimper as she anticipated seeing someone creeping along behind her, but again no one was there. The short street in front of her was empty too, a pothole-dotted stretch of asphalt faded to grayness. Two other houses faced each other from opposite sides of the street, but to her amazement they were in even worse shape than the place she was fleeing. One had a large hole in its gabled roof. The landscape of desolation and decay made her feel as if she'd unknowingly stepped through a portal into a post-apocalyptic world.

On any other street in just about any other neighborhood anywhere in the world, her nudity would make her feel vulnerable and self-conscious, but after all she'd been through, it was hard to care about such things. That was especially true on a street as utterly deserted as this one seemed. She nonetheless felt compelled to walk with her arms crossed over her breasts as she continued down the street toward an intersecting two-lane road leading to points unknown. There were no other houses on the other side of that street, only another dense stand of tall trees. She had no clue how far she was from anything resembling actual civilization, but she felt she had to keep heading toward that other road. No other obvious route out of this place was currently available to her.

She picked up the pace and was maybe twenty yards from the intersecting street when she heard the rumble of an approaching engine. The sound was coming from somewhere beyond the field of tall grass to her right. She stopped in her tracks, seized by a pair of disparate, conflicting impulses. There was the part of her that wanted to run toward the sound and reach the intersecting street before the driver of the vehicle could zoom by without noticing her, which struck her as a distinct possibility. She feared missing out on a chance at being carried away from this place far more quickly than she'd dared to imagine.

Then there was the far less optimistic voice in her head screaming at her to run into the field and drop down out of sight before the driver could spot her. This impulse was fueled by memories of the night of her abduction, when she'd been transported here in a brown van. Whether the van actually belonged to her captors or they'd stolen it, she did not know, but she had to assume they had access to automotive transport when they wanted it.

This could be them returning from some outing. An excursion

into town for supplies, perhaps, or they might have been out hunting for fresh victims. Or maybe they'd merely wished to escape the stifling confines of their putrid house for a time by going on a scenic country drive.

She glanced toward the field again and felt the tension in her body as she leaned in that direction. The sound of the engine became more distinct, louder, no longer a distant rumble. Within seconds the vehicle would either drive past the entrance to blighted Millhaven Road, or it would slow down and turn in, a development that could still easily be either ominous or innocent. The unused street did, after all, offer a convenient turning around point for anyone in need of doing so. A car slowing down—as this one was now definitely doing—didn't necessarily signal anything sinister.

In the end, indecision kept her rooted to the spot.

A whine rose up in her throat and she trembled as the nondescript brown van from the night of her abduction turned in and rolled slowly up the road toward her. She whimpered as she took a couple of instinctive steps backward, stopping and turning when she heard someone chuckling behind her.

Trixie was standing in the road about a dozen yards away.

Gripped in her hands was an aluminum baseball bat with fraying old tape wrapped around the handle. The girl had crept up on her fast while she was distracted by the sound of the approaching engine.

The van came to a stop and one of the doors flew open.

Trixie grinned as she raised the bat. "You naughty bitch. What are you doing out of your cage? I bet Wormie's worried sick missing you."

She raised the bat higher and took a step toward her.

Melissa screamed and ran into the field.

As she stumbled her way through the tall grass, the thought came to her that this brush with freedom had never been anything more than a carefully orchestrated game. The truth of this was clear in the way they laughed and whooped it up as they gave chase. They were having fun with her, playing with her emotions in the cruelest way they'd conceived of yet. The worst part was she'd known something like this was a possibility from the beginning, but they'd allowed her to get far enough away to start really believing she might escape. Her eyes overflowed with bitter tears as she continued staggering forward. She heard them getting steadily closer and knew she had no hope of eluding them, but the drive to survive would not allow her to stop running until they took her down.

She heard wild, gleeful laughter right behind her.

Trixie again.

"Where do you think you're going, Slaggie? Don't you know this is your wedding day? You can't leave your bride standing at the altar. Have some fucking respect, for fuck's sake."

Melissa had no clue what any of that madness was supposed to mean, but the others cackled at the deranged wit of their now thoroughly indoctrinated new member. She stumbled again and nearly fell but managed to right herself in time for the barrel of the baseball bat to crack across her shoulders. She screamed again and pitched forward, landing face down on the muddy ground. A last-ditch attempt at rising up and resuming her flight ended when the bat struck her again, this time in the lower back.

She cried out and fell face down in the mud again.

This time she sensed them standing arrayed around her, and she rolled onto her back, cringing at the sight of the leering faces hovering above her. Trixie touched the tip of the bat to her chin and took a practice swing before glancing at Ursula. "Should I fuck her up some more?"

Ursula shook her head. "Nah. We want her alive for the wedding, right?" She glanced at her brother, her leering grin giving way to a scowl of disdain. "What are you waiting for, you useless shit? Snatch her ass up and throw her in the van. We gotta start getting ready for the nuptials."

Calvin scooped her up and carried her back to the road. He threw her into the back of the van, climbing in after her and sitting on her back while Ursula got in behind the wheel. An instant later, Trixie climbed into the front passenger seat, and then they were driving back up the street toward Dead End House.

TWENTY-THREE

BEING INSIDE THE ELKMONT POLICE station for the first time in four years was a surreal and disquieting experience for Nancy Kincaid. She'd last been here for a meeting with the police chief, the mayor, and the lead detective in her daughter's case. The purpose of that meeting was to coordinate how they would handle a planned press conference on the one-year anniversary of Lara's disappearance, which was happening later that afternoon. No new information was shared with her on that day because none had been uncovered.

There'd been no solid leads in the case since day one, she was told. The few tips that trickled in were almost always identifiable as being without merit. That was bad enough, but the insinuations regarding her daughter were worse. She was asked again and again if Lara had ever talked about running away and starting a new life elsewhere, as well as whether she could accurately be described as "alienated" or "disaffected." The intent behind these questions was never explicitly stated, but what the cops were getting at was clear enough.

They believed it was at least remotely possible that Lara had killed Kevin Malone and had taken off to avoid being sent to prison. This was pure bullshit, but the situation was complicated by gossip spread among conservative elements of the community, including members of Kevin's family. They described Lara as a wicked temptress who'd led a good God-fearing Christian boy astray. There were even suggestions that she'd sacrificed him in the name of the devil before leaving town with a traveling satanic cult.

Absolute nonsense.

The police never went anywhere near that far with their insinuations, but knowing they were open to the idea of Lara being complicit in some way was infuriating. The ridiculous notion contributed greatly to Nancy's sense of disillusionment, as did the false front of investigatory optimism evinced by the officials at the press conference.

She stopped asking the detectives for updates in the case, and after a while they ceased contacting her, dropping any pretense of actively investigating Lara's disappearance. The Malones continued to spread their malicious gossip, but over time that faded into the background.

Nancy washed her hands of it all.

The gossip *and* the useless local cops.

She'd thereafter vowed to never again voluntarily set foot in the Elkmont police station. The old memories associated with it were too painful. She'd hoped the passage of years would alleviate those feelings of unease, but this was revealed as a false hope almost from the moment she stepped through the door. Everyone she encountered either ignored her or treated her with thinly disguised disdain. There was nothing openly confrontational in any of the behavior, but the underlying sense that she wasn't welcome wasn't hard to miss.

The lead detective in Lara's case in the early stages was a man named Travis Davis. He'd become Elkmont's acting police chief a few months ago, replacing the previous chief after that man was forced to resign in the wake of a sex scandal. This made Davis an even busier man these days, but he'd reluctantly agreed to an afternoon meeting with Nancy.

A meeting she was now walking out on, frustrated and barely able to contain her fury after enduring fifteen minutes of sneering contempt from Davis. The man scoffed at the ideas she presented, calling them ludicrous and a waste of his time. The way he repeatedly snorted disbelieving laughter throughout her stammering attempt to explain what she saw as the obvious connections between her daughter's case and the recent disappearance of Brady Whitmore was shocking. He'd been so much more respectful—even deferential—toward her years ago. It was like he wasn't even the same man anymore.

She felt humiliated and angrier than she'd been about anything in a long time. Before entering the station, she'd expected to encounter some level of pushback and skepticism once she started laying out the theory, but not for a moment had she anticipated anything like this happening. She was treated like a child, or like a silly bubble-headed woman lacking the intellectual capacity to understand why what she was saying was so stupid.

Once she was back behind the wheel of her Mitsubishi, she vented some of her rage by screaming and pounding the steering wheel with her fists. This went on for a few minutes and drew the attention of a few people passing through the parking lot outside the station. The long look one uniformed man gave her as he walked by at an extremely slow pace brought the fit of rage to an end, replacing anger with a tingling sense of fear. The man was still staring at her as she started her car and drove out of the parking lot.

She felt only moderately better as she put some distance between herself and the station. This whole thing was something she hadn't wanted to do in the first place. She believed Lara was dead and could never be returned to her, and that there was no point in reopening all the old wounds. That is, until Sterling and his persuasive young friend showed up and started filling her head with dangerous ideas. Ideas that seemed crazy at first, but then became steadily more compelling as the theory was spelled out for her in methodical fashion.

The theory wasn't proof of anything. It was based on hearsay, some surface similarity between the two cases, and the fact that Lara had "dated" Brady for about a minute when they were in high school. The hearsay stemmed from Agatha's conversations with two of Brady's friends. She tracked them down on social media and met them in person. One of them, a young man named Paul Costa, referenced a brief obsession Brady had harbored in the early weeks and months following Lara's disappearance. He'd believed her fate was somehow tied to the infamous "Dead End House." According to his friend, Brady had even tried convincing the cops to look into it.

Then, also according to Costa, he'd abruptly dropped the idea, never once mentioning it again in the years that followed.

Again, it was proof of nothing, but put all together, the idea of a

Dead End House connection tickled something inside Nancy's brain. She knew it was unlikely the old house on Millhaven Road held the answers to the questions that had haunted her for years, but the possibility must at least be worth looking into.

Right?

After some debate, it was decided she alone should present the theory to the police. The reasoning behind this approach was straightforward. After his years on the street, Sterling's reputation was not a good one. To understate. He was considered a public nuisance, and the cops would not be inclined to view anything he had to say in a favorable light. Agatha would be viewed with nearly equal skepticism due to her youth. She was also new in town and had only entered their lives within the last week.

Doing this alone was an intimidating thing, but she worked up the nerve to attempt it by telling herself she was doing it for Lara. Doing it for the memory of her only child, who didn't deserve to be forgotten. It'd taken a lot to make herself do this, to step so far outside anything resembling her comfort zone of the last few years. Yet she'd done it.

Only to be laughed at.

Just thinking about it made her scream again.

She was still fuming over it as she turned down the street leading to her house and pulled into the driveway. After allowing herself a few moments to calm down, she got out of the car and went into her house. Instead of immediately announcing her return, she eased the front door shut and locked it. She was still processing everything that had happened and felt consumed with anxiety at the prospect of telling Sterling and Agatha all about it.

She removed her high-heeled shoes and carried them with her as she walked out of the foyer and through the living room and into the kitchen. The last she'd seen of Sterling and Agatha had been in there. They'd been seated at the little dining table, talking and having coffee as she was getting ready to leave, but they were not there now.

The house itself was eerily quiet.

She stood in perfect stillness in the kitchen for a few moments, the straps of her heels still dangling from her upraised fingers as she strained to detect sounds of any kind. All she heard was the hum of the refrigerator, followed within seconds by the sound of the air-conditioning kicking on again.

She was on the verge of heading out back to see if her guests might be lounging on the patio when she heard something else in the house. She furrowed her brow as she walked out of the kitchen and into the downstairs hallway, moving as quietly as she could manage on her bare feet. The fully furnished but rarely used spare bedroom was at the end of the hallway. She knew the sound was emanating from it before she reached the door, which stood open a crack. It took every ounce of will she had not to gasp out loud when she put an eye to the slim opening and saw what was happening in the room.

Sterling sat at the edge of the bed with his pants down around his ankles. His head was tilted back and his eyes were closed. The girl was kneeling in front of him on the carpeted floor. She was clad only in the black tights she always wore. Her slender, pale hands were gripping Sterling's thighs and his cock was in her mouth. Sterling's weathered face was contorted in an expression of the purest ecstasy. The soft moans issuing from his slack mouth were what had drawn her in this direction. He was trying his best to be quiet, with only moderate success.

They'd expected her meeting with the police chief to last far longer than it actually had, thus granting them a seemingly safe window in which to have an erotic interlude. That much she understood. What she decidedly did *not* understand was pretty much everything else about what she was seeing. The girl had only just turned nineteen. She was beautiful. Her ex-husband was in a far more presentable state than he'd been in years, but he was still quite obviously a beaten down old bum. It made no sense. A girl like this could have anyone she wanted, and she picked Sterling? Why? Just thinking about it made her brain feel on the verge of exploding.

As if sensing her presence on the other side of the door, Agatha turned her head slightly in that direction while keeping Sterling's cock in her mouth. She saw the eye peering in at her through the crack and smiled. She then popped his dick out of her mouth and gave it a long lick up the length of its underside to the tip. Still keeping his eyes closed, Sterling gave a much louder moan and clenched at the bedspread. Agatha took his long member back into her mouth and became more aggressive in her ministrations.

It was too much.

Everything she'd been through with the police this afternoon and now this.

Nancy felt something break inside her with an almost audible snap.

Sterling was no longer her husband and she had no interest in ever rekindling anything with him, but she'd come to believe he might be capable of some level of redemption. He'd made her believe in that by speaking with real passion about his desire to finally discover the truth about their daughter's fate.

Now this.

In *her* fucking house.

The level of disrespect was unparalleled.

She backed away from the door and padded back down the hallway to the kitchen, where she set her heels on the table and spent a few moments feeling close to hyperventilating. She imagined waiting here for them to finish and then attempting to have the conversation she'd anticipated on the ride home. The one in which she would tell them all about her humiliation at the police station. She'd imagined how they would offer support and comfort.

What a fucking joke.

Everything felt like a joke now.

The idea she might ever find out what had happened to Lara. The concept of redemption of any kind. The notion that people in positions of authority and trust might actually want to help her.

Her whole goddamn life was nothing but one giant fucking joke.

She stood shaking in the kitchen another moment or two longer as a wave of molten rage engulfed her.

Then she snatched a butcher knife from a wood block on the counter and raced out of the kitchen and down the hallway to the spare bedroom. Agatha was still on her knees in front of Sterling when she kicked the door open and rushed into the room, but she was up on her feet and backing away from her an instant later. Nancy unleashed a shriek of rage and chased the more agile girl around the room. Agatha hopped over the bed and tried making a break toward the door, but Nancy doubled back and put herself in the way. Sterling sat blinking in confusion on the edge of the bed, his erect cock wet with the girl's saliva.

His eyes widened as he finally noticed the knife. "Nancy, what are you doing? Put that thing down."

"Fuck you."

She took another run at Agatha, but this time the girl was ready for her. One of her hands clamped tight around Nancy's wrist, and they grappled with each other, the knife hovering between them as they moved in a circular way, repeatedly banging against the walls and various pieces of furniture.

Sterling got up and tried to intervene, but he tripped over the pants bunched around his ankles and stumbled against Nancy's back. This drove her toward Agatha with a greater level of force than she'd managed before, but at the last possible instant the girl was able to twist her wrist away from her. The point of the knife punched into Nancy's flesh just below the sternum, the blade penetrating almost up to the handle as Sterling fell to the floor. Nancy knew almost right away the wound was a mortal one, the knife having been driven upward into her heart.

Agatha met her gaze. "You stupid woman. Look what you've done. It was just a fucking blowjob."

Nancy opened her mouth to scream.

But she had no strength left for that.

Agatha held on to her as she sagged slowly to the floor. Then she pried Nancy's fingers off the handle of the butcher knife, pulled the blade out, and cast it aside. Nancy was dimly cognizant of Sterling wailing in anguish in the background as the girl started talking again, but by then she was already starting to fade and it was all just noise that no longer mattered.

She sighed a final breath and was gone.

TWENTY-FOUR

THE SCREAMING WAS COMING FROM somewhere nearby, but the sound stirred no sense of alarm in Lexie. She felt detached from the physical world during the occasional moments of foggy wakefulness that came between extended periods of unconsciousness, barely capable of coherent thought. The one idea she kept returning to every time her eyes fluttered open was the feeling she must not still be alive, that any faint sense of self remaining was only a spiritual echo of the person she'd been. She was a ghost that hadn't yet managed to detach from its pitiful physical shell and pass on to the world beyond.

The screaming didn't matter because it emanated from the realm she was in the process of departing. It was a product of the pain and terror of a living being. Hearing it did strike a faint chord of sorrow within Lexie's fading spirit, but she consoled herself with the knowledge of her pending liberation. Soon she'd be all the way gone from here, and the same would be true of this other person before much longer. All this suffering was only temporary, mere prelude to the glorious and redeeming transition to come.

She was still thinking along similar lines right up to the moment when someone peeled the damp netting away from her face. The intrusion of bright sunshine made her squint and sent a sharp dagger of pain through the center of her skull, a sensation that brought with it a soul-crushing realization. She was still alive and her ordeal was not yet over.

The sun outlined the form of a person kneeling next to her on the ground, but she could not immediately discern who it was. She squinted harder and the finer details of the face looming above her slowly came into focus. The terror she'd lived with for so long did not return as the moment of recognition arrived, but only because this person had not directly harmed her during her time inside Dead End House. This was the guy with the greasy long hair who'd briefly come into the living room that first night, the one the others had refused to acknowledge.

The strap of a vintage instant camera was draped around his neck, the camera itself hanging to chest level. It was the kind where a photo would emerge through a slot at the bottom. She flinched as the man touched her face and gently moved her head, first to one side and then to the other. Her one good eye opened wider in response to the touch, her heart beating faster in dread of what this man might do to her in the coming moments. She didn't fear him as intensely as the others, but she knew better than to think he was safe.

There was a weird, inexplicable dynamic at work between this man and the rest of them. He did not seem to participate in the vile deeds they perpetrated, but as far as Lexie was concerned, this in no way absolved him of responsibility. He moved freely among them with no apparent trace of fear. Still, perhaps his reluctance to commit acts of direct physical harm hinted at some small capacity for empathy or even mercy.

She whimpered in as pitiful a manner as she could manage, an easy thing in her current condition. The man tilted his head as she made this sound, his gaunt features shifting in a way that indicated deep curiosity if not actual compassion. She whimpered again and tried speaking to him from behind the layers of duct tape.

He smiled and raised the camera, clicking a button in front after placing the viewfinder against one of the thick lenses of his glasses. Seconds later, a whirring sound accompanied the emergence of a square piece of instant film from the slot at the bottom. After peeling away and discarding an attached piece of paper, he showed her the image of her face. She stared at it in incomprehension for a time, unable at first to associate what she was seeing with any internal image she'd ever held of herself.

Then she began to sob.

The long-haired man began to peel more of the netting away from her body, tugging it down nearly to her knees. He raised the camera again and took multiple additional pictures, showing her the results each time. His expression remained neutral as she experienced fresh surges of distress upon seeing the images of her marred and maimed flesh. One of her nipples had been sliced away and the wound cauterized, something she hadn't been cognizant of until this moment. How that was possible she did not know, but the evidence that it had happened was undeniable.

Louder screaming rang out from somewhere closer than before, so sharp and clear it had to emanate from somewhere outside rather than from inside the house. The long-haired man turned his head and stared off toward the side of the house for a moment.

Then he tugged the netting back up over her body, ignoring her squeals of protest as he draped it over her face again. He got to his feet and moved swiftly away from her. The next thing she heard was the screen door opening and shutting.

The long-haired man was gone, but to her great regret, her reawakened state of full cognizance remained. It would have been better to stay in that state of drifting detachment until she was dead, but for now at least she wasn't being allowed that luxury. With nothing else around to distract her for the time being, her mind returned to memories of the storm.

The sense of absolute helplessness that had gripped her during those long, lonely hours was horrible. The hard rain striking her body felt akin to being endlessly pelted with rocks. She thought there'd never be an end to it. Even when she kept her head turned to the side, the water continually got inside her semi-clogged nostrils. Blowing air out to keep the passages at least partly open became a constant battle, one she seemed perpetually on the verge of losing.

The frequent explosively loud cracks of thunder made her feel like she was trapped outdoors in a war zone. She screamed behind the duct tape every time lightning lit up the entire sky. The fear of getting struck by one of the arcing bolts was with her the whole time. It came to seem inevitable not long after the storm began in earnest, but somehow it never happened.

At some point, after enduring hours of this while also being struck by the occasional piece of whirling debris, she lapsed into unconsciousness. She wouldn't have thought it possible until after the storm was over, but it happened. Intermittent periods of brief wakefulness ensued, but the gaps between them became longer, and when they did occur, they were characterized by that sense of foggy detachment. As she reflected on these things, she thought again of that illusory feeling of having become a ghost, one still mired in the process of moving on to the spirit realm.

How she wished that'd been true.

About ten minutes after the long-haired weirdo disappeared into the house, the screen door opened again. She heard voices she recognized, faint at first but steadily getting louder as they came toward her. As they drew nearer, she did her best to remain as still as possible.

Maybe they'd go away if they thought she was dead.

Moments later, she sensed them standing over her.

"Do you think she's dead?"

Trixie's voice.

Ursula laughed. "Well, let's have ourselves a look-see."

She knelt at Lexie's side and pulled the netting away from her face.

Lexie didn't flinch as she held her breath and persisted in her attempt to remain absolutely still. She couldn't see them because she'd closed her good eye. During the several ensuing silent seconds, it occurred to her to wonder whether a dead person's eyes would remain shut. Wouldn't an eyelid relax at the point of death like other muscles in the body?

Fuck.

Ursula laughed. "Bitch is playing possum."

She stood up and stomped on Lexie's stomach.

Lexie's eyes snapped open.

Air whistled in and out of her nostrils as she screamed behind the duct tape. The blow to her stomach was not a measured one, intended only to force her to abandon her ruse. It'd been delivered with maximum force, with a severity more than sufficient to reignite raw agony in seemingly every wound she'd absorbed. This was especially the case with her fractured ribs. Each labored breath was accompanied by the torturous sensation of splintered bone shards driving into her lungs. This time the feeling was worse than ever, probably because the original injury had not yet had time to fully heal.

She was still screaming when Ursula stomped on her stomach a second time. This blow felt harder than the first, almost as if someone had dropped an anvil on her midsection. She squealed and twisted at her bonds as she squirmed miserably on the ground.

Ursula lifted the hem of her raggedy white dress and removed a hunting knife from a sheath strapped to her thigh. Upon seeing it, Lexie believed she was on the cusp of finally being put out of her misery. Anticipation of the sharp steel invading her flesh as it sliced her throat open made her tremble in terror, but once again, that was only instinct. She felt ready to welcome death, readier than she'd ever been, and though she knew the pain would be terrible, at least it wouldn't last long. Then she could be a ghost for real, or just be nothing, if that was how it actually worked. Either way, she'd be at peace.

The woman knelt next to her, but instead of opening her throat with the knife, she used it to saw through the layers of duct tape encircling the bottom part of her head. In the process, the blade sliced into her face. The pain this caused was not pleasant, but it was soon rendered irrelevant by the instant massive relief of being able to breathe through her mouth again. She sucked in great, greedy gulps of air, temporarily not caring about the way her splintered ribs jabbed at her lungs. There was more pain, a brighter burst of it, when Ursula tore the duct tape away, ripping out some of the hair at the back of her head. This was also meaningless in the face of that overwhelming relief.

Ursula tapped the tip of the knife against Lexie's chin, pricking her flesh. "I haven't heard a 'thank you' yet."

The obscene absurdity of being forced to thank her torturer for some minor act of dubious mercy was nothing new to Lexie by now. She'd been coerced into doing it countless times. As usual, she suppressed any impulse to speak with defiance, responding in the required way. "Thank you."

Ursula smiled.

Then she glanced over her shoulder at Trixie. "Go fetch the stuff we left on the stoop."

Her gaze returned to Lexie as the other girl hurried back toward the house. "You look like shit, you know that?"

This wasn't exactly a revelation.

Lexie said nothing.

Ursula chuckled. "Yeah, you was pretty once, but not no more.

You got transformed, made ugly. I've turned a lot of pretty girls into ugly ones, but you might be on your way to becomin' my most disgustin' creation yet. You've got a ways to go before you're uglier than Wormie, though. Christ, that bitch looked like a livin' goddamn nightmare."

A question occurred to Lexie, one that had been in her head often over the last few weeks. It'd gone unasked because she was so focused on getting through all the terrible things happening to her, but she knew if she didn't ask now, her curiosity might never be satisfied. "I thought your brother was the one who did all the killing and torturing. Are all the stories wrong?"

After glancing over her shoulder, Ursula leaned in close, her voice dropping to a conspiratorial whisper. "Come on, girl. You're smarter than that. You know as well as I do, that bellowin' idiot ain't the real Crazy Calvin. For one thing, he ain't the right age by about forty goddamn years. That should've tipped you off from the start. The real deal is locked up in the nuthouse, just like you always thought. He's probably senile and shittin' his drawers every night."

Lexie's brow furrowed "But why—"

Ursula placed a finger against her lips. "Shush, now. That's just between you and me. I think I hear your sister comin' back."

Lexie hadn't heard anything, but sure enough, Trixie came into view seconds later. She'd returned with a long-handled axe and the propane torch canister.

"I got the stuff." She paused a beat. "Ma'am."

Ursula didn't look at her as she tugged more of the netting away and went to work with the knife again, this time cutting through the lengths of nylon rope securing Lexie to the stakes. "Good girl."

As soon as she was finished, she stood up and lifted the hem of her dress, returning the knife to the sheath. She took the axe from Trixie, who set the propane canister on the ground.

Ursula moved out of the way as Trixie knelt next to Lexie and took hold of her left wrist, the one that wasn't broken and useless, and stretched her arm out so it lay flat on the ground. Both women did these things as if enacting the steps of a prearranged plan, each with their own role to play in the forthcoming next atrocity.

Ursula moved in close.

Panic surged inside Lexie as she saw the heavy head of the axe hanging in the air, poised to strike. "No! It's the other one that needs to go."

Ursula smirked. "You still don't understand shit, do you?"

Her face contorted as she brought the axe down with a loud grunt of exertion. The blade chopped through Lexie's wrist, severing her hand from her arm in one clean, ruthlessly efficient blow. Blood jetted from the wrist stump, staining the ground red before beginning to pool at the bottoms of Trixie's sneakers. Lexie raised the arm higher and tried to reach for her sister, who yelped in dismay as blood sprayed across her face, getting in her mouth and in her eyes. She got up and stumbled away from her mutilated twin, shrieking and spewing profanity as she frantically attempted to wipe the blood from her eyes. The effort was semi-successful, but she also managed to smear the blood across most of her face in the process, which prompted another tirade of shrieking annoyance.

Ursula stood doubled over with laughter for a few moments as she watched the histrionic display. Then she heaved a big breath and made an attempt to collect herself. "Calm down, bitch. It ain't like it's the first time you've been bled on."

Trixie made a sound of disgust. "But it got all in my fucking *eyes* this time!"

Ursula shrugged. "That'll happen now and again. Now get over here and start helpin' before I get mad."

Trixie continued grumbling at a lower volume as she snatched the propane canister off the ground. "Okay, okay, sorry."

All this was happening on another plane of existence, something glimpsed through the distorted lens of an interdimensional camera or some other arcane viewing device. Or so it felt to Lexie during those moments of stunned detachment. Nothing felt real. She stared at her wrist stump and felt only an odd fascination as blood continued to pump out of the wound, spurt after spurt, a strangely beautiful phantasmagoric fountain.

The sense of detachment ended when her sister applied the blue-red propane flame to her wound, the sizzling agony shocking her back to reality. She screamed and tried sitting up, but Ursula stepped on her chest and held her in place.

As the flame continued to cook and blacken her flesh, Lexie sniffled and met Ursula's smirking gaze. "Why?"

Ursula smiled. "It's like I said. You still don't understand shit, not even after all that's been done to you. Why would I ever lift a fuckin' finger to help you? This here's a process of desecration. A dark tribute in the name of the unholy one. That bad arm of yours? I'm gonna let you keep that one."

"Just kill me."

Ursula shook her head. "Nope. The proper desecration of a human being should be as drawn out as you can make it. That's a lesson I learned early on from Grannie Alma, one I took to fuckin' heart. Sometimes a desecration will drag on for years. I don't think that's gonna be the case with you, though. You're getting used up too fast." She laughed. "There's just somethin' about you that makes you extra fun to hurt."

Trixie chuckled as the whoosh of the propane torch abruptly ceased. "That's the goddamn truth."

Lexie looked at her blackened forearm and experienced a new level of bleak hopelessness. The blood had ceased pumping, but the cooked state of her flesh distressed her even more than the formerly free-flowing blood. Because her other arm was already useless, she'd been robbed of any remaining ability to do anything for herself. She wouldn't be able to feed herself or drink water unless it was poured into her mouth, unless they intended to have her take her gruel and water out of bowls on the floor like a dog. As soon as the latter thought entered her head, she knew it was exactly what would happen. It was the logical next step in the slow and methodical stripping of her dignity. In her desecration.

She sobbed.

Ursula took her foot off Lexie's chest. "All right, let's get the bitch back inside. We've got work to do before the wedding."

They hauled her off the ground and started dragging her back toward the house.

TWENTY-FIVE

MELISSA WAS NOT RETURNED TO the basement after her failed escape attempt. She was, instead, brought into the main part of the house and carried up to the second floor. This was after she was dragged screaming and thrashing out of the van. She'd been consumed with a sense of wild desperation driven by the certainty that she'd never see the outside world again if she allowed these maniacs to take her back inside. Her struggling continued all the way across the barren front yard to the porch, where Calvin set her down long enough for Trixie to clobber her upside the head with the baseball bat.

The blow didn't knock her out, but it did render her woozy enough to cease screaming and struggling. At that point, Calvin scooped her up again and carried her inside. As soon as he started up the stairs with her slung over his shoulder, she figured she was again being installed in the unfurnished room where she'd spent the first few days of her imprisonment at Dead End House. The one that reeked of human waste and had chains bolted to the walls.

They walked right by the open door to that dark, desolate space, though, and continued down the upstairs hallway. At the point where she'd once assumed the hallway ended, it branched off to the right and extended for a shorter distance. Closed doors to other rooms she hadn't known existed stood opposite each other in this shorter section of hallway. The door to the room on the left opened with the expected loud creaking of hinges.

Calvin carried her into the room and dumped her on the floor with his customary lack of regard for human comfort, but the landing was softened somewhat by the presence of a rug covering the creaky floor planks. The room was furnished in the manner of an ordinary bedroom, albeit one frozen in time, unchanged from the long-ago days when this house had functioned more like a normal home. It might have been a house of horrors even back then, for all she knew, but evidence of a comparatively more mundane period in its existence was plentiful in this room.

A four-poster bed with a sagging canopy occupied the largest percentage of space. Other furnishings included a nightstand, a tall dresser, a wardrobe that stood next to the dresser, a vanity table, and a recliner. Also present was another of those old-fashioned floor model televisions, like the one she remembered seeing downstairs. It stood against a wall opposite the foot of the bed. One wall was adorned with a large multi-colored tapestry of a vaguely psychedelic design. Thumb tacked to the wall above the vanity table was a faded poster of someone called Peter Frampton. Judging from his look, he'd either been a famous musician or movie star several decades ago. A slatted pair of accordion-style doors marked the likely location of a closet. The room was lit by a pair of oil lamps. One rested on the nightstand while the other sat atop the dresser.

Melissa sensed this had once been the bedroom of either a teenage girl or a very young woman. Something catastrophic had happened here, inducing a strange state of stagnation. The latter insight was largely a product of intuition and nothing else, but she was convinced it was correct.

Ursula snatched the baseball bat away from Trixie as they entered the room. She touched the end of the bat against Melissa's chin and sneered. "You're gonna hang out in here while I take care of some other business. I ain't gonna tie you up or nothin', but Calvin's gonna watch over you and make sure you behave. If you don't, he's got my full permission to fuck you up any way he sees fit." She laughed in a softly insidious way. "Short of killin' ya, that is."

Melissa resisted the urge to push the bat away as she met Ursula's hateful gaze. "I swear I won't try anything," she said, wincing at the way speaking sparked pain. The pain was a consequence of that blow to the head, and she worried she might have suffered a hairline fracture to her jaw. "Just tell your fucking brother not to rape me."

Calvin grinned in his crooked way and made a sound of snuffling amusement.

Ursula snorted. "The boy's had his bone in all your fuckin' holes how many times now? What's it matter at this point?"

Melissa tilted her head back slightly as she felt the pressure of the bat against her chin increase. She knew speaking up this way made another beating more likely, but she didn't care. It wasn't like she still had anything meaningful left to lose. Other than her life, of course.

"Just tell him not to do it. I know he'll listen to you. He always does, even if he gets mad about it. If you do, I won't scream or fight. I'll go along with anything you tell me to do."

Ursula sneered. "Bitch, you'll do anything I say anyway."

"That's true. The difference is that if you do this for me, I won't resist doing anything you want, no matter how fucking disgusting it might be."

Ursula pursed her lips as she appeared to give the matter some thought.

She exchanged a glance with Trixie.

Then she smiled in her usual smirking way and shrugged. "You know what, bitch? You're on. We'll see how serious you are about that in a little while." The look on her face hardened as she glanced at her brother. "Don't try any dirty stuff with this one while we're gone, boy. Ya hear me?"

Calvin made a loud noise indicating discontent and stomped a foot on the floor. A floor plank under the rug made a splintering sound. Another roar of discontent followed, and for a moment he appeared on the verge of going into full meltdown mode, but then Ursula waved the bat around and yelled at him to shut his mouth. He whimpered and cringed away from the bat, holding his hands up in a protective gesture.

Ursula lowered the bat and shifted to a placating tone. "If it makes you feel any better, you can play with Closet Girl until we get back."

Melissa frowned.

Closet Girl?

Calvin's demeanor changed in dramatic fashion the instant his sister uttered these words. He clapped his hands together twice and grinned broadly as he laughed in his idiotic, piggish way.

Ursula nodded. "Yeah, I thought you'd like that." Her head swiveled back toward Melissa, and she raised the bat again, pointing it at her. "As for you, you best be true to your fuckin' word and be a meek little bitch, because if you can't do that, my brother gets to do what he wants."

Melissa grimaced. "You don't have to worry about that."

Ursula laughed. "Hell, I don't have to worry about a single goddamned thing, least of all your busted-up scrawny ass. We'll be back shortly. In the meantime, you two have fun. Or should I say, you three."

Ursula and Trixie giggled as they went out the door, shutting it behind them.

Melissa was still on the floor at that point, raised up on her elbows. As soon as the door clicked shut, she sat fully up and looked at Calvin. "This knuckle-dragging idiot thing you've got going on is an act, isn't it? I mean, it has to be. Right?"

The leering, shit-eating grin faded slowly from his misshapen face, and after a few moments of staring blankly at her, he spoke clearly in her presence for the first time. "Does it matter?"

Melissa gaped at him in surprise.

What she'd expected was for him to ignore her impromptu query, but instead she got clearly enunciated words.

It was kind of mind-blowing.

"Okay, so hold on, you can talk like a normal person? No actual speech impediment?"

Calvin stared at her for another stretch of silent moments, his lumpy features again betraying nothing of his inner feelings, which Melissa now realized must be much more complicated than she'd ever imagined.

Consumed with the desire to know more, she asked him additional questions, but Calvin ignored them all. When she fell silent, he grunted and traipsed heavily across the room to the closet, where he ripped open the accordion-style doors and stepped aside. Melissa made a sound of instinctive disgust upon glimpsing the human form in the closet.

The closet was not of the modern walk-in style that featured lots of space. It had a depth of perhaps three feet and was crowded with moth-eaten dresses and other garments dangling from hangers. The clothing items were pushed as far as possible toward one end, allowing just enough room for Closet Girl at the other end. That she was the one Ursula had referred to was not in doubt.

She sat with her knees pulled up to her chest and her back against the narrow side wall. Her slender body existed in a state of near-emaciation, a condition Melissa now recognized as common among the girls kept in this place. She'd lost a considerable amount of weight during her own time here, and it was obvious this poor creature had been a captive of the monstrous inhabitants of Dead End House for a far longer period of time. She was missing all her extremities, only scarred nubs remaining where there'd once been hands and feet. Also missing were her eyes and teeth. Much of her flesh was marred by a roadmap of welts, bruises, and assorted scars.

Visible amidst all the damage were traces of tattoos she'd gotten during her previous existence as a free person in charge of her own life. A few tufts of limp blonde hair protruded from an otherwise shorn scalp also marred by scarring. The scarring had that melted look Melissa associated with the cheap propane torches that were among Ursula's favorite instruments of torture. A thick leather collar encircled the girl's slender neck. Clipped to the collar was a long lead, the other end of which was tied to the rod overhead.

Calvin reached into the closet and unclipped the lead from the collar, the girl stirring as she sensed him doing this. She groaned as he lifted her off the floor, backed out of the closet, and carried her over to the four-poster bed. There was no attempt at resistance or speech from the girl, not even the feeblest effort to prevent him from doing what she must know was coming. The same thing she'd undoubtedly endured countless times already.

Melissa's eyes misted as she watched Calvin position her over the edge of the bed, with her ass turned upward.

"Calvin, don't."

He didn't respond or even glance at her as he undid the buckles holding up the top of his coveralls. She tried pleading with him a few more times while he pushed the coveralls down to his ankles, exposing his erect prick. Each of these additional entreaties was also ignored.

Melissa turned her head away, unable to watch as Calvin lowered himself to the girl from the closet, cringing at the sound of the semi-rhythmic grunts that followed. She experienced a crushing wave of guilt, knowing the vile act being perpetrated right in front of her was a direct result of the arrangement she'd made with Ursula. It didn't matter that this wasn't an entirely fair characterization of the situation. This was the fault of the bad people keeping them here. *They* were the ones doing all this evil shit. Not her and not Closet Girl, nor any of the other unfortunates who'd been imprisoned in this disgusting place. Not even Wormie, who'd probably been a decent person once upon a time.

From somewhere outside, someone else started screaming.

Melissa slapped her hands over her ears and whimpered, overcome by a fervent wish to banish the sickening sounds of horror forever. Like all her other wishes since being brought to this place, it went unheeded.

TWENTY-SIX

Five years ago

THE NEXT PERSON TO VISIT Lara in the hellish upstairs room was Alma Wilcox. Days had passed since the strange act of self-torture Ursula had committed by sitting in the nail chair, which had been removed from the room shortly afterward. She was again thirsty to the point of miserable desperation and would welcome any opportunity to chug down another jug of tainted water, even if it meant having to swallow more of Calvin's revolting ejaculate. Her need for it was so severe she'd resorted to loudly beseeching her tormentors for relief, a campaign that started several hours before Alma came in to see her.

This was in defiance of one of the strictest rules of the house. Screams were expected when they were in the room with her. They were a natural consequence of inflicting harsh physical punishments. In that context, all of them loved hearing the anguished sounds that came out of her mouth. Audible noise of any kind was forbidden when they were out of the room. Disturbing the "peaceful" environment inside the house was considered an inexcusable nuisance, one that would not be tolerated under any circumstances. It was a laughable notion, the idea of peace existing in a place like this, but they were serious about it. The vicious beatings she'd taken in response to her early violations of the rule were testament to that. Once she came to understand how savage and merciless the beatings could become, she made a determined effort to refrain from further violations. She wasn't a masochist. There was nothing about her that enjoyed being caned, whipped, strangled, and burned.

Today, though, she was breaking the rule.

Her need for liquid sustenance was such that she simply couldn't take it any longer. The atmosphere in the house was more oppressive than ever, the heat level rising steadily in recent days. Summer was coming. She felt like she couldn't breathe, a feeling she knew would only worsen as the days continued to get longer and hotter. Water, even a little, would alleviate the situation, make her feel like she could get through to the next day without suffocating.

At last, she heard a sound of approaching footsteps from out in the hallway. She knew right away it must be Alma, because the tread was heavy and plodding. It couldn't be Calvin, because although he too had a heavy tread, he generally moved at a faster pace than this, whereas Ursula's lighter, barefoot tread was barely detectable at all.

The heavy footsteps stopped.

A key slid into the door lock and rattled.

Then the door swung open and Alma entered holding a long candle wedged into a silver candlestick. The candle didn't provide the same level of illumination as the lanterns Ursula favored, but the light was enough to discern the grim set of the old woman's features. "About had it with your racket, girl."

Chain links clinked as Lara rose slowly from the floor and maneuvered herself into a sitting position. She forced open her dry, cracked lips and croaked a single word: "Water."

Alma laughed. "Lordy. That's what all the noise is about? Tell me, girl, what makes you think you deserve anything at all? You're not respecting the rules of the house. Maybe you need your tongue taken out."

"No. Please, listen. I'm sorry about all the noise, I really am, but I am beyond fucking desperate. There's literally nothing I wouldn't do for a little water. I'm serious."

A softer chuckle from the old hag this time. "Yeah, I heard about that. Said you swore you'd skin a person alive or eat a baby's heart. I told Ursula I think you're probably all talk. That if it came down to it, you wouldn't have it in you to do a thing like that."

Lara hardened her expression. "I fucking meant it. Bring me somebody. *Anybody*. Give me a hammer and a knife. Anything at all. And I'll do shit that'll make even you twisted fuckers cringe. I goddamn swear I will. Just give me water."

Alma smirked. "You know what, girl? We're gonna see if you can back up that big talk. There's this sweet young thing we've got caged up in the basement. Pretty sure Calvin's gone and knocked her up. Got all the signs and whatnot. Her belly's getting bigger even though she gets hardly any grub at all. Think you're up to cutting the little tadpole out of her?"

The idea made Lara's stomach clench in revulsion, but she maintained her fierce expression and said, "Fucking bring her to me. But give me water first."

Alma grinned in a disturbingly devilish way. "Oh, you'll get a drink before you do the work, but it ain't gonna be water."

The intensity of Lara's thirst made her face twitch. "I don't understand. I *need* water."

"And you'll get it. *After* you've done the work." Her grin became an anticipatory leer as she came a step closer. "But that don't mean I ain't gonna let you have a drink first."

Lara frowned. "I still don't understand."

Alma came another step closer, the candle flame flickering as she moved. "It's real simple. Lie flat on your back and open your mouth wide so I can fill it with piss."

Lara's stomach clenched again. For a second or two, she considered telling Alma to go fuck herself. The prospect of swallowing this hideous woman's urine sickened her, but the reality was she'd be subjected to some far worse act of sadistic punishment for the act of defiance. Another aspect of the situation to consider, one rooted in the bleakest form of pragmatism, was that what Alma proposed *would* diminish her thirst. Urine, after all, was composed primarily of water. Knowing that wouldn't make enduring this any less sickening or humiliating, but it would help her get through it.

Alma smirked. "Don't think it over too long. I might rescind the offer."

The chains clinked again as Lara stretched out on the floor. "The only thing I'm thinking over is how much I'm gonna enjoy the look on your face when I cut the fetus out of that bitch in the basement and eat it."

Alma chuckled. "Nothing would please me more."

After setting the candlestick on the floor, she positioned herself above Lara, planting one large, swollen foot to either side of her head. She lifted the hem of her tattered pink muumuu and slowly lowered herself to the floor, taking some moments to adjust her positioning after her knees touched the floor. The woman's pelvic area hovered inches above her face during these last few seconds, allowing her enough time to take a big breath and open her mouth wide. Then she felt the soft folds of the vagina settle against her face, the woman's large thighs enveloping her head. Alma wiggled atop her for a moment, groaned in a way that was tinged with sexual arousal, and began filling Lara's mouth with piss.

The acidic taste was as sickening as she'd imagined, but she forced herself to swallow every drop, as by that point there was no viable alternative. She could either drink it all down or choke on it. Also not pleasant was the way she felt engulfed by the woman's stale sweat and body odor. The worst part of the entire ordeal, however, was how the weight pressing against her face inflamed the throbbing pain caused by her fractured cheekbone. The agony worsened sharply every time Alma wiggled, which happened frequently.

The urine came out in a flood at first, forcing her to swallow rapidly many times, but it soon slowed to a trickle and then, mercifully, ceased. There was relief in that, but it was short-lived, ending when she realized the woman was not yet interested in dismounting from her face. She wiggled her groin against her and made groaning noises. What she wanted was obvious, if disheartening. The sooner she got on with it, though, the sooner it'd be over. So she went to work with her tongue and it wasn't long before those groans became squeals of ecstasy.

At last, after what felt like forever, the woman climbed off her with another loud groan, this one a product of exertion and satisfaction. She smoothed the front of her muumuu and waddled away from Lara, groaning again when she knelt to retrieve the candlestick.

She went to the open door and paused there. "I'll be back directly. I think it's time to see if you can back up your big talk."

The door remained open as she walked out of the room, a sure indication she meant what she said. They never left the door open or unlocked if they intended to leave her alone for any significant stretch of time. She felt stirrings of dread, knowing she was likely only minutes away from being compelled to participate in an atrocity.

The depth of her disgust over what she'd been made to do was such that she needed a few minutes to realize she was no longer miserably thirsty. She'd still welcome a large jug of untainted water to flush the piss taste away, but the sense of desperation that had consumed her for most of the day was undeniably in partial retreat.

As she'd suspected, she wasn't left alone for long. Some ten to fifteen minutes after Alma's departure, she heard footsteps out in the hallway. More than one set of them, judging from the continuous creaking of the floorboards. There was another sound as well, one almost entirely obscured by the noisy creaking.

Someone was sobbing. A woman.

Until that moment, Lara had existed in a state of temporary semi-denial. She knew an experience in unspeakable horror was forthcoming and there was nothing she could do to forestall it, but she'd put up a mental wall to shield herself from it until the last possible moment.

That wall crumbled as Alma and Calvin came into the room.

Cradled in Calvin's arms was the slender nude form of a young woman who'd been through hell. Almost every inch of her skin bore the gruesome evidence of prolonged extreme torture. Her ears and nose were gone. Something heavy like a railroad spike had been pounded through the center of her feet in order to create holes large enough to admit a length of chain. The chain had been threaded through both holes and secured in the middle with a padlock. Her feet were swollen and inflamed, the edges of the wounds oozing pus and tinged green. The infection gave off a foul odor that matched the room's baked-in stench of human waste. Her emaciated form was awful to gaze upon, but perhaps worst of all was the swollen belly. As Lara had feared, Alma hadn't been lying about her condition. Calvin allowed her to slide out of his arms and snorted in his piggish way when she hit the floor and cried out in pain.

This time Alma brought with her a pair of lanterns instead of her usual candlestick. These she set on the floor before walking back out of the room only to return moments later with a cloth sack and an antique cast iron key ring with one key attached. She dropped the sack and it hit the floor with a heavy thump.

She looked at Lara and grinned, flashing her assortment of rotting, jagged teeth. "All right, girlie. Sit your ass up. It's showtime."

Lara made a concentrated effort to shut off all emotion. It was her only hope of making it through this.

The chain links clinked as she got herself into a sitting position.

Alma came closer. "Hold out your hands."

Lara did as she was told.

Alma unlocked the shackles binding her wrists and cast them aside. Then she gave her the key and said, "Get them other ones off your feet and get to work. No point dawdling. Everything you'll need is in the sack. You can do it fast or do it slow, your choice." She grinned again, chuckling. "You'll earn yourself some brownie points by dragging it out and putting on a real Satanic horror show, though."

Lara unlocked the shackles and removed them from her ankles, flinging them across the room. "I don't ever want to wear those again."

Alma sneered. "That's gonna depend on you. You'll need to really impress me if that's what you want."

The doomed woman writhed miserably on the floor, her head turning until she could see her fellow prisoner, the one who'd become her designated executioner. It was hard to read any specific emotion in that ruined countenance, but Lara imagined she wished only for a swift end to her suffering.

She wouldn't be getting it.

Lara reached for the cloth sack and pulled it closer, feeling its heavy weight as she dragged it across the floor planks. She upended the sack, dumping out its contents. After examining the various implements for a moment, she picked up a hunting knife, one with a long, serrated blade. One could easily eviscerate another human being with a blade like this one. A time would come when she would utilize it, but that time was not now.

She put the knife down and picked up a heavy mallet, testing its weight. The woman from the basement made pitiful mewling sounds. Lara went to her on her hands and knees, raised the mallet, and brought it crashing down against one of her feet, right at the point of infection.

There were no soft mewling sounds now.

Only a howl of the purest agony as the woman sat bolt upright.

Another swing of the mallet caught her in the face, causing her to flop backward.

Lara frowned as she glanced at the open door. "Where's Ursula? Seems like she should be here for this."

Alma nodded. "You're right, she should be, but the girl's been feeling sickly. Don't you worry none about that, though. You've still got work to do."

Once again, Lara did as she was told.

And she kept at it for a long, long time.

TWENTY-SEVEN

CALVIN SPENT SO MUCH TIME abusing the girl from the closet that Melissa was forced to emerge from her state of willful oblivion. The screaming from somewhere outside had finally stopped by then, but Calvin was far from finished with the girl. In addition to all the expected varieties of sexual violation, he strangled her to the point of semi-consciousness several times, only to remove his hands from her throat and revive her with slaps and punches each time. After tiring of that, he picked her up and slammed her against the wall. Then he picked her up and did it again. And again. He also devoted a lot of time to twisting her arms behind her back, exerting enough pressure to induce significant pain without quite causing the bones to snap.

The girl endured all of it because she had no choice. Missing her extremities, she had no means of resisting or fighting back. Because all her teeth were gone, she couldn't bite his cock when he put it in her mouth. Even screaming seemed beyond her. The only noises she made were little gasps and moans, along with some weak mewling.

Although she'd kept her head turned away early on, Melissa felt compelled to watch at various points. She started actively wishing for the girl to die the second time Calvin slammed her against the wall. It was amazing to her—and not in a good way—that the human body could endure that level of extreme abuse and still not expire. She imagined in many cases this degree of physical trauma would be more than enough to kill a person, while some other people might possess an abnormal level of natural resilience. To her supreme misfortune, it seemed that Closet Girl fell into the latter category.

At one point while Calvin was amusing himself by twisting the girl's limbs, Melissa wandered over to the open closet and peeked inside. She encountered the expected odor of human waste, but it wasn't quite as severe as she'd feared and soon enough, she saw why. Someone had cut a rough circular hole in the floor that was several inches in diameter. The hole was surrounded by a ring of smeared shit. Whether the waste that fell through it went down to the basement or elsewhere was unclear, but the hole's purpose was obvious. It was a poop chute, a further way of reducing the need to ever take her out of the closet for anything other than inflicting abuse.

Staring at it and thinking about the endless misery of the girl's existence made Melissa wish she had a knife. She would sneak up on Calvin while he was distracted and stab him as many times as it took to put an end to the monster's existence. Then she'd put an end to Closet Girl's misery. Even in a fantasy scenario, she couldn't fathom wanting to save the woman's life. What would be the point of being removed from this hellhole only to spend years or decades living in such a decimated condition? The horror would go on and on in her head forever. She'd probably end up begging someone to blow her brains out. No, Melissa would spare her that if she could, but unfortunately, she had no access to a knife or any other kind of weapon.

She turned away from the closet and crossed the room to the nightstand, where she pulled open the top drawer and took a look inside, discovering several interesting items. These included a long lock of black hair with a blue ribbon tied around it, a pile of old letters in envelopes, an issue of *Tiger Beat* magazine, a faded Polaroid photo of a good looking boy with long hair cut in a feathered style, and an Elkmont High yearbook from 1977. The boy had been photographed wearing a Black Sabbath t-shirt.

The letters were all stamped with postmarks from the mid-1970s.

DEAD END HOUSE

On the back of the Polaroid was an inscription that read TOMMY-N-URSULA 4-EVER. She spent several minutes staring at the inscription in a deepening state of confusion. There was little doubt the photo dated from the time of the letters, but that made no sense because she was positive the Ursula she knew hadn't been born yet back then. Her exact age had always been difficult to determine because her facial features were so lumpy, but there was no way she was more than thirty.

Melissa removed the yearbook from the drawer, flipping it open after sitting on the bed. She found herself staring at a page of black-and-white student photos. The book had opened easily to this page in the middle, likely because it was the most visited page in the volume. At the end of the second row of pictures from the bottom was an image of the same boy from the Polaroid. His name was Tommy Duncan, and he'd been a senior at Elkmont in 1977. In this photo, he was wearing a Led Zeppelin t-shirt. A big music fan, apparently. After staring at the boy's smiling visage for a minute or two, she flipped to the back of the book and found the page with Ursula's photo, gasping when she saw it.

"Oh my God."

Ursula Wilcox in 1977 was a breathtakingly gorgeous young woman with sculpted cheekbones, a delicately angular jawline, pouting lips parted ever so slightly to reveal rows of perfectly straight white teeth, and the kind of eyes people wrote songs about. Big eyes you could get lost in. Her beauty was so luminous the images of the other kids on the same page paled by comparison. She looked like she was from a different planet from the rest of them, a goddess among unremarkable boys and girls.

That settled it.

There was no way in hell *this* Ursula Wilcox was the same person who'd been tormenting her for weeks. She'd adopted this girl's name for some reason and she lived in the same house the girl from the photo had once called home, but they were definitely different people.

What the fuck?

The longer she stared at the picture, though, the more she did begin to detect faint hints of familiarity. She puzzled over this long enough to become frustrated, unable to determine what was sparking the feeling, but just as she was about to flip to the front of the book and read the inscriptions there from the original Ursula's high school friends, the feeling intensified. It was something about the shape of the girl's eyes. She spent another frustrated few moments studying that part of her face when it came to her.

No. No fucking way.

She shook her head, only vaguely aware of Calvin at last returning the girl to the closet. At the edge of her vision, she saw him clip the lead back to her collar and shut the door, but all she could think about was the dawning certainty that the wreck of a woman she'd known as Alma Wilcox had once upon a time been the girl in this photo.

What the actual fucking fuck?

How did this gorgeous creature turn into *that* hideous thing? It was almost inconceivable, yet it appeared to be true. Melissa supposed there was a chance the sense of familiarity had a different explanation. If the disgusting hag who called herself Alma was an actual blood relation of the goddess in the photo, that could account for vague similarity in facial structure. She might be exactly who she said she was, or she could be some other unknown member of the Wilcox clan.

She told herself these things several times, but she knew what she felt in her gut. Alma was Ursula, and somehow over the years she'd undergone a radical transformation that wasn't merely due to the passage of time. She could guess at some of the contributing factors because they were so obvious. Living in squalor. Growing up in an environment that fostered derangement. A long period of being subjected to the same kind of horrific abuse she would later visit upon countless others. Subsisting on a diet that often included the devouring of human flesh. And perhaps more than a bit of deliberate self-ruination.

She looked up and saw Calvin looming over her, watching her with interest. "What the hell is going on in this house? Why are you all pretending to be people you're not?"

He looked for a moment like he might respond in some way, but then his eyes flicked toward the door.

There were footsteps coming down the hallway.

Calvin snatched the yearbook from her hands, put it back in the drawer, and closed it. He made eye contact with her and shook his head in an adamant way, which Melissa took as a clear indication that she should keep what she'd learned to herself.

She decided she would. For now.

Calvin moved away from the bed as the footsteps drew closer.

DEAD END HOUSE

Trixie entered the room ahead of Ursula—or the person currently using that name, at any rate—who entered carrying a ratty old wedding dress on a hanger.

Ursula shot a smirking glance at Calvin. "Out of the room, ya fuckin' retard. Time to go fetch you-know-who. Go on, get. And close the door on your way out."

Calvin grumbled in response, but he started toward the door anyway, his eyes darting in Melissa's direction one more time before he walked out of the room and closed the door.

Once he was gone, Ursula said, "Time to get ready for your big day. On your fuckin' feet, bitch. Now."

Melissa rose from the bed with a weary sigh. Participating in the farce of a ceremony they were planning was pretty much the last thing in the world she wanted to do, but the choice wasn't hers. They spent several minutes getting her into the ill-fitting dress, adjusting the fit with numerous safety pins and a belt cinched around the waist. The dress smelled as awful as it looked, as if they'd dredged it out of a sewer, and it was of an antiquated style no modern bride would choose.

After they were finished, Trixie and Ursula spent some time gushing over her in mocking tones, saying how "beautiful" and "radiant" she looked. Melissa endured all of this without comment, knowing the worst parts of this deranged charade were undoubtedly still ahead of her.

She was not wrong.

TWENTY-EIGHT

AN ATTIC DOOR WAS HANGING open in the short section of hallway outside the bedroom, with the attached foldable ladder extended to the floor. As she followed Ursula out of the bedroom, the enigmatic long-haired man Melissa had glimpsed briefly on previous occasions climbed the ladder steps and disappeared into the dark opening in the ceiling. She assumed he was another family member, but she'd never seen him converse or interact with anyone else in the house.

Ursula circumvented the ladder without comment and continued down the hallway. Melissa was right behind her, but she couldn't help throwing a quick glance up at the ceiling as she moved past the ladder. She heard the man moving around up there, but she couldn't see anything through the opening. Trixie was the last one out of the room, holding up the long train of Melissa's wedding dress as she trailed along behind her.

Once they started moving down the longer section of hallway,

DEAD END HOUSE

Ursula cupped her hands around her mouth and loudly announced the start of the wedding procession. A moment later, someone downstairs started playing "Here Comes the Bride" on a chintzy sounding keyboard, the kind designed for use by small children. The music continued for the duration of the process, repeating the main instrumental part again and again as the procession arrived at the end of the hallway and started down the disquietingly creaky stairs.

Calvin was waiting for them in the foyer. He was clad in his usual coveralls, only he'd now also stuffed himself into a tuxedo jacket that was at least one size too small for him. The jacket was the kind with a long tail, and as with the wedding dress, Melissa was certain several decades had passed since the last time anyone had worn it to any type of formal event.

As Melissa arrived in the foyer, Calvin held out the crook of his arm for her in the manner of an usher at a real wedding while someone in the living room continued to pound the keys of the chintzy keyboard. Knowing it was expected—and she'd probably be punished for not playing along—she accepted Calvin's proffered arm, allowing him to guide her out of the foyer and into the living room.

Alma was parked in her wheelchair in front of the sagging old couch. The toy keyboard was in her lap, and her fat fingers ceased crashing against the keys as Calvin guided her to a stop in the center of the room. Unlike the last time Melissa had seen the woman, she wasn't nude, having donned a filthy pink muumuu for the occasion. Up close, the similarity to the girl in the yearbook photo became even more obvious. She was otherwise completely unrecognizable, but those eyes were exactly the same.

Despite her intimate knowledge of the inhuman beast the woman had become, Melissa felt a flicker of sadness. The utter destruction of the original Ursula's rare natural beauty was a tragic thing, a terrible, senseless waste. She couldn't comprehend how the woman had allowed it to happen. Anger soon replaced sadness, however, as she reminded herself the same thing was in the process of happening to her. She believed that if she were able to escape this place and have the chance to recover, she might yet retain some diminished level of beauty. The severing of her ear was the worst thing done to her thus far in terms of marring her looks, but she knew it would not end there. After another couple weeks here—if that long—she might end up looking like the horror show currently strapped into the Bad Girl Chair.

The right arm of the naked girl in the chair ended in a nub of blackened flesh. The burned flesh had a recently cooked smell, strong and pungent in the way of a sirloin steak left on the grill for too long. Her other arm looked almost as bad, swollen to a hideous degree at the wrist and discolored almost up to her shoulder. The limb looked like it was dying, which meant it probably wouldn't be long before the infection spread throughout her body and killed her. She was missing an eye and much of her bare flesh was marred in the ways typical of the girls imprisoned here for any significant stretch of time. One notable difference was that she appeared to have been burned with propane torches more often than most. There were melted patches of skin all over her body. The girl looked up at her and trembled, but said nothing. Melissa had been made to sit in the Bad Girl Chair once during her initial period of confinement to the main part of the house. For hours. Even after all the horrendous things she'd been through since then, it remained her most miserable experience in this wretched place.

Atop the floor model television was a medium-sized box covered in wrinkled pink wrapping paper that didn't appear new. A bow of the same color was pinned or taped to the top of the box.

Alma looked Melissa up and down, then began gushing over her in a mocking manner that was a lot like the way Trixie and Ursula had acted after getting her into the dress upstairs. She doubted it was a coincidence. Every aspect of this so far was part of a prearranged plan.

Trixie approached the girl in the Bad Girl Chair and slapped her. "Where are your manners, cunt? Aren't you going to tell the bride how beautiful she looks?"

The girl in the chair whimpered and looked at Melissa. "Y-you look . . . b-b-buh . . . beautiful."

Then she began to sob.

Trixie laughed and slapped her again.

After that, she dropped into the girl's lap and began to grind against her like a dancer in a strip club giving a customer a lap dance. The girl in the chair moaned loudly in agony, but Alma and Calvin responded with hoots of approval. Ursula put her fingers in her mouth and did a wolf whistle.

This went on for at least a full minute, ending when Alma raised her voice to cut through the commotion. "All right, y'all, that's enough. Time to get on with the ceremony. Calvin, go bring the other one in here. Holler when you're about to enter."

Calvin walked out of the room, disappearing through the nearby hallway entrance. Some grunts of exertion could soon be heard coming from the direction of the kitchen. As soon as Calvin unleashed a bellow signaling his readiness, Alma again began playing "Here Comes the Bride" on the toy keyboard.

Trixie came over and squeezed Melissa's arm, leaning close to whisper in her ear. "I'm so happy for you, Slaggie. This is such a magical day, getting hitched to the woman of your dreams. You're so lucky."

Melissa didn't bother saying anything to that.

She stood rigidly facing Alma, her stomach churning with dread.

After another few moments, Trixie turned her head and gasped in mock appreciation as Calvin came back through the archway into the living room. Her eyes widened and she put a hand to her mouth. "Oh my gosh, look at Wormie. She looks positively ravishing."

Melissa glanced in that direction and felt the churning in her gut intensify. The dead woman was being held upright by Calvin, who was gripping her underneath her arms. The corpse had been shoved into a plain white frock, in lieu of a more formal wedding dress. Her head was lolling stiffly to one side and there were maggots squirming in one of her eye sockets. The missing bottom lip looked even worse now, the weeks of decay making the facial anomaly stand out in a far more hideous way than before.

Alma again ceased banging on the keyboard as Calvin maneuvered Wormie's corpse into position alongside Melissa. Trixie remained at Melissa's other side while Ursula took up a similar position next to Wormie. A period of relative silence ensued, lasting until the strange long-haired man came into the room. A vintage camera attached to a strap dangled from his neck. No one other than Melissa so much as glanced at him, but she nonetheless had the impression they'd been waiting for him to arrive.

Alma smiled. "Y'all, we are gathered here today to join Wormie and Slaggie in unholy matrimony. This here special couple has gotten to know each other in ways not many others ever do. Their bond is the kind that lasts forever and ever, even after death, because it's been forged in the glorious fires of Hell. They already know how much they love each other, but the time has come to make it official. Slaggie, do you take Wormie to be your awful wedded wife?"

It took Melissa a moment to realize she was expected to respond.

She shuddered in recognition of the eager way everyone in the room was staring at her. Even the wretch in the nail chair was watching her with apparent interest. The long-haired man raised his old camera and pointed it at her.

She cleared her throat. "Yes. I do."

There was no point in not playing along. She'd be made to comply one way or another, and defiance would only result in more pain.

Alma looked at the corpse. "And do you, Wormie, take Slaggie to be your ball and chain forever and ever?"

There was another brief period of silence.

Melissa again glanced around at everyone assembled in the room. She looked at Wormie and saw a fly emerge from her nose and move across her cheek. The silence went on long enough to make Melissa seriously consider answering on Wormie's behalf just to put an end to it.

Alma, however, interjected before that became necessary. "She said yes. The rest of y'all heard that, didn't ya?"

General noises of assent followed.

The girl in the Bad Girl Chair laughed in a way that made her sound close to cracking up. The sound was deep anguish tinged with a degree of morbid amusement only available to those who are already doomed. "She didn't say anything. She's *dead*. Dead people don't talk, you assholes."

Trixie took a step in the girl's direction, but Alma held up a hand, stopping her. "Don't pay that one any attention. She's bitter because she knows nobody's ever gonna love her like Wormie and Slaggie love each other. She's too damn ugly. Now who's got the rings?"

Ursula stepped forward at that point, extending a hand to Melissa, who almost laughed when she looked at the woman's upturned palm. The "rings" were fashioned from cheap twist ties, the kind used to seal loaves of bread in plastic bags. She plucked them from Ursula's hand, slid one on the ring finger of her left hand, which happened to be one of the three digits still remaining on that hand. Grimacing as she took hold of one of Wormie's hands, she lifted it up and slid the twist tie ring onto one of her fingers. It immediately slid off again after she let go of the dead woman's hand, but no one seemed to notice or care. It was enough, apparently, that she'd gone through with the pretense of the ring exchange.

Alma clapped her hands together and exclaimed, "I hereby pronounce you wife and wife! You may now kiss the bride."

A silent beat elapsed

They were all looking at her in that expectant, eager way again.

Melissa suppressed a groan.

Fuck.

They'd already made it clear what was expected of her, and it was just as clear there'd be no getting around it.

She turned toward Wormie, cupped her rotting face in her hands, and pressed her lips against what remained of the dead woman's mouth. This was disgusting, but it was no worse than some of the other things she'd already been forced to do to the corpse. She hoped nothing would crawl out of Wormie's mouth and into her own before she could break the clinch. The squirming maggots in that eye socket an inch away from her own face disgusted her more than the kiss.

She was easing herself away from Wormie when the flash cube attached to the long-haired man's camera went off with a loud pop. A whirring sound accompanied the ejection of a square-shaped piece of paper from the slot at the bottom of the camera.

Trixie squealed in excitement. "Congratulations, Slaggie! I'm so thrilled for you. I wish I could find someone to love me as much as you love Wormie. It's so inspiring. Like, even with all the bad stuff happening in the world today, true love can still prevail. Gives me hope for the future."

She was laying it on extra thick now, the blandly optimistic platitudes a deliberate contrast to the ugly reality of the situation, accentuating the dark truth rather than obscuring it. The leering way Trixie uttered the words drove the point home even more firmly. Everything about this ghoulish mockery of a wedding ceremony was a cruel joke, an elaborate piece of staged entertainment rather than a true expression of anything profound or sacred. She wished she could lash out at them, even if only in a verbal way, but that wasn't an option.

Ursula went over to the television and retrieved the box covered in pink wrapping paper, a sly smile gently curving her mouth as she subsequently presented it to Melissa. "We got a little something for you."

Alma harrumphed. "It's from *all* of us."

Ursula rolled her eyes. "That's basically what I fuckin' said."

A shrug from Alma. "I just want her to know."

Ursula pushed the box into Melissa's hands. "Go ahead, open it."

She couldn't help frowning as she eyed the box with trepidation. Whatever it contained, there was zero chance it wasn't something deeply fucked up. These were people with diseased imaginations. Almost anything could be in the box. Human body parts. A pile of shit. A dead animal. She trembled at the thought of opening the box only to be confronted with another snake, a prospect that struck her as distressingly plausible in light of recent experiences. Only this time it might not be a non-venomous one. She gave the box a light shake, ready to drop it in an instant if anything hissed or rattled inside it. Nothing like that happened, but she remained wary.

Ursula scowled. "There ain't anything in there that's gonna bite you."

Trixie grinned. "Not this time. We promise. So go ahead, open it."

Promises from these people were hard to trust, but Melissa knew she again had no choice but to do as they wanted. She removed the bow and tore away the old wrapping paper, revealing an aged cardboard box. The crumpled top flaps were not taped shut. She pulled them open, reached inside, frowned for a moment as her fingers curled around an object of a familiar shape with an odd texture. Wads of tissue paper tumbled to the floor as she extracted the object from the box. Someone giggled as the box slipped from her fingers.

Her "wedding gift" was a strap-on rubber dildo attached to a black harness. She was holding it by the artificial phallus, her expression registering confusion as she spent a few moments gaping at it. The crazies gathered with her in the room tried their best to restrain their mirth, but a few additional helpless giggles slipped out.

Melissa shook her head. "I don't understand. What do you expect me to do with this?"

Alma snorted laughter. "Ain't it obvious? Now that you're hitched, it's time to consummate the marriage."

Melissa frowned. "What?"

"It means you're gonna fuck Wormie right here in this room," Trixie said, laughing as she waggled her eyebrows. "And we're gonna watch while you do it. Hell, we might even join in. Ain't that right, Grannie Alma?"

Alma nodded. "That's right, Trix-a-licious. Now somebody get our bride out of that dress and into that prick harness."

Ursula and Trixie converged on Melissa at the same time. Her instinct was to flinch away from them, but she made herself stay still, knowing resistance remained pointless. What they wanted seemed clear. She'd be made to mount the corpse and simulate intercourse with it by penetrating the dead flesh with the strap-on dildo. It was a nauseating notion, but Trixie had already forced her to lick the dead woman's vagina on a previous occasion. This would be bad, but it couldn't possibly be any worse than that. She'd comply in the desired way, as usual, enduring it until it was over, and that would be that.

The belt was removed from her waist and cast aside, and after that the girls set about removing all the safety pins. This process required several minutes because they'd used a lot of them, but the instant it was complete, the stifling, foul-smelling dress was removed from her body. The relief she felt was considerable, as being cinched into so constricting a heavy garment in this hotbox of a house was uncomfortable in the extreme. She remained unsure of how much time had passed since her abduction, but she felt certain that summer was not yet over. The sweltering heat inside the house was almost too much to take. Her entire body was dripping with perspiration.

Ursula helped her into the strap-on device, adjusting the angle of the phallus a few times as she fastened the straps. She endured this without protest, still luxuriating in the relief of no longer being in the wedding dress. It wasn't until Ursula took her by an arm and steered her over to the Bad Girl Chair that she started to become truly alarmed.

"Hold on. Why are you—"

Ursula punched her in the lower back. "Shut the fuck up."

She turned Melissa roughly about and shoved her down into the lap of the girl in the chair. The girl beneath her howled in agony, her body jolting as if she'd received an electric shock.

Melissa's instinct was to rise, but Ursula leveled a forefinger at her face and said, "Don't you fuckin' dare. Stay right the fuck there." A corner of her mouth twitched. "You want to lose that other ear, bitch? Because that's exactly what's gonna happen if you don't do as you're told."

The girl beneath her was sobbing and quivering nonstop.

Melissa felt bad for her, but not bad enough to risk incurring more of Ursula's wrath. "Okay. Whatever you say."

Ursula smirked. "Damn right."

At Ursula's direction, she adjusted her position atop the whimpering girl, leaning back against her and pushing the lower half of her body forward enough to cause the dildo to stand at a perfectly vertical angle. Several times she saw the blackened nub at the end of the girl's right arm twitch and try to raise up off the nail points embedded in the armrest, only to be restrained by a strap. It was pitiful and sickening at the same time. As with Closet Girl, she wished she could put this poor thing out of her misery, but it just wasn't possible.

Trixie disappeared through the hallway entrance while this was happening and was gone from the room for a few minutes. When she returned, it was with a brown jar of some oily substance. She smiled as she approached the Bad Girl Chair. "Time to get you lubed up and ready for your blushing bride."

She scooped a handful of what was either lard or tallow out of the open jar and slathered it all over the dildo. Before she was finished, she'd used multiple handfuls of the stuff to ensure that the phallus was as slicked-up as possible.

Ursula stood smirking nearby, her arms folded beneath her breasts as she observed this process. "Reckon you know what's coming next, huh?" She glanced at her brother. "Hey, dumbshit, get Wormie over here."

Calvin grumbled in response, but he complied with this directive. He'd been holding Wormie's corpse upright the entire time, and now he shuffled his way over to the Bad Girl Chair. When he got there, he turned her around and raised her up into the air. Obeying Ursula's instructions, Melissa took hold of the phallus and held it steady, guiding it into Wormie as Calvin lowered the corpse onto her. She heard a wet squelch as the dildo entered the dead woman's vagina. Once he was sure he had Wormie positioned atop her in a more or less stable way, he backed away and stood between Trixie and Ursula. Alma scooted her wheelchair closer and leaned forward in it, the eyes that were the only recognizable trace of the girl she'd once been projecting eagerness.

The long-haired man who never spoke or interacted with the rest of them moved a little closer and raised his camera again.

Melissa turned her head and looked at all of them over Wormie's shoulder. "Now what?"

Ursula sneered. "It's like you were already told, girl, this is the consummation of your marriage. The thing is, you're gonna have to do all the work, Wormie not being up to it for obvious reasons."

There were more giggles in response to this statement.

Ursula moved a step closer. "You're gonna fuck your bride, bitch. Grab her by the hips and thrust your fake cock up into her. Then keep doing it until I tell you to stop. That easy enough to understand?"

Melissa sighed. "Yeah."

She once again did as she'd been told, only she grabbed hold of Wormie by the waist instead of by the hips. The corpse in her lap was a heavier weight than she'd anticipated, and she had to constantly work at exerting enough strength to maintain the required up thrusting rhythm. At one point she started feigning moans of sexual ecstasy when Ursula screamed at her for not sounding like she was enjoying it enough. This contrasted with the agonized moans of the girl beneath her in a way the ghouls directing her through this lurid scene seemed to enjoy.

At first Melissa tried disconnecting herself from the sounds and sensations of the other girl's agony, believing she could get through this by focusing only on what she'd been told to do. It soon became apparent this would not be possible. The girl's agonized moans grew louder, and she frequently begged Melissa to stop, not seeming to get that it wasn't up to her. It happened often enough to become irritating, and Melissa eventually responded by working harder to feign an intense state of arousal. She began grinding against the girl beneath her, causing the sounds of her suffering to intensify as she raised the volume of her own moaning. She got so into her performance it took her several minutes to notice Ursula and Trixie had started enthusiastically groping and making out with each other. Alma had pulled up the hem of her pink muumuu and had thrust a hand between her massive thighs. Her head was lolling around and she was moaning louder than any of them. Calvin had removed the ill-fitting tuxedo jacket and was starting to undo the buckles of his coveralls.

The wedding was on the verge of turning into a redneck psycho orgy. That things had developed in this direction was far from shocking. After more than a month of being held captive by these freaks, she knew there was no bottom to their depravity. Taboos did not exist in this place. There were no lines they would not cross. Acts of incest and necrophilia were just the tip of the iceberg. Ursula had taunted her with tales of impregnated captives and forced births, implying that this might be her ultimate fate if she managed to stay alive long enough. Any spawn produced was likely to be eaten, something Ursula assured her had happened several times. It was a rare delicacy they all enjoyed immensely.

Hearing about these things was one of many reasons she was glad Calvin had largely stayed away from her after her first few days of captivity. The rest of them abused her with great enthusiasm on a regular basis, but at least they weren't capable of planting a baby in her womb. Well, there was also the long-haired guy, but he gave every appearance of being uninterested in directly participating in any form of abuse. All he cared about, it seemed, was moving wordlessly among the rest of them, observing and taking the occasional picture before disappearing. She might yet wind up pregnant, but she felt confident he wouldn't be the one to knock her up.

All the grinding and thrusting began to take a toll after it'd gone on for an extended time. Her back and all the muscles in her pelvic region were feeling the strain, with every movement requiring a greater level of exertion while becoming steadily more painful. It didn't help she was having to continually fight to hold Wormie's corpse upright. The dildo was moving more easily inside her than it had in the beginning. She had the impression there was now an additional form of lubricant, suggesting that something inside Wormie had ruptured. There was a wetness in the region of her own groin that hadn't been there before, which enhanced the impression.

At the same time, she remained aware of the effect her ceaseless gyrations were having on the girl beneath her. The nail points were being driven deeper into her flesh, the movements also causing them to shred the flesh in ways that didn't happen when one was merely sitting still in the chair. After a while, the girl's loud moaning gave way to weaker whimpering. The only intelligible word she could utter by that point was "please" in a voice so soft only Melissa could hear it.

Hearing the girl's endless suffering tormented Melissa to such an extreme degree that she redoubled her efforts to shut out the sounds. She tried so hard that she began to feel mentally adrift, connected to the blood drenched reality of the world around her only by the thinnest of threads. The drifting sensation caused her to lose her good, solid grip on Wormie's waist, and the next time Melissa did one of those hard upward thrusts, the corpse became dislodged, sliding off the dildo and tumbling to the floor. Full awareness returned the instant this happened, along with a spike of dread at the prospect of being punished for allowing this to happen. Then she saw the dildo and part of the harness were now coated with a layer of an oily blackness. A twinge of nausea made her feel close to throwing up, but because it'd been so long since she'd last eaten, there was little in her stomach left to expel.

She looked around and saw Calvin had lifted Alma out of her

wheelchair and placed her on the couch, positioning himself above her in a way that allowed him to aggressively fuck her in the mouth, while she clutched at his straining calf muscles and groaned. How he was able to keep going like that after spending so much time repeatedly violating Closet Girl, Melissa did not know. Ursula and Trixie were entwined together on the floor, moaning and writhing. The long-haired guy was the only one still clothed, unsurprisingly. He was standing near the foyer, still taking pictures with his vintage camera.

Then Ursula belatedly noticed Wormie had become dislodged and was now sprawled on the floor in front of the Bad Girl Chair. She disengaged herself from Trixie and approached the chair. The set of her flushed features still conveyed a state of intense arousal as she looked first at the dildo and then at Melissa's face.

She smiled. "Do you think you're done now?"

Melissa did not think that.

She didn't believe there'd ever be an end to this descent into psychosexual madness, not until she was dead or freed from this place. She also knew that pleading for mercy or temporary relief from the insanity would accomplish nothing positive.

The exact opposite was her only hope.

She forced a smile of her own. "I hope I'm not done."

Ursula stepped over the corpse and dropped to her knees in front of the Bad Girl Chair. After a moment of intense eye contact with Melissa, she began a long, slow process of licking every speck of the mixture of substances from the dildo, including lumpy bits of what might have been bugs or shredded pieces of flesh. Or both. When she was finished, she got to her feet, smiling and wiping her mouth with the back of a hand as she held Melissa's gaze again. Then she turned around and lowered herself, groaning as the dildo slid easily into her. Melissa grabbed onto her and made sounds of arousal.

This time there was nothing fake about them.

And the redneck psycho orgy went on and on.

TWENTY-NINE

HOURS HAD PASSED SINCE NANCY Kincaid's violent death and the woman who called herself Agatha Winchester could not calm down. She had periods of sitting and fidgeting at the table in the kitchen, tugging at her hair and bouncing her leg. Often she would get up and pace all around the house, pausing now and then to peek outside through various windows, hiding behind curtains in hopes of not being noticed by anyone passing by. She was convinced the police would somehow know a crime had been committed, and that they were about to come swarming into the house, knocking the door down with a battering ram like in an action movie.

The one part of the house she did not venture into during this period was the spare bedroom. Nancy's lifeless body was something she hoped to never set eyes on again. She vacillated between feeling sickened by what had occurred and angry with the dead woman for having returned home so early without warning. She'd expected a phone call after the meeting at the police station. That was one thing.

DEAD END HOUSE

The bigger thing by far was the early return. They'd believed she'd be gone at least another half hour to an hour. Most of what she felt, however, was an overriding sense of horror.

This was only supposed to have been a fun little adventure, a means of amusing herself at the tail end of the summer. Less than a week remained until she was due to return to her community college teaching job in neighboring Barlow County. She'd sought to fill that time in her usual manner of presenting a false version of herself to total strangers.

Interesting things often happened when she did this, ranging from brief romantic flings with men and women to drawing people into a variety of harmless little schemes. Small-time swindles that separated her targets from a small amount of money. Getting people to believe in and feel excited about the ideas she put in their heads before ghosting them forever was the worst thing she'd ever done until today. Today was a disaster of epic proportions.

There was an element of tragic irony involved as well, because until the deadly encounter with Nancy she'd believed her latest escapade might result in something of tangible value for someone other than herself. Quite by accident, she'd stumbled her way into connecting with people haunted for years by an inexplicable disappearance. She became emotionally invested in a genuine way, convincing herself she could help Sterling and Nancy uncover the truth about their daughter. It'd been like stepping into the pages of a mystery novel, which made it extra exciting, because reading old paperback mysteries had been a passion of hers since childhood. The opportunity to play a key role in unraveling a real-life mystery excited her.

The main question confronting her now was what could she possibly do to extract herself from this situation and avoid incarceration. Was that even possible? She didn't know. All she did know was she'd rather die than go to jail. She was too cute and too interesting for prison. Society needed unusual and creative people like her out and roaming about freely, circulating amongst the vast population of boring normal people while sowing seeds of benign chaos.

Such had always been her philosophy, at any rate, but now she was wondering if there might have been hidden flaws in this whimsical self-opinion all along. Sowers of benign chaos were not supposed to stab anyone to death. Kind of negated and made a joke of the whole "benign" part. It also didn't matter that it'd been a semi-accidental killing committed in the course of defending herself. The end result was the same.

It *looked* like a murder.

Therefore, the cops would probably treat it like one.

She stalked back into the kitchen and went to the refrigerator, yanking the door open and glaring at its sparse contents again. "I can't believe the woman doesn't have booze in her house. Not even any fucking beer. Christ, I need a drink so bad."

Sterling's only response was a whimper.

Jars of condiments rattled as she threw the refrigerator door shut.

She went to the table and pulled out a chair, sitting down. "You need to pull yourself together and help me think of a way out of this."

Sterling was seated at the opposite side of the table. He took his hands from his face, revealing a tear-streaked visage. "I can't believe she's dead."

"Oh, yeah? Well, how about you take a walk back down the hall and look inside that fucking room. I promise you, she's fucking dead, and we need to figure out a way to cover our tracks."

Sterling sniffled and wiped tears from his face. "How can you be so cold, Agatha?"

She grunted. "I'm not being cold. I didn't want that to happen, but it did and nothing's going to change that. I get that you're upset. I get that you cared about her. But we have to deal with reality and start thinking about ourselves. I don't know about you, but I'd really rather not spend the rest of my life in jail."

Sterling wiped away more tears. "I'm sure if we just explained things the right way, the cops would see it was a terrible accident."

"I don't want to talk to the police. Like, at all. Things would come out that might make me look bad."

Sterling frowned. "I don't understand. It *was* an accident. If they don't believe me, they can strap me to a lie detector. There's no reason to fear the truth."

Agatha sighed. "You don't get it. What happened to Nancy is bad enough, but I have other reasons to worry."

"Like what?"

Her laugh was fraught with bitterness. "In the absence of a dead body, most of it would be minor stuff the police wouldn't give a shit about, but because someone has been killed, there's a chance they might have a harsher than normal view." She pursed her lips and shifted in the chair, recrossing her legs. "There's a small chance I could be connected to a series of petty crimes."

Sterling shook his head. "That's ridiculous. You're so young. Cops don't care about small-time juvenile shit."

She laughed in a bitter way. "Oh my God, there's so much you don't understand. I mean, there's no way you could have known, but almost everything I've ever told you about myself is a lie."

Sterling's expression was a study in undiluted incomprehension. Even now, the idea she might have willfully deluded him in any form would not take shape in his head. It was crazy. This man on the surface was nothing but human wreckage. He should be jaded to the core, incapable of putting any degree of faith in another person, and yet he'd done just that with her. Beneath all the damage lurked an unlikely vestige of innocence.

One she was about to crush forever.

He sighed. "I don't . . ."

She nodded as he trailed off. "You don't understand. I know. I'm sorry, but the truth is I'm kind of a piece of shit. I like to insert myself in the lives of total strangers, usually only for a little while and usually only to mess with them. Hardly anything I ever say is the truth."

Sterling stared at her in silence for a moment, a new wariness in his expression. "What lies have you told me then?"

The shift in his demeanor didn't frighten her. It only made her sad. She'd hurt him and she hated that. What made it worse was knowing the hurt was only going to deepen.

She took a deep breath and let it all out. "Agatha Winchester is a made-up name. Agatha is from Agatha Christie, my favorite writer, and Winchester comes from a TV show I like. Also, I don't live in Elkmont. I'm just here on an extended visit."

Sterling scratched the side of his head, his look of confusion deepening. "But your apartment . . ."

She shook her head. "Not mine. I'm apartment sitting for a friend who's vacationing in France this summer. It's not something that actually needed doing, but I talked her into it, telling her I'd welcome a temporary change of scenery. What I was really after was a place where I could safely pursue new marks and have some fun before disappearing."

Sterling frowned. "Marks?"

She nodded. "Yeah. Marks. Gullible people likely to believe the bullshit I tell them."

A look of anger crossed Sterling's face. "Gullible people, eh? So nothing you told me is true? Not a single goddamn thing?"

She shifted in the chair again, fidgeting as her nervousness increased. "First of all, I hope you get that I'm telling you all this now because I want to be real with you from this point forward. When I came up to you on the street, I had nothing in mind but playing another of my stupid games, no goal other than messing with a stranger I figured I'd never see or talk to again after that day. Then you fucking fainted on me and everything changed. You told me about your daughter and I got wrapped up in it. I sincerely wanted to help you solve that fucking mystery. I really thought we could do it, but now . . ."

She waved a hand in the direction of the hallway.

The implication was obvious.

Minutes of silence elapsed.

Sterling laced his fingers together and stared at his hands, frowning harder than ever.

Then he raised his eyes and met her gaze. "I want to believe the part about wanting to help. I think I *do* believe that, which means I can let some of this other shit slide. So you're a small-time con artist? So what? It's not like I'm some kind of saint. Then there's the matter of your age. People would take that into account when judging your actions."

She spluttered laughter.

Sterling looked annoyed. "I don't see what's funny here."

She sighed. "I'm sorry if this is disillusioning in any way, but you have not actually been having sex with a hot nineteen-year-old chick. I just happen to have the kind of face and body that allows me to pass for one."

Sterling grunted. "How old are you then?"

"Twenty-eight. Almost twenty-nine."

He shook his head. "I just don't get it. Why trick people and make up stories about yourself?"

She shrugged. "There's no real point in trying to explain it. I barely even understand it myself. It's something I've always done, going back to when I was a little kid. I just thought you should know before we do anything rash like getting the authorities involved."

Sterling groaned in exasperation.

He got up from the table and went over to the refrigerator, pulling the door open to peer inside. "She really doesn't have any beer in here."

"Told you."

Sterling slammed the door shut. "Goddammit!"

She gave him a wary look. "You okay? You're sounding a wee bit unhinged all of a sudden."

He laughed and rubbed his chin. "Oh, you think so? My ex-wife is dead. Stabbed to death. You talk about wanting to cover our tracks, but there's no getting around that. Even if we buried her body somewhere and cleaned up all the blood, her disappearance would be suspicious as hell. Then there's the matter of her meeting with the chief of fucking police today. And who knows what she told that son of a bitch. They'll probably come looking for us first thing as soon as they realize she's gone missing."

The last bit further heightened her already elevated sense of unease. "I do wish we had some idea of what was said at that meeting. She said she'd leave us out of it for now, but there's always a chance she let something slip."

Sterling nodded. "There's also the fact your car's been parked out front all damn day. People in neighborhoods like this are always on the lookout for things that don't belong. Someone might've taken a picture or written the plate number down."

Somehow she hadn't considered that until now.

Fuck.

She got up and started pacing around the kitchen again, the knuckles of her right hand wedged between her teeth as she tried not to freak out.

Fuck, fuck, fuck!

The car wasn't hers, but it didn't matter. It belonged to her friend and could easily be linked back to her.

What the hell am I gonna do?

Then she came to an abrupt stop in the middle of the kitchen, the solution coming to her with lightning bolt quickness. It was so simple and obvious. She and this man had only the most tenuous of connections. Washing her hands of all of this and leaving him here to deal with the situation on his own was the only thing she could do. Going that route would require her to abandon any pretense of noble intent, but she was kind of past that point already anyway.

Sterling could tell the cops whatever he wanted. That was the beauty of it. It didn't matter because the cops hated him. Nothing he told them would be taken seriously. Yes, there was lingering concern about what Nancy might have said to the chief, but the woman had seemed clear in her intent to leave them out of it prior to the meeting.

It was unlikely she'd mentioned either of them.

And "Agatha" still hadn't told Sterling her real name.

She considered simply grabbing her purse and walking out without another word. The urge to do this was so strong that for a moment she was right on the edge of snatching her purse off the table.

Then she remembered the one crucial thing she'd forgotten.

The knife. The fucking knife. Shit.

The knife had been in Nancy's hand at the moment of penetration, but for no good reason she could think of, "Agatha" had pulled the blade out after she was dead. Her fingerprints were on that handle, possibly imprinted in blood. It'd been nothing but unthinking impulse, some deluded fading belief that the woman might still be saved despite the mortal wound. She'd been rattled in the immediate aftermath of violent chaos, understandably, but now she was left with a dire complication in need of solving.

Sterling regarded her with a look of curiosity mixed with lingering wariness.

But mostly curiosity, she was pretty sure.

"I can see the wheels spinning in your head. Have you come up with an idea?"

She nodded. "I think so. I'm sorry, I know this will be painful, but we need to go have one more look at Nancy."

He grimaced and shook his head as fresh tears welled in his eyes. "No. No fucking way. I can't."

Drawing on the skills she'd developed over a lifetime of getting people to believe in things that were not true, she was able to convince Sterling of the necessity for one last look at the death scene. This involved repurposing and spewing out a lot of scientific stuff about forensics she'd gleaned from reading mystery novels and watching cop procedurals on television. Stuff about blood spatter patterns, the wound angle, and the position of the body on the floor. There might even have been a seed of truth in the things she was saying, but it didn't matter, nothing changed what she now knew she had to do. Her earnestness convinced Sterling.

They returned to the room.

Sterling broke down the instant he saw his ex-wife's corpse again. He became so distraught he didn't notice when she picked up the butcher knife. His eyes were screwed shut from the force of his anguish, and she was close enough to him that she could easily have rammed the knife straight into the hollow of his throat. Bury it deep enough to inflict a fatal wound and yank it back out within the space of about a second.

Something roughly like this had been the basis of her quickly formulated plan. By closing his eyes, Sterling had even gifted her with the perfect opportunity to get it done fast and with relative ease, but now that the moment was at hand, she was having trouble psyching herself up to go through with it. The problem was that she wasn't a killer by nature. She was far from morally pure, but she did possess a conscience. The gulf between fatally stabbing a person by accident and purposely killing another person was vast. She was no longer sure she possessed the necessary sense of ruthless self-preservation.

At first Sterling only looked confused when he opened his eyes, but then he noticed the bloodstained blade and frowned. "Were you planning on stabbing me?"

She opened her mouth, but no words came out.

She had no idea what to say. Denial was pointless. Words were pointless. She had no doubt he could clearly read the truth in her expression. Had anyone on earth ever looked guiltier than she did in this moment?

She didn't think so.

Sterling reached for the knife.

She jerked it away and stabbed him in the arm.

The blade opened a big gash in the meaty underside of his forearm. He cried out in pain and flinched away from her. The blade was shaking harder than ever and she was struggling to hold onto it. Sterling almost immediately made another grab for it. His hand closed around the blade and she ripped it away from him, slicing open his palm and eliciting a louder shriek of pain. This time he staggered away from her and nearly tripped over Nancy's corpse. While he was busy righting himself, she rushed forward and stabbed him in the stomach. Twice. The blade sank in a few inches each time. Instinct propelled him away from her, and this time he did stumble over the body, falling to the floor.

"Agatha" didn't know whether she'd wounded Sterling severely enough to kill him. The long blade hadn't gone all the way in like it had with Nancy, so maybe he'd survive. She stared at him in disbelieving horror for a moment as he writhed and moaned on the floor, unable to comprehend how this had happened. She'd been so close to talking herself out of hurting him at all.

Sterling whimpered and glanced up at her through his tears. "I can't believe you did this. I trusted you."

She nodded. "Yeah. I'm sorry, but that was stupid of you. I'm getting out of here."

He moaned and raised a shaking hand. "Please . . . help me . . ."

She walked out of the room and staggered down the hallway. In the kitchen, she snatched her purse off the table and snapped it shut after shoving the knife inside it. All she was thinking was that she'd get rid of it at some point after she managed to calm down. Never mind all the other ways she might still be linked to what had happened here.

Outside night was falling. She'd been here far longer than she'd realized, but she was glad of the approaching darkness. There was no one moving about in the street, which was good, but any nosy neighbor peeking outside might not be able to see her clearly in the faint, dying rays of twilight. It'd probably also prevent any such person from seeing the blood on her hands.

She hurried across the yard to her friend's car, fumbling with the keys for a few maddening seconds before finally getting the door open. More than once she choked back the urge to screech in frustration. Once she was finally in the car and ensconced behind the steering wheel, her nerves cost her another precious few seconds as she repeatedly jabbed the key at the ignition slot and missed. This time she did scream, but then the key finally went in and she heaved a huge sigh of relief.

Let's get the fuck out of here.

She started the engine and reached for the gear shifter.

And that was when the flashing blue lights popped up behind her.

THIRTY

THE ORGY SEEMED ENDLESS TO Melissa as it was happening, but in actuality it ran out of steam in less than an hour. After Ursula had her first go at it, Alma and Trixie took turns riding the strap-on dildo. Though her sounds of arousal were loudly expressed, there was something rote and performance-like in Trixie's outward behavior during her turn. Melissa sensed the girl was only doing what was expected of her rather than responding to any genuine urge to wallow in sexual depravity.

Alma announced her intention to take a turn after watching Ursula mount up for a briefer but no less energetic second ride. She needed help mounting the dildo, with Ursula and Trixie working together to lift her up and guide the fake phallus into her body. This wasn't easy, because they were barely able to squeeze her bulk into the space between the chair's nail studded armrests. At the moment of first penetration, she unleashed a scream, a sound so loud that Melissa couldn't help but cry out in response.

This was misinterpreted by Alma as a signal of her own excitement, which had the effect of intensifying the way the woman bucked against her. The chair creaked and groaned under the strain, and Melissa spent much of that time convinced it would soon collapse from the pressure. She had a hard time breathing while Alma screamed and screamed and rode the dildo with the tenacity of a rodeo cowboy clinging tight to a bucking bronc. It was a miserable and uncomfortable experience, and she could only imagine how exponentially worse it must be for the mutilated girl whimpering steadily beneath her.

At long last, the woman ran out of energy and sagged against her in the chair. Melissa prayed this meant she was finished, but she made no request to be lifted off the chair. Every few moments, she wiggled her hips slightly and moaned a little, making it clear she was still enjoying the way the phallus felt inside her. After a seeming eternity, the woman let out a long sigh and requested assistance. This time it was Calvin who came to her aid, and he was able to lift her up and return her to the wheelchair without help from anyone else.

At that point, a strong sense the orgy was at an end descended. It wasn't anything anyone needed to say. It was just done. With the exception of Alma, everyone was getting back into their clothes. The older woman spent much of her time undressed anyway, donning one of her old muumuus only on rare occasions. Considering how oppressively hot the the house was, Melissa had to wonder why any of them ever bothered wearing clothes during the summer when indoors.

After belatedly realizing Wormie was no longer on the floor at her feet, she looked around and saw the corpse was now propped up on the couch. After weeks of rotting away in the basement, it'd been looking rough even prior to the forced coupling, but now it was in much worse shape. The head was tilted forward at a precipitous angle, the neck having snapped at some point, either during the dildo ride itself or when the corpse slid off and hit the floor. Maggots had spilled out of the eye socket and now were squirming all over the front of the torso. The space between her legs was a black, goopy mess.

Melissa became aware again of the twist tie still affixed to the ring finger of her left hand. The ridiculous thing struck her as perhaps the most appropriate symbol possible of their deranged union, cheap and disposable. She frowned at the claw appearance of her hand as she rubbed at the twist tie with the ball of her thumb. The pinkie and forefinger were missing, removed weeks ago with a meat cleaver wielded by Ursula. It was difficult to reconcile the pain and terror of those moments with the genuine sense of sexual excitement Ursula had stirred within her today. The feeling simultaneously shamed and mystified her, and she wondered if she might now have become infected with the same terminal sickness of the mind and spirit that consumed these other people.

The twist tie came free of her finger with the slightest of tugs. She held it cupped in her hand until realizing she wasn't being observed. Then she cast it to the floor, hoping the gesture wouldn't earn her a reprimand. Nothing happened, in part because the others were listening to Alma yammer away about feeling famished.

The girl seated beneath Melissa on the Bad Girl Chair uttered her first intelligible words in some time, her voice so soft and weak she doubted anyone else heard them. The girl was begging her to get up. Melissa made no move to rise from the chair. Surreptitiously removing the joke of a "ring" was one thing, but standing without the express permission of her tormentors wasn't something she had any intention of doing.

Calvin rolled Alma out of the living room and then into the hallway leading to the kitchen, where, presumably, her hunger would receive some form of satiation. Only at that point did Melissa realize there was no longer any sign of the long-haired man. He'd disappeared along with his camera at some vague point during the orgy.

Ursula and Trixie remained in the living room.

After quietly observing her a moment or two longer, Ursula beckoned to Melissa with the crook of a finger. "Come here."

Melissa rose from the chair and went to the woman. She maintained an outward appearance of relative calm, but on the inside she was in a fragile state, walking the fine line between maintaining her composure and falling apart. The cumulative trauma of having endured so many assaults against her body and mind made her believe another was likely to happen as soon as she was within striking range. Another slap or punch to the face at the very least was what she expected, but neither of those things happened.

Instead, Ursula draped an arm over her shoulders and turned her so she was facing the pathetic wreck of a woman still ensconced in the Bad Girl Chair. "Take a good look at that useless cunt. What do you think of her?"

Melissa grunted. "Not much."

Trixie groaned in exasperation. "Holy shit, who cares what this bitch thinks about anything? Shouldn't we get Slaggie and Wormie back down to the basement? They must be chomping at the bit to get on with their honeymoon."

Ursula glared at her. "You're doing that thing again where you're talkin' to me like you think we're equals. That could be bad for your health if you keep it up."

Trixie flinched at her harsh tone. "I'm sorry. It won't happen again."

Ursula gave Melissa's shoulder a squeeze. "Pardon the interruption. Block that shit out of your head and focus on the bitch in the chair. Tell me what you see."

"A pile of fucked-up, ugly ass shit."

Describing a fellow sufferer in so callous a way pained Melissa, but her focus had to remain on her own best interests. She'd selected her words with a high level of cold calculation, reminding herself she was dealing with a psychopath who reveled in the denigration of others. Emulating that attitude felt like the right thing to do.

Ursula laughed. "That's the damn truth, but you know what? She ain't always looked this fucked-up. Matter of fact, this gal was one fine bitch when she first got here. Now tell me something else. How long ago do you think that was?"

Melissa studied the girl's battered and scarred body again, allowing herself time to assess the full scope of the physical damage in a more thorough way. A lot of the wounds and bruises seemed fresh, but there were so many it was hard to imagine they'd all been inflicted within a short frame of time.

She shrugged. "Six months? Maybe a little longer."

Another laugh from Ursula. "Nah, you're way off. She and her sister showed up here less than a week after we snatched you from the carnival."

The revelation stunned Melissa. She didn't know exactly how long she'd been here, but it couldn't have been much more than a month, maybe a month and a half at the most. The extreme level of brutalization the girl in the chair had been subjected to in so short a time was almost inconceivable, but she believed Ursula was telling the truth. She had no reason to lie or exaggerate about something like this.

She shook her head. "Holy shit."

Ursula moved away from Melissa and positioned herself at the side of the Bad Girl Chair. "Most folks would probably look at this bitch and say we've already done the worst we could do to her short of killing her. Which leads me to my next question. Do you want to be put in the basement again?"

Melissa shook her head. "I'd do anything to get out of that."

Ursula smirked. "Really? Anything?"

"Yes, anything at all," came Melissa's unhesitating reply.

Ursula again gave her a silent once-over before responding. "You know what? I think maybe I believe you, but we're gonna put it to the test. Come up with some new and interesting kind of hell to put this bitch through, something we haven't done a hundred times already. Then do it to her. Impress me with how fucked up you can get." She raised a hand and slapped it down against the top of the bound girl's head, prompting a moan. "If you can do that, you'll never have to stay in the basement again. That sound like something you wanna try?"

Melissa studied the pale, tear-streaked face of the girl in the Bad Girl Chair. She had to think of her as something other than a human being, but not necessarily a mere object. She was an equation, a problem in need of solving, a means by which her life could be improved if she came up with the right answer.

Several minutes passed largely in silence as she stared at the girl and pondered the dilemma.

Trixie signaled her impatience with a derisive snort. "She's stalling. No way this bitch comes up with anything good. She doesn't have it in her."

The corners of Melissa's mouth lifted almost imperceptibly as she made eye contact with Ursula. "The nails that were used to make that chair . . . are there more of them?"

Ursula nodded slowly. "A lot, yeah. What do you have in mind?"

"Have you ever seen *Hellraiser*?"

The inscrutable look on Ursula's face concerned her for a moment, right up to the moment when she began to laugh. "Damn, girl. I thought Trixie might be right about you until just fuckin' now, but goddamn. Shit, yeah, let's turn this bitch into a Pinhead."

Trixie made noises of petulant disapproval, but before she could verbalize any complaints a series of loud knocks rattled the front door.

Melissa flinched at the unexpected sound, her heart racing as a jolt of adrenaline hit her system. Not once during any of her time spent in this place had she heard anything like this strident knocking. It was an insistent sound, one imbued with knowledge of someone being inside to hear it. She was gripped by an almost impossible to resist impulse to scream for help. The only thing that held her back was seeing how calm Ursula remained even as the series of knocks recurred, an insight followed by belated realization that there was a deliberate pattern to the knocks. A code.

Ursula looked at her and smiled. "Save your breath."

The smirk on her face as she walked out of the living room and into the foyer made it clear she knew the exact contents of Melissa's thoughts in that moment. At the door, she undid a series of heavy-duty locks and tugged hard on the doorknob to pull the warped, ill-fitting door out of the frame. A series of splintering creaks and cracks ensued, some nearly as loud as gunshots.

She stepped out of the way as a beefy man in a rumpled suit entered. The man in the suit was followed into the house by a scrawnier man, one who moved with a shambling gait as he clutched at his abdomen. His shaking hands were stained with blood. A wheezing breath accompanied his every shuffling step forward, and the weathered features of his face were contorted with pain. Right behind this second man was a gorgeous young woman with flawless pale skin and black hair, fear evident in the way her eyes kept darting everywhere. The last person through the door was a man in the uniform of an Elkmont police officer.

Melissa recognized none of them but knew immediately they were *not* here to help.

The man in the rumpled suit started talking, but Ursula ignored him, becoming fixated on the bleeding man seconds after he'd walked through the door. She intercepted him on his way to the living room, grabbing him by an arm and turning him toward her.

He whimpered and clutched his stomach tighter, the blood continuing to spill out between his fingers.

Still holding fast to his arm, Ursula squinted, studying his face with an expression of disbelief. Tears gleamed in her eyes. "Daddy?"

The single word was uttered with more heartfelt vulnerability than Melissa had ever imagined hearing from the woman.

The man wobbled on his feet and stared blearily at her. Then his eyes rolled back in his head and he collapsed to the floor.

Abandoning all pretense of being Ursula, Lara Kincaid screamed and dropped to her knees at her father's side.

THIRTY-ONE

Five years ago

ON A WINDY DAY IN early June, Lara Kincaid opened the screen door at the back of the house and stepped out onto the little concrete stoop. She carried with her a jug of Alma's awful homemade hooch. Its high alcohol content more than compensated for what it lacked in taste. After seating herself at the edge of the stoop, she opened the jug and took a big gulp of the nasty concoction. She grimaced as the taste filled her mouth, like usual, but she was slowly getting used to it, the amount she was able to consume growing day by day. A time was likely coming when she'd be swilling the stuff like water. She considered it a necessary part of adapting to her new life as a willing resident of Dead End House.

She no longer had fantasies of escape or rescue. Any notion she'd had of resuming her previous life or fitting in with regular society again ended the day she cut a fetus out of a screaming live woman's womb. A fetus she subsequently cooked in a pot on the wood burning stove prior to eating it. The unborn child had been further along in its development than she would've imagined based on its mother's emaciated frame. It'd made for a surprisingly substantial meal, one she'd devoured in the presence of the mother, who'd amazingly still been clinging to life at that point. After she'd had her fill of baby meat, she poured the pot of boiling water into the woman's open abdominal cavity. Even *that* didn't kill her, and she was forced to finish her off by smashing the heavy pot against her skull until it cracked open and her brain matter leaked out.

Nope. No coming back from that at all.

Even if she'd been able to compartmentalize all that and seal it away forever in a dark corner of her mind, there was the matter of the way she looked now. Not only was she no longer pretty, she was disfigured, her facial structure altered forever by the beatings with the pipe wrench. She supposed it was possible a plastic surgeon could improve the situation somewhat, but it seemed unlikely. She was also missing a couple of fingers and several teeth. Dental implants could maybe fix the latter, but there was nothing to be done about the fingers.

There was no way around the undeniable truth. She'd been turned into a *freak*, a thing to be shunned and pitied. In high school, she'd played the part of the bad girl rebel, which was quite a different thing altogether. That was a choice, a matter of lifestyle and wardrobe, subject to being discarded in favor of new choices at any point. Choices no longer available to her. She couldn't bear the thought of returning to society and being an object of scorn, pity, and ridicule, of normal people staring at her and whispering. Or laughing. Not everyone would be that cruel, she supposed, but plenty would be *exactly* that cruel and even worse. She knew this because she'd already experienced it firsthand, having accompanied Calvin to the nearby M&K Market twice on supply runs.

The M&K Market was the closest thing this part of town had to a proper grocery store. It wasn't even half the size of the Kroger and Publix stores frequented by her parents, but it had most of the staples, including the yeast and sugar Alma required for her hooch. The building was rundown and there was no jaunty pop music playing over the store intercom. The aisles were narrow and crowded with people she would have considered seedy or dangerous a few months ago. Most of these people ignored her because they clearly had their own issues to worry about, but each time she'd been whispered about and snickered at by a different set of young people. She couldn't help wondering what kind of treatment she'd receive in a more upscale setting.

Her hunch was it'd be much worse.

It was best to not even ponder such theoreticals.

That old life was *done*. Period. End of story.

Her trips to the market had provided the starkest possible proof of this. She'd noticed the prominent placement of the missing persons flyers on utility poles and elsewhere, including one inside the entrance to the store. Yet there'd been not even the slightest flicker of recognition in the eyes of the people who saw her there. And why would there be?

She wasn't really Lara Kincaid anymore.

She took another big swig of the cheap hooch. She was determined to get to a point where she could tolerate drinking the foul-tasting stuff all day long because staying smashed all the time was the only coping method available to her. Without some means of taking the edges off reality she wouldn't be able to do all the vile things now required of her.

The drinking made her think of her father, who was a high-functioning lush, a maintenance drinker who imbibed at a steady level throughout every day. He was always a little tipsy at the minimum, but there were times when he got bombed out of his mind. It was especially embarrassing when it happened in public, like if they were out dining at a restaurant. He didn't get belligerent or abusive for the most part, just loud and obnoxious without being cognizant of it. She'd adopted her rebellious, beer-swilling high school persona in part as a response to his behavior. To some degree, it'd only been an act, at least in the beginning. She liked the way alcohol made her feel as long as she felt like she could control it, and for the most part that hadn't been a problem. Now, however, moderating her intake wasn't even a consideration.

She couldn't help wondering how her parents were doing.

It'd been roughly three months.

Were they still looking for her?

Was *anyone* looking for her?

Did they even think she was still alive?

She figured her mom and dad had been out of their minds with worry in the early days and weeks following her disappearance, but was that still the case? This was something she thought about a lot. Sometimes she'd try putting herself in their place, imagining herself as the mother of a missing child. Every time she did that, it was almost impossible to imagine ever getting over it, but maybe that wasn't how it worked in real life. Maybe the reality was that time kept passing no matter what kind of tragic shit happened and sooner or later you were left with no choice but to get on with things.

To get back to *life*.

Her eyes got a little misty as she thought about it. She put up a mental dam against the emotions swelling inside her, shutting them down as she took yet another big swig of hooch. The people who lived here—who'd put her through this hellish transformation—would never get to see her tears again. That was the one solemn vow she'd made to herself after being freed from the chains.

She was nothing special.

That was something else she knew beyond a goddamn doubt. A lot of abducted girls had passed through this house over the years. Some, Calvin went out and snatched himself while others just showed up at the front door, almost like religious zealots offering themselves up as sacrifices. Still others were funneled to them by corrupt members of the police force. Junkies, whores, and runaways, the disposable segments of society.

All of them had people who were missing them and who wondered what had become of them. People whose hearts would ache at the thought of their loved ones suffering the kind of degradation inflicted upon these girls every day. And what would those people think of her now that she'd become an active participant in perpetuating that same brand of degradation? Would they understand or have any shred of sympathy at the thought?

She snorted humorless laughter.

I don't fucking think so.

She was raising the jug for another swig when she saw a figure emerge from the distant line of trees. The open area behind the house was a large one, and the figure was too far away to discern anything clearly about it at first, but she was not concerned. Locals stayed away from Dead End House, and morbid sightseers were unlikely to approach it from that direction. Even without this knowledge, she would've been unconcerned.

She already had a pretty good idea who this was.

Her guess was proven correct minutes later as the figure continued across the field toward the house, details becoming discernible as he neared the midpoint between the house and trees. He was in his usual coveralls and a long handled tool of some kind was propped over his shoulder. In another minute or so, she realized the tool was a shovel.

Psyching herself up to talk to him when he got close enough, she gulped down more of the hooch.

"What you been up to out yonder, Calvin?"

The words didn't feel right in her mouth. She was still learning to talk in the less educated sounding way the one in charge desired, sliding in and out of the different speech patterns. When he didn't respond immediately, she tried again.

"You hear me, boy? Ya fuckin' deaf or somethin'? Whatcha been doin' with that shovel?"

By then he was only about ten feet away.

He looked at her and responded in his usual unintelligible way, the grunts and hoots that made him sound like a dumb version of the Wookiee from *Star Wars*. As he got closer, he veered toward the concrete stairwell, probably with the intention of stashing the shovel in the basement.

She got up and put herself in front of him before he could do that. "Hold up, dude," she said, dropping her voice to a point just above a whisper. "Knock that shit off. It's just you and me out here. Nobody can hear us. Seriously, what were you doing?"

He stared at her for a moment, his own lumpy features unreadable.

Then he shrugged and said, "I buried you."

She frowned. "What?"

He nodded. "I buried you. The other you. The last Ursula. She died while you were asleep."

This part of it wasn't unexpected.

After weeks of committing various acts of self-harm, the physical condition of the woman who'd assumed the role of Ursula Wilcox years earlier had deteriorated to an alarming degree. In recent days, she'd been conscious only intermittently, feverish and suffering from hallucinations. Several of the self-inflicted wounds had become infected and she'd resisted any attempt by others to clean and treat them. It'd become obvious she was trying to kill herself, but what Lara hadn't been able to understand at first was why she was doing it in such a deliberately slow fashion.

Now, however, she believed she knew why.

She'd been punishing herself. For all her sins, all the acts of torture and murder. For all the atrocities. She'd done it because she deserved it, and because no one else was going to do it. Lara grasped this on an intellectual level, but it wasn't something she could see herself ever doing, no matter her level of self-loathing.

The part of it that did surprise her was the burial.

"Why dig a grave? Why not cut her up and use the meat and stuff like we do with the others?"

This earned her another silent moment of expressionless scrutiny.

Then Calvin grunted. "Because she was special. Because I wanted to and because they said I could." He started to move past her, but stopped and turned toward her, leaning closer as he whispered again. "Don't ever ask me about her again. Ursula isn't dead. *You* are Ursula. Understand?"

He didn't wait for her to respond, brushing past her as he moved toward the stairwell. Seconds later, she heard the creak of the basement door opening, a sound followed by the whimpering of the girl currently kept in the cage down there.

Lara returned to the stoop and sat down.

She drank more hooch and stared at the distant tree line. A large bird of prey swooped across the sky, cawing loudly.

I am Ursula Wilcox, she thought. *I am the craziest, meanest bitch on the whole damn planet, and anybody who fucks with me better watch out.*

She didn't fully believe it yet, but one day she would.

She had no other choice.

She drank until the jug was empty.

Then she got to her feet, feeling a little wobbly at first from the booze, but when she felt steady enough, she went on inside. There was a new girl up there in the second-floor bedroom, which smelled like shit. Lara decided she'd go see her and work a little harder at becoming someone else.

THIRTY-TWO

THE MAN IN THE SUIT removed his blazer and held it slung over his shoulder, revealing a handgun in a shoulder rig. He unknotted his tie and popped open the first few buttons of his shirt.

"Christ, it's hotter than a boiler room in here," he said, his face flushed red and shiny with perspiration. "Don't know how you crazy fuckers stand it. I've only been here a minute and already I feel like I'm about to pass out."

There was no immediate response to these comments. This was at least in part due to Ursula's histrionic expression of grief over the man who'd fallen dead to the floor shortly after entering the house. She was still on her knees next to him, clutching at his bloodstained shirt and wailing with abandon. She'd called him "Daddy" and her extreme emotional reaction to his demise seemed to confirm the family connection. The confusing thing was that in all her time here not once had anyone referenced a Wilcox family father figure. It stood to reason there'd been one once upon a time, but Melissa had assumed he was long out of the picture, dead or perhaps in jail. Or perhaps she wasn't a true Wilcox family member at all, in addition to not being the original Ursula.

The uniformed cop who'd followed the rest of them into the house looked at Melissa and snickered. "Hey, Chief, check that one out. She's got herself a plastic dick."

Melissa had guessed already that the man in the suit was some kind of plain clothes cop, possibly a detective, but the uniformed one had called him "Chief" and she had to wonder if he might actually be Elkmont's new chief of police. She didn't recognize him, but the resignation of the previous chief in the wake of a sex scandal had been big local news in the months immediately prior to her abduction. Something to do with taking advantage of female prisoners.

The possibility gave rise to a new level of despair. It was an emotion she'd experienced to varying degrees throughout her imprisonment here, but now it fell over her like a dark shroud, snuffing out forever even the slightest possibility of hope. She thought about all the time she'd spent fantasizing about being rescued by a team of cops swarming this miserable pit of Hell and felt an urge to spew bitter laughter. Well, representatives of local law enforcement had finally shown up, but they were clearly not here in the role of saviors.

The probable chief smirked as he looked her over. "Ain't even close to the craziest thing I've seen here, Eddie, believe it or not." He glanced at the rotting corpse on the couch and grimaced. "That ain't either, but it's a closer thing. Y'all might want to think about burning or burying that one. Jesus."

It wasn't immediately clear to whom the latter remark was directed. Ursula was still lost in her grief, sobbing loudly and clutching at the body of her father. Alma and Calvin were still out of the room, and despite Trixie's indoctrination into the clan, she was still on somewhat of a short leash and not in a position to speak with authority about anything.

The girl in the nail chair groaned and leaned as far forward as the straps holding her in place would allow. "Please . . . help . . . I'm being kept prisoner. They're . . . torturing me."

Tears spilled down her cheeks.

Officer Eddie and the chief glanced at each other.

Then they burst out laughing.

The chief winked at the miserable girl. "No shit, honey. I never would've guessed."

More laughter from the so-called public servants.

Alma came waddling into the living room through the hallway entrance, drawn in by a degree of curiosity strong enough to inspire a rare instance of locomotion from one room to another without the aid of her wheelchair. She was still devoid of clothing, and there were several pieces of partially masticated food spilling out of the corners of her mouth.

"What in tarnation is all this ruckus about?"

Calvin followed her into the room and positioned himself well away from everyone else, exuding a degree of nervousness unusual for him. Melissa attributed that to the presence of multiple strangers who were not here under duress. Not all of them, anyway.

The chief glanced at Alma and cringed. "Christ, woman, put on some clothes."

Alma wiped the bits of food off her jowly face and pushed them back into her mouth, swallowing the whole mess in a single big gulp. "Eat my ass. It's too hot for clothes. Who's the dead sumbitch on the floor?"

Before the chief could respond, Ursula surged to her feet and angrily swiped tears from her face as she turned to face the rest of them. "He's my daddy. My real daddy from my old life. Who did this to him?"

The chief's smug grin vanished and he hooked a thumb in the direction of the stylishly dressed but terrified goth girl. "That one right there did the stabbing. Caught her literally red-handed, with blood on her hands and the knife in her purse." The look on his face took on a grimmer cast. "And, well, I hate to break it to you this way, but your ma is dead, too."

Ursula held her hands stiffly at her sides, her face twitching as she struggled to hold in her rage a few moments longer. She was still staring right at the goth girl, who was weeping steadily and shaking her head. "Did this same bitch kill her, too?"

The chief nodded. "Looks that way. We found your mother in the house right after we nabbed Wednesday Addams here. Had just dropped by intending to have a friendly little chat about some things we discussed earlier today. Nothing important." He chuckled. "Anyway, she'd been stabbed right through the heart, from the looks of it. Figured we'd let you dispose of the bodies however you see fit. Better for us, see, if this whole mess just goes away."

The goth girl let out a louder sob, her breath hitching as she struggled to speak. "It's . . . it's . . . n-not wh-what . . . it sounds like. I . . . I . . ." She wiped tears from her face with a shaking hand. "It was . . . an ac-accident. I . . . sw-swear . . . please . . ."

Ursula leveled a withering look of rage-fueled disdain at the girl a moment longer.

Then she looked at the chief and held out her hand. "Give me your gun."

The goth girl wailed in anguished despair. "No, no, no, please. You don't understand. You must be Lara." She swallowed hard and pressed ahead with determination now, anxious to be heard and understood before the worst could happen. "You look so different now, not like the old pictures at all, but you must be. I was trying to help your parents find you. I swear to God. Then things got all fucked up and I never meant for any of this to happen. Please, you have to believe me."

The goth girl's plaintive plea for understanding failed to move Ursula. Or Lara. Whatever the hell her name actually was, she was still holding out her hand and staring straight at the chief. "Give me your fucking gun."

The chief was hesitant.

He stared at her open palm, frowning hard as he scratched at the back of his head. "Well, now, I'm not sure how good an idea that is. I mean, go ahead and ice the bitch if you want. Doesn't make any difference to me, but I can't let you murder anyone with my registered service weapon. I can't risk that coming back on me. Anyway, don't y'all prefer to do things the slow way, with torture and maiming and all that? Ain't that more along the lines of what she deserves?"

Lara shook her head. "Not this time. This requires a fucking execution. Give me your gun."

The chief did some more hemming and hawing, still hesitating.

Then another male voice intruded: "Give it to her."

All heads turned toward the long-haired man, who was now standing under the high archway demarcating the border between the foyer and the living room. He'd materialized from seemingly nowhere, as was often the case when he put in one of his infrequent appearances.

The chief and the long-haired man locked eyes for a moment. No further verbal communication occurred, but there was a tangible sense of some silent acknowledgement passing between them. The chief's demeanor changed perceptibly, the smirking joviality disappearing. As soon as she saw this shift occur, Melissa knew Lara would get what she wanted.

And she was right.

The scuzzy long-haired man was an enigma to her. She didn't understand how his mere presence could unsettle a man of the chief's stature and authority so easily. Yet there was no denying the obvious. For whatever reason, the chief feared this man. He didn't even try to argue with him.

Instead of handing over the gun from his shoulder rig, he knelt for a moment and lifted the cuff of a trouser leg, revealing a snub-nosed revolver in an ankle holster. He took this gun out of its holster and offered it to Lara. "That's my spare piece. Unregistered and untraceable. Hell, you can even keep it. I'll get another one."

Lara took the gun and pointed it at the goth girl. "You're right, I don't look like I did. That's kinda what happens when someone with a pipe wrench uses your face as a fuckin' pinata. Now get on your goddamn knees."

The goth girl whimpered as tears gushed from her bleary eyes. "No, please. I'll do anything you want. Anything at all. Just please don't kill me. Please, I'm begging you."

Lara sneered. "You're still not on your knees. You've got about three seconds to do as you're told before I shoot you where you stand."

This time the girl did as she was told, coming a few steps closer before dropping to her knees right in front of Lara. She looked up at her through shiny, beseeching eyes, hands clasped together in penitence. "Please. I'm begging you."

Lara placed the gun's muzzle against the girl's forehead. "You already said that. What people like you never get is it doesn't matter how much you beg. It ain't changing shit."

The girl's entire body trembled as she wept and struggled to say something else. In the end, she was too terrified to intelligibly articulate a final, desperate plea, surrendering to uncontrollable sobbing.

Melissa flinched at the big boom of the gun's concussive report as Lara squeezed the trigger. The bullet drilled a hole all the way through the goth girl's head, blood flying out of the exit wound in back like a strong spurt of water from a hose. Then her body slumped to the floor and didn't move.

This was another grim first for Melissa. She'd witnessed and personally experienced a wide range of horrific things during her time in this place, but until this moment she'd never seen the life blasted out of a person, extinguished with such blunt finality in the space of about a second. Seeing it happen offended something primal within her, striking her as obscene and wrong, the power of a god held in human hands.

She barely had time to start processing it before Lara swung her arm about and squeezed the trigger again, shooting the chief in the face. The bullet punched through the bridge of his nose, making his eyes bulge in their sockets as he staggered backward a step or two before collapsing to the floor. Officer Eddie backed into the foyer, fumbling with his gun as he tried and failed to draw it cleanly free of the holster.

Lara shot him twice, once in the belly as he started to turn and make a break for the open door, then another time in the back. His knees hit the foyer floor with an audible crack, and he remained in that position several seconds longer as he tried reaching behind his back, the shaking fingers of his right hand seeking the bullet hole. What he hoped to accomplish by doing this was unclear, but he was still at it when the long-haired man approached him from behind, gripped the sides of his head, and broke his neck with a single brutal twist.

Melissa's ears were still ringing from the multiple gunshots as Alma started spewing angry invective at Lara for shooting the policemen. Given what had just happened, her fury was understandable. Some sort of arrangement had existed between the now deceased chief and the Wilcox clan, that was obvious, but surely that was null and void in the wake of the man's murder.

Alma's furious ranting continued until Lara's arm swung around again, aiming the revolver at the older woman's face. "They had that coming for bringing my daddy here instead of taking him to the hospital." She sneered. "We all get what we deserve sooner or later. Even you."

She cocked the revolver's hammer.

The long-haired man spoke again. Just a single word. *"Don't."*

There was something different about the man's voice as he enunciated the single syllable, the timbre of it crackling with palpable dark energy. *Occult* energy. Hearing it raised goosebumps on Melissa's arms and made her knees go weak. Something curdled inside her, a feeling that made her want to find a dark, lonely space to crawl into and never emerge from again.

She wasn't surprised when she felt piss running down her legs.

DEAD END HOUSE

A moment of frozen stillness prevailed in the room until Lara sighed and said, "Fine. Jesus Christ, the Savior, please forgive me for my sins and let me see my momma and daddy in Heaven."

She put the barrel of the revolver in her mouth and squeezed the trigger one last time.

THIRTY-THREE

THE BACK OF URSULA'S HEAD blowing out in a shower of blood, brain matter, and skull fragments was one of the most joyous sights of Lexie's life. She was in a state of near delirium as the result of the endless process of torture, humiliation, and mutilation she'd endured, floating between periods of searingly painful lucidity and dissociation. In the moments leading up to Ursula's demise, however, she felt anchored to reality and able to appreciate the momentous nature of what was happening.

She started laughing shortly after some of the DNA fragments hit her in the face and chest, delighted that she'd outlasted the evil witch who'd taken such great pleasure in subjecting her to endless misery. The circumstances of how it'd come about were somewhat less satisfactory. No one had made Ursula get on her knees and beg for mercy. There'd been no turning of the tables, no opportunity to make her pay for all the terrible things she'd done. She'd chosen her own exit and it'd been an act of defiance, which was less than ideal. There was a lot about all of it she didn't understand, including the matter of her actual identity, but in those rapturous moments following her death, none of that mattered much. The chance to bear witness to the woman's destruction was far more than she'd expected.

The others resumed talking after the shock of the moment passed, but Lexie's expression of mirth continued unrestrained. She found reserves of energy she hadn't known were still available to her and kept on laughing. The force of it caused her additional pain, the nail points digging into her flesh again and again as her body quaked with laughter, but she no longer cared about that. She didn't enjoy the pain, but consoled herself with the knowledge it wouldn't last much longer.

Death, however, was forever, and Ursula, or whatever, was never going to laugh at anything again. Her days of reveling in sadistic cruelty and taunting her victims were finished. She would never get to complete Lexie's process of so-called degradation.

Good. Burn in Hell, bitch.

She was still laughing when Calvin started dragging the corpses out of the house one at a time. He started with Ursula, taking her out of the living room through the hallway entrance. She turned her head and kept laughing as she watched the body slide across the floor, leaving a trail of blood and brain goop in its wake. The laughter continued even after the corpse of her tormentor disappeared from view. She was experiencing what she recognized would probably be the last moment of pure giddiness she'd ever know, thus she made no attempt to stop or restrain herself when both her sister and the large older woman started screaming at her to shut the fuck up. The laughter didn't stop even after Trixie started punching her in the face. It was funny how frustrated her sister was getting, her screaming increasing in volume with each blow she delivered, each one of which failed to silence her. At that point she became determined to continue laughing until she drew her final breath.

She did it too, laughing throughout Calvin's extended process of removing the corpses from the house. He was gone for a longish period between dragging away each corpse, somewhere between ten and fifteen minutes every time. Maybe longer. It took a while, yet still the laughter continued, more softly than in the beginning, her body no longer quaking from the force of it, but she remained committed to her determination to never stop. She was still laughing quietly even after the rest of them left the living room and went upstairs.

After carrying away the rotted corpse of the one they'd called

Wormie, Calvin returned one last time. She felt a tingle of fear as he came to her and started undoing the straps binding her to the Bad Girl Chair, but still she laughed, her final sad smile still lifting the corners of her mouth.

He lifted her out of the chair and carried her out of the house. It was dark outside as he transported her across the vast backyard toward the distant line of trees. She looked up at the stars in the sky and laughed. It was a beautiful late summer evening, so different from her last night outside. What had that been, only a day ago? It was so hard to tell anymore. There were no clouds in the sky and everything was still, with only the gentlest of breezes to caress her flushed face.

Calvin breathed heavily as he carried her into the dark woods, the tops of the tall trees blotting out the starry sky. He was big and strong, but the strain of transporting so many bodies over such a distance was a lot even for him. She felt the occasional scrape of low-hanging branches across her face and legs as he bulled his way through the dense woods. Still she laughed, trembling with it as she absorbed all these additional little jabs of pain.

Eventually they emerged into a clearing and she was again briefly able to enjoy the lovely sight of all the twinkling stars above her. Then he heaved her into a pit filled with all the other bodies. The landing was painful and caused her to cry out, but after that the soft, almost inaudible laughter resumed. She'd landed between the bodies of the plain clothes cop and the man Ursula had called daddy. The pit was not a new excavation of earth. She looked around and saw bone and skull fragments, as well as lumpy gray piles of what might have been ashes. Tears filled her eyes as she continued to force out the laughter. She kept at it even as Calvin began to douse her and the pile of fresh corpses with gasoline. She didn't stop even as he lit a match and tossed it into the pit.

The pain she experienced as flames engulfed her broken and battered form transcended even the worst agonies she'd experienced inside and outside of Dead End House, but even so she managed one last gasp of laughter. Then she screamed, but the sound was short-lived as the fire was sucked into her lungs and burned out her breath. Her last conscious thought was of her sister and how much she hated her. She harbored not one ounce of forgiveness in her heart.

Calvin watched her die.

Then he turned away from the pit and started the journey back toward the house.

DEAD END HOUSE

~

All Melissa wanted was to run out of the house and keep on running. The warped front door was still standing wide open, an invitation that felt nigh impossible to resist. The old order inside Dead End House was on the verge of collapsing. Or perhaps that was a false perception, based on the oddly unconcerned demeanor of the long-haired man.

The bizarre thing about this was how he was projecting this palpable sense of powerful, malevolent energy with no visible effort. He was just standing there, his posture as relaxed as always. There was no evidence of tension in his lean, lanky frame. The closest he'd come to seeming bothered about anything was when he'd issued his one-word command to Lara, quelling her lethal intentions toward Alma.

Even that had required only a small effort of will. All he did was look at her and utter the one syllable, putting an immediate end to it. The air in the overheated room still felt charged with electricity, a lingering side effect of his brief verbal intervention. The power continued to radiate from his every pore, and the strange thing was how he looked no different than before. There'd been no obvious radical physical transformation. He was still the same scruffy late middle-aged dude on the outside, the kind of guy who wouldn't look out of place haunting the racks of a used record shop or mingling with the other oldsters at a nostalgia rock show.

And yet she already had all the proof she could ever need that this man was not ordinary. Melissa knew he could bend her to his will as easily as he'd influenced Lara in her last moments. Even the girl's final act of defiance now struck her as something the long-haired man had allowed to happen and was not—as she would've preferred to believe—an indication of cracks in his power. She was positive Lara would still be alive if it was what he'd wanted. Either he'd granted her a fleeting moment of bloody grace for inscrutable reasons of his own, or he'd judged her and found her lacking in some way, no longer a suitable conduit of the evil Dead End House existed to perpetuate.

The maimed girl in the Bad Girl Chair was still in the midst of her fit of mad laughter when the long-haired man wordlessly walked out of the living room and into the foyer, where he stopped and stood near the foot of the staircase as he addressed the rest of them as a group for the first time.

"The house has fed well and is satiated. Blood has flown in abundance and the time of rebirth has finally arrived. Join us."

He waved a hand toward the stairs.

The implication seemed obvious.

Melissa and Trixie looked at each other, an odd sense of something that wasn't quite camaraderie but was adjacent to that feeling forming between them. This was a girl who'd cut off Melissa's ear and tortured her in gleeful fashion, but they had something in common. They were recent arrivals to this place and were still outsiders, even Trixie despite her willing embrace of the clan's sadistic ways. There was a feeling they were in this together now, regardless of how much they hated each other.

Trixie grunted, a sound of resignation. "Fuck it. Come on, girl."

She clasped hands with Melissa and they walked into the foyer.

Upon arriving at the bottom of the staircase, Trixie looked at the long-haired man and said, "Okay, we're going upstairs, I guess. Do you want us in any particular room or . . ."

He said nothing as she trailed off, but Alma waddled up behind them and said, "We're going into the attic. That's where it happens."

Melissa glanced at her. "Where *what* happens?"

Alma smiled. "Elucidation and enlightenment. *Rebirth.* Just wait and see. Y'all are gonna have to help me up that damn ladder, though."

Trixie groaned. "Of course. Don't fall on me, bitch."

They started up the creaky stairs, a procession that moved with stultifying slowness with Alma in the lead, huffing and puffing with each labored step. The long-haired man followed in their wake, still not speaking. They were about halfway up when the open front door of the house began to close, the warped wood groaning in loud protest as the heavy door slammed into the frame. This was followed by the sound of a series of locks clicking shut.

Melissa didn't glance back once as this happened, not yet willing to acknowledge the reality of the impossible thing she'd undoubtedly see—the door closing and the locks engaging with no visible human assistance. The air in the house again crackled with strange, unnatural energy.

After what felt like a long time, the group reached the second-floor landing and continued down the hallway, turning right at the juncture. In the shorter stretch of hallway, the attic door was already hanging open, the foldable ladder extended to the floor.

Alma placed one large, swollen, purplish foot on the bottom step and groaned as she tried heaving herself up to the next one. At this point, Trixie and Melissa were resigned to the arduous process ahead of them, and they worked together to push Alma up the ladder. The bulk of the responsibility fell on Trixie as she was the one with fully intact hands. Melissa merely supported her weight as best she could.

After they were finally able to propel Alma through the dark opening in the ceiling into the attic, Trixie and Melissa stepped up into the dark space with her and found each other's hands again. It was impossible to see anything, the light from the hallway lanterns below being so faint. The steps of the ladder creaked as the long-haired man came up behind them. They heard his footsteps on the floor as he entered the attic and moved past them. Melissa glimpsed the outline of his back an instant before it was swallowed by the thicker darkness deeper in the attic.

One thing that surprised her was the atmosphere inside the attic, which she'd imagined would be even more suffocatingly hot than the first and second floors of the house, but that was not the case. There was even a slight coolness to the air. Then she heard a loud thunk as a switch was thrown and she squinted against the array of electric lights that came on. The illumination was courtesy of strings of red and orange bulbs wrapped around the rafters. A whirring sound accompanied a rush of fresh cold air that swept through the space.

That there actually was functioning electricity and air-conditioning in this part of the crumbling abode was merely the first in a string of revelations. A large red pentagram was painted on the floor, and the paint looked fresh, still wet. It took Melissa longer than it probably should have to realize the "paint" was actually blood. One of the walls was almost entirely covered with Polaroid photographs depicting an astonishing range of bloody atrocities. Melissa recognized a few of the faces in the photos—the more recent ones—but many others were strangers, people she'd never seen.

A high percentage of the pictures were old. She saw an image of a nude woman nailed to a cross in what looked like the backyard. Another showed a woman with her stomach torn open and her guts and organs arrayed around her on the floor. There were images of decapitations and obvious acts of necrophilia. Another of the older photos showed the original Ursula in her prime, slicing open the throat of another young woman. She had a huge grin on her face, and her nude torso was bathed in blood. Still another of the older photos showed a large man she assumed was the original Calvin. He was operating a gas-powered chainsaw and was pushing the whirring blade through the top of a teenage girl's head. On and on the images of horror went, stretching from one end of the long wall to the other, an overwhelming panorama of lurid abominations.

Dangling from the attic's vaulted ceiling was an iron cage of a medieval design. The long-haired man went to a wheel crank mounted on another wall, and as he turned it, the hanging cage began to lower. Trapped inside it was Closet Girl, who mumbled and moaned and moved about awkwardly, the stumps of her limbs slipping repeatedly through the slats at the bottom of the cage.

Melissa felt pity for the nameless, sightless girl, but she also felt no inclination to help her. On top of everything else, her captors appeared to be actual Satanists, and not of the harmless playacting variety. These people were the real thing, and somehow they'd tapped into some genuine vein of dark power. She knew without doubt she was incapable of defying that power, and that any such attempt would incur the wrath of an evil capable of crushing her in an instant.

The long-haired man stopped turning the crank as the iron cage reached the floor. From a hook on the same wall, he took a single long key of an ancient design and went to the cage, unlocking it. He opened the rusty door, reached inside, and grabbed Closet Girl by an arm, hauling her roughly out, and dumping her on the floor at the edge of the pentagram.

Alma stepped into the center of the pentagram and looked at Melissa and Trixie. "I reckon y'all know what's about to happen here, at least part of it."

Trixie nodded. "Well, this all appears devil-related, so I'm guessing a blood sacrifice?"

Alma smiled. "Smart girl. Tonight we're completing a process that started a long time ago . . ."

She went on to explain that a number of the dark lord's acolytes had occupied positions of high power in Elkmont for many years, going at least as far back as the 70s. Politicians and lawmen, shadowy figures who brokered shady deals behind closed doors. They all worked together to further the glory of Satan, with Dead End House as the focal point of their efforts. In addition to the victims that the inhabitants of the house sought out and procured on their own, they were fed a regular supply of sacrifices by the powerful. The more blood it was fed, the greater the dark power inside the house became.

The house was lent additional strength through the power of local legend and the fear generated by the tales of the horrors that had occurred within its walls. The house itself became like a living thing, and as a living thing it possessed an awareness of its own history, as well as a desire to uphold and perpetuate that history. Thus, after a long dormant period, the process of renewal was begun. The long-haired man took the original Ursula in after she was granted compassionate release from prison following a long illness doctors had pronounced as terminal. An illness that was later held at bay by an endless flow of innocent sacrificial blood.

He returned her to Dead End House and she assumed the role of her deceased mother, taking her name and transforming herself physically. New, younger replacements for Calvin and Ursula were found, people who were coerced and brainwashed into adopting those roles through a brutal and unrelenting process of transformation. Thus, the Wilcox family was reborn and resumed its bloody work.

Tonight was the final phase in the process of rebirth.

Tonight the dark lord would reward them for all they'd done in his name.

It all sounded completely insane.

And yet Melissa believed every word of it.

Alma/Ursula stepped close and looked her in the eye. "Do you want to be one of us?"

"Yes."

She meant it, too.

The pulsating dark energy was a scary thing, but it was not without allure. She felt a burgeoning sense of excitement as she felt it seep inside her, suffusing the wounded parts of her psyche and making her feel strong. She no longer had any desire to return to her old life. The last remnants of that feeling had been swept away in these last few minutes.

Dead End House was her home now, the place where she truly belonged.

Trixie squeezed Melissa's hand, letting her know she felt all these same things. "You already know my answer, Ursula."

Ursula smiled. "I've known it from the start. From the moment I set eyes on you."

At her direction, they took hold of Closet Girl and dragged her into the center of the pentagram. The eyeless girl moaned and squirmed, but Melissa held onto her arms while Trixie sat astride her closed legs to prevent thrashing. Ursula went to a table in a dark corner of the attic and returned moments later with a tool that appeared to be a hybrid of a cleaver and a knife, long and wide with a curved and wickedly sharp blade.

She groaned as she dropped heavily to her knees at Closet Girl's side. Then she went to work with the tool, ripping open the girl's belly with gleeful abandon. The blade rose and fell, rose and fell, chopping and chopping into organs and guts, shredding them as blood and pieces of meat flew everywhere. Trixie and Melissa grinned and giggled as the flying blood painted their faces. They gobbled handfuls of shredded Closet Girl meat. Ursula grabbed handfuls of goopy organ bits and smeared them all over her face, breasts, and belly, then down between her legs, moaning in ecstasy.

The long-haired man removed his clothes and joined in as the second orgy of the day commenced.

Then, just as the writhing and moaning tight circle of entwined, bloody bodies reached their most frenzied state of delirious ecstasy, Ursula began to violently convulse. The rest of them disengaged and watched as the spasms continued and intensified, Ursula's body rising up from the floor and smashing back down again over and over. After at least a minute of this, an unseen force raised her up again and set her on her feet. She began to claw at her face, tearing the flesh away in huge bloody ribbons. A series of popping and cracking sounds ensued, her skeletal frame and musculature coming apart as she continued tearing away at the dying outer shell of her former self, the diseased and bloated self. She kept at it until she emerged fully from the bloody suit of her old skin.

Ursula kicked free of the pile of gore and stood naked and renewed before them, young and perfect again, reborn in the glory of Satan.

Melissa fell to her knees in front of her and bowed in worship.

Trixie did the same right next to her.

The long-haired man peeled away his own flesh suit.

Moments later, a young and rejuvenated Tommy Duncan clasped hands with Ursula Wilcox, the girl he fell in love with in 1977, the year they both pledged their souls as eternal servants of evil.

Bryan Smith is the author of numerous novels and novellas, including *Depraved*, *68 Kill*, *The Unseen*, *Slowly We Rot*, *Last of the Ravagers*, and *Kill For Satan!*, which won a Splatterpunk Award for best horror novella of 2018. He won a second Splatterpunk Award in 2020 for *Dirty Rotten Hippies and Other Stories*. He is also the co-author of *Suburban Gothic*, written with Brian Keene. A film version of *68 Kill* was released in 2017. He lives in TN with his dog Mac. Signed copies of his books are available at https://bryansmithhorror.bigcartel.com

Other Grindhouse Press Titles

#666__*Satanic Summer* by Andersen Prunty

#091__*Graffitti Tombs* by Matt Serafini

#090__*The Hands of Onan* by Chris DiLeo

#089__*Burning Down the Night* by Bryan Smith

#088__*Kill Hill Carnage* by Tim Meyer

#087__*Meat Photo* by Andersen Prunty and C.V. Hunt

#086__*Dreaditation* by Andersen Prunty

#085__*The Unseen II* by Bryan Smith

#084__*Waif* by Samantha Kolesnik

#083__*Racing with the Devil* by Bryan Smith

#082__*Bodies Wrapped in Plastic and Other Items of Interest* by Andersen Prunty

#081__*The Next Time You See Me I'll Probably Be Dead* by C.V. Hunt

#080__*The Unseen* by Bryan Smith

#079__*The Late Night Horror Show* by Bryan Smith

#078__*Birth of a Monster* by A.S. Coomer

#077__*Invitation to Death* by Bryan Smith

#076__*Paradise Club* by Tim Meyer

#075__*Mage of the Hellmouth* by John Wayne Comunale

#074__*The Rotting Within* by Matt Kurtz

#073__*Go Down Hard* by Ali Seay

#072__*Girl of Prey* by Pete Risley

#071__*Gone to See the River Man* by Kristopher Triana

#070__*Horrorama* edited by C.V. Hunt

#069__*Depraved 4* by Bryan Smith

#068__*Worst Laid Plans: An Anthology of Vacation Horror* edited by Samantha Kolesnik

#067__*Deathtripping: Collected Horror Stories* by Andersen Prunty

#066__*Depraved* by Bryan Smith

#065__*Crazytimes* by Scott Cole

#064__*Blood Relations* by Kristopher Triana

#063__*The Perfectly Fine House* by Stephen Kozeniewski and Wile E. Young

#062__*Savage Mountain* by John Quick

#061__*Cocksucker* by Lucas Milliron

#060__*Luciferin* by J. Peter W.

#059__*The Fucking Zombie Apocalypse* by Bryan Smith

#058__*True Crime* by Samantha Kolesnik